ROGER ZELAZNY

KNIGHT OF SHADOWS

AVON BOOKS ◆ NEW YORK

AVON BOOKS
A division of
The Hearst Corporation
105 Madison Avenue
New York, New York 10016

Copyright © 1989 by the Amber Corporation
Cover illustration by Tim White
Published by arrangement with the author
Library of Congress Catalog Card Number: 89-34658
ISBN: 0-380-75501-7

Published in hardcover by William Morrow and Company, Inc.; for information address Avon Books.

First Avon Books Printing: September 1990

AVON TRADEMARK REG. U.S. PAT. OFF. AND IN OTHER COUNTRIES, MARCA REGISTRADA, HECHO EN U.S.A.

Printed in the U.S.A.

RA   10   9   8   7   6   5   4   3   2   1

This book is for John Douglas

KNIGHT OF SHADOWS

I

Her name was Julia, and I'd been damn certain she was dead back on April 30 when it all began. My finding her grisly remains and destroying the doglike creature which I'd thought had killed her were pretty much the way it started. And we had been lovers, which I suppose was how things had really commenced. Long before.

Perhaps I could have trusted her more. Perhaps I should never have taken her on that shadow-walk which led to denials that took her away from me, down dark ways and into the studio of Victor Melman, a nasty occultist I later had to kill—the same Victor Melman who was himself the dupe of Luke and Jasra. But now, perhaps—just barely—I might have been in a position to forgive myself for what I'd thought I'd done, for it seemed that I hadn't really done it after all. Almost.

That is to say, I learned that I hadn't been responsible for it while I was in the act of doing it. It was when I drove my knife into the side of the mysterious sorcerer

Mask, who had been on my case for some time, that I discovered that Mask was really Julia. My half brother Jurt, who's been trying to kill me longer than anyone else in the business, snatched her away, and they vanished then, immediately following his transformation into a kind of living Trump.

As I fled the burning, crumbling Keep there at the Citadel of the Four Worlds, a falling timber caused me to dodge to my right, trapping me in a cul-de-sac of crashed masonry and burning beams. A dark metal ball flashed past me then, seeming to grow as it moved. It struck the wall and passed through it, leaving a hole one could dive through—a hint I was not slow in taking. Outside I jumped the moat, using my Logrus extensions to knock aside a section of fence and a score of troops, before I turned back and shouted, "Mandor!"

"Right here," came his soft voice from behind my left shoulder.

I turned in time to see him catch a metal ball, which bounced once before us and dropped into his extended hand.

He brushed ashes from his black vest and ran a hand through his hair. Then he smiled and turned back toward the burning Keep.

"You've kept your promise to the Queen," he remarked, "and I don't believe there's anything more for you here. Shall we go now?"

"Jasra's still inside," I answered, "having it out with Sharu."

"I thought you were done with her."

I shook my head.

"She still knows a lot of things I don't. Things I'll be needing."

A tower of flame began to rear itself above the Keep, halted and hovered a moment, heaved itself higher.

"I didn't realize," he said. "She does seem to want

control of that fountain fairly badly. If we were to snatch her away now, that fellow Sharu will claim it. Does that matter?"

"If we don't snatch her away, he may kill her."

Mandor shrugged.

"I've a feeling she'll take him. Would you care to place a small wager?"

"Could be you're right," I said, watching the fountain continue its climb skyward, following another pause. I gestured toward it. "Thing looks like an oil gusher. I hope the winner knows how to cap it—if there is a winner. Neither one of them may last much longer, the way the place is coming apart."

He chuckled.

"You underestimate the forces they've generated to protect themselves," he said. "And you know it isn't all that easy for one sorcerer to do in another by sorcerous means. However, you've a point there when it comes to the inertia of the mundane. With your permission . . . ?"

I nodded.

With a quick underhand toss he cast the metal ball across the ditch toward the burning building. It struck the ground and with each bounce thereafter it seemed to increase in size. It produced a cymballike crash each time it hit, entirely out of proportion with its apparent mass and velocity, and this sound increased in volume on each successive bounce. It passed then into the burning, tottering ruin that was the near end of the Keep and for several moments was gone from sight.

I was about to ask him what was going on when I saw the shadow of a large ball pass before the opening through which I had fled. The flames—save for the central tower from the broken Fount—began to subside, and a deep rumbling sound came from within. Moments later an even larger circular shadow passed, and I began to feel the rumbling through the soles of my boots.

A wall tumbled. Shortly thereafter part of another wall fell. I could see inside fairly clearly. Through the dust and smoke the image of the giant ball passed again. The flames were snuffed. My Logrus vision still granted me glimpses of the shifting lines of power which flowed between Jasra and Sharu.

Mandor extended a hand A minute or so later a small metal ball came bouncing our way, and he caught it.

"Let's head back," he said. "It would be a shame to miss the end."

We passed through one of the many gaps in the fence, and sufficient rubble filled the ditch at one point for us to walk across on it. I spent a barrier spell then, to keep the re-forming troops off the premises and out of our way for a time.

Entering through the broken wall, I saw that Jasra stood with her back to the tower of fire, her arms upraised. Streaks of sweat lined her face zebra through a mask of soot, and I could feel the pulsing of the forces which passed through her body. About ten feet above her, face purple and head twisted to one side as if his neck were broken, Sharu hung in the middle of the air. To the untutored he might have seemed magically levitated. My Logrus sight gave me view of the line of force from which he hung suspended, however, victim of what might, I suppose, be termed a magical lynching.

"Bravo," Mandor stated, clapping his hands slowly and softly together. "You see, Merlin? I'd have won that bet."

"You always were a better judge of talent than I was," I acknowledged.

". . . and swear to serve me," I overheard Jasra saying.

Sharu's lips moved.

"And swear to serve you," he gasped.

She lowered her arms slowly, and the line of force which held him began to lengthen. As he descended toward the Keep's cracked floor, her left hand executed a gesture similar to one I had once seen an orchestra conductor employ in encouraging the woodwinds, and a great gout of fire came loose from the Fountain, fell upon him, washed over him, and passed on down into the ground. Flashy, though I didn't quite see the point . . .

His slow descent continued, as if someone in the sky were trolling for crocodiles. I discovered myself holding my breath as his feet neared the ground, in sympathetic anticipation of the eased pressure on his neck. This, however, did not come to pass. When his feet reached the ground, they passed on into it, and his descent continued, as if he were an occulted hologram. He sank past his ankles and up to his knees and kept going. I could no longer tell whether he was breathing. A soft litany of commands rolled from Jasra's lips, and sheets of flame periodically separated themselves from the Fountain and splashed over him. He sank past his waist and up to his shoulders and slightly beyond. When only his head remained visible, eyes open but unfocused, she executed another hand movement, and his journey into the earth was halted.

"You are now the guardian of the Fount," she stated, "answerable only to me. Do you acknowledge this?"

The darkened lips writhed.

"Yes," came a whispered reply.

"Go now and bank the fires," she ordered. "Commence your tenure."

The head seemed to nod at the same time it began sinking again. After a moment only a cottony tuft of hair remained, and an instant later the ground swallowed this, too. The line of force vanished.

I cleared my throat. At the sound Jasra let her arms

13

fall and turned toward me. She was smiling faintly.

"Is he alive or dead?" I asked, and then added, "Academic curiosity."

"I'm not really certain," she responded. "But a little of both, I think. Like the rest of us."

"'Guardian of the Fount,'" I reflected. "Interesting existence."

"Beats being a coatrack," she observed.

"I daresay."

"I suppose you feel I owe you some gratitude now, for my restoration," she stated.

I shrugged.

"To tell you the truth, I've other things to think about," I said.

"You wanted an end to the feud," she said, "and I wanted this place back. I still have no kind thoughts toward Amber, but I am willing to say we're even."

"I'll settle for that," I told her. "And there is a small loyalty I may share with you."

She studied me through narrowed eyes for a moment, then smiled.

"Don't worry about Luke," she said.

"But I must. That son of a bitch Dalt—"

She continued to smile.

"Do you know something I don't?" I asked.

"Many things," she replied.

"Anything you'd care to share?"

"Knowledge is a marketable commodity," she observed, as the ground shook slightly and the fiery tower swayed.

"I'm offering to help your son and you're offering to sell me the information on how to go about it?" I inquired.

She laughed.

"If I thought Rinaldo needed help," she said, "I'd be at his side this moment. I suppose it makes it easier to hate me if you feel I lack even maternal virtues."

"Hey, I thought we were calling things even," I said.

"That doesn't preclude hating each other," she replied.

"Come on, lady! Outside of the fact that you tried to kill me year after year, I've got nothing against you. You happen to be the mother of someone I like and respect. If he's in trouble, I want to help him, and I'd as soon be on good terms with you."

Mandor cleared his throat as the flames dropped ten feet, shuddered, dropped again.

"I've some fine culinary spells," he remarked, "should recent exertions have roused some appetites."

Jasra smiled almost coquettishly, and I'd swear she batted her eyelashes at him. While he makes a striking appearance with that shock of white hair, I don't know that you'd exactly call Mandor handsome. I've never understood why women are as attracted to him as they usually seem to be. I've even checked him out for spells on that particular count, but he doesn't wear one. It must be some different order of magic entirely.

"A fine idea," she responded. "I'll provide the setting if you'll take care of the rest."

Mandor bowed; the flames collapsed the rest of the way to the ground and were damped therein. Jasra shouted an order to Sharu, the Invisible Guardian, telling him to keep them that way. Then she turned and led us toward the downward stair.

"Underground passage," she explained, "to more civilized shores."

"It occurs to me," I remarked, "that anyone we encounter will probably be loyal to Julia."

Jasra laughed.

"As they were to me before her and to Sharu before me," she replied. "They are professionals. They come with the place. They are paid to defend the winners, not to avenge the losers. I will put in an appearance and make a proclamation after dinner, and I will enjoy their unanimous and heartfelt loyalty until the next usurpation. Mind that third step. There's a loose flagstone."

So she led us on, through a section of fake wall and into a dark tunnel, heading in what I believed to be a northwesterly direction toward the area of the Citadel which I had investigated somewhat on my previous journey this way. That was the day I had rescued her from Mask/Julia and taken her back to Amber to be a coatrack in *our* citadel for a while. The tunnel we entered was totally dark, but she conjured a darting dot, bright in its will-o'-the-wispiness, which preceded us through the gloom and the damp. The air was stale and the walls were cobwebby. The floor was of bare earth, save for an irregular patch of flagstones down its middle; there were occasional fetid puddles at either hand; and small dark creatures flashed past us—both on the ground and in the air—every now and then.

Actually, I did not need the light. Probably none of us did. I held to the Sign of the Logrus, which provided a magical way of seeing, granting a silvery, directionless illumination. I maintained it because it would also give me a warning against magical effects—which might include booby trap spells about the premises or, for that matter, a bit of treachery on Jasra's part. One effect of this seeing was to note that the Sign also hovered before Mandor, who, to my knowledge, has never been much into trust either. Something cloudy and vaguely Pattern-like also occupied a similar position vis-à-vis Jasra, completing the circle of wariness. And the light danced on before us.

We emerged from behind a stack of barrels into what appeared to be a very well-stocked wine cellar. Mandor paused after six paces and carefully removed a dusty bottle from the rack to our left. He drew a corner of his cloak across its label.

"Oh, my!" he observed.

"What is it?" Jasra inquired.

"If this is still good, I can build an unforgettable meal around it."

"Really? Better bring several to be sure then," she said. "These go back before my time—perhaps before Sharu's time even."

"Merlin, you bring these two," he said, passing me a pair. "Carefully, now."

He studied the rest of the rack before selecting two more, which he carried himself.

"I can see why this place is often under siege," he remarked to Jasra. "I'd have been inclined to have a go at it myself had I known about this part."

She reached out and squeezed his shoulder.

"There are easier ways to get what you want," she said, smiling.

"I'll remember that," he replied.

"I hope you'll hold me to it."

I cleared my throat.

She gave me a small frown, then turned away. We followed her out a low doorway and up a creaking flight of wooden stairs. We emerged in a large pantry and passed through it into an immense, deserted kitchen.

"Never a servant around when you need one," she remarked, casting her gaze about the room.

"We won't be needing one," Mandor said. "Find me a congenial dining area and I'll manage."

"Very well," she replied. "This way then."

She led us through the kitchen; then we passed through a series of rooms till we came to a stairway, which we mounted.

"Ice fields?" she asked. "Lava fields? Mountains? Or a storm-tossed sea?"

"If you are referring to a choice of views," Mandor responded, "give me the mountains."

He glanced at me, and I nodded.

She conducted us to a long, narrow room, where we unfastened a series of shutters to behold a dappled range of round-topped peaks. The room was cool and a bit dusty with shelves running the length of the near wall. These held books, writing implements, crystals, magnifying glasses, small pots of paint, a few simple magical instruments, a microscope, and a telescope. There was a trestle table at the room's middle, a bench on either side of it.

"How long will it take to prepare this?" Jasra asked.

"A minute or two," Mandor said.

"In that case," she said, "I would like to repair myself somewhat first. Perhaps you would also."

"Good idea," I said.

"Indeed," Mandor acknowledged.

She led us to what must have been guest quarters, not too far away, and left us with soap, towels, and water. We agreed to meet back in the narrow room in half an hour.

"Think she's planning something nasty?" I asked as I drew off my shirt.

"No," Mandor replied. "I like to flatter myself in thinking that she would not want to miss this meal. Nor, do I feel, would she want us to miss seeing her at her best, having so far seen her at something less than that. And a possibility of gossip, confidences..." He shook his head. "You may never have been able to trust her before and may never again. But this meal will be a Time-out if I'm any judge."

"I'll hold you to that," I said as I splashed and lathered.

Mandor gave me a crooked smile, then conjured a corkscrew and opened the bottles—"to let them breathe a little"—before he tended to himself. I trusted his judgment, but I hung on to the Sign of the Logrus in case I had to duel with a demon or avoid a falling wall.

No demons sprang; no masonry toppled. I entered the dining room behind Mandor and watched him transform it with a few words and gestures. The trestle table and the benches were replaced by a round table and comfortable-looking chairs——the chairs so situated as to provide a good view of the mountains from each. Jasra had not yet arrived, and I was carrying the two wine bottles whose respiration Mandor found most appealing. Before I could even set them down, Mandor conjured an embroidered tablecloth and napkins; delicate china, which looked as if it had been hand decorated by Miró; finely wrought silverware. He studied the tableau a moment, banished the silverware, summoned a set with a different pattern. He hummed as he paced and regarded the layout from various angles. Just as I moved forward to place the bottles on the table, he summoned a crystal bowl filled with floating flowers as a centerpiece. I took a step backward then as crystal goblets appeared.

I made a small growling noise, and he seemed to notice me for the first time in a while.

"Oh, set them there. Set them there, Merlin," he said, and an ebony tray appeared on the table to my left.

"We'd better check to see how the wine is holding up, before the lady arrives," he said then, pouring some of the ruby fluid into two of the goblets.

We sampled these, and he nodded. It was better than Bayle's. By far.

"Nothing wrong there," I said.

He rounded the table, went to the window, and looked out. I followed. Somewhere up in those mountains, I supposed, was Dave in his cave.

"I feel almost guilty," I said, "taking a break like this.

There are so many things I should be tending to—"

"Possibly even more than you suspect," he said. "Look upon this less as a break than a retrenchment. And you may learn something from the lady."

"True," I replied. "I wonder what, though."

He swirled his wine in his glass, took another small sip, and shrugged.

"She knows a lot. She may let something slip, or she may feel expansive at the attention and grow generous. Take things as they're dealt."

I took a drink, and I could be nasty and say my thumbs began to prickle. But it was actually the Logrus field that warned me of Jasra's approach along the hall outside. I did not remark upon it to Mandor, since I was certain he felt it, too. I simply turned toward the door, and he matched my movement.

She had on a low over-one-shoulder (the left) white dress, fastened at the shoulder with a diamond pin, and she wore a tiara, also of diamonds, which seemed almost to be radiating in the infrared range amidst her bright hair. She was smiling, and she smelled good, too. Involuntarily I felt myself standing straighter, and I glanced at my fingernails to be certain they were clean.

Mandor's bow was more courtly than mine, as usual. And I felt obliged to say something pleasant. So, "You're looking quite . . . elegant," I observed, letting my eyes wander to emphasize the point.

"It is seldom that I dine with two princes," she remarked.

"I'm Duke of the Western Marches," I said, "not a prince."

"I was referring to the House of Sawall," she replied.

"You've been doing homework," Mandor noted, "recently."

"I'd hate to commit a breach of protocol," she said.

"I seldom use my Chaos title at this end of things," I explained.

"A pity," she told me. "I find it more than a little . . . elegant. Aren't you about thirtieth in the line of succession?"

I laughed.

"Even that great a distance is an exaggeration," I said.

"No, Merle, she's about right," Mandor told me. "Give or take the usual few."

"How can that be?" I asked. "The last time I looked—"

He poured a goblet of wine and offered it to Jasra. She accepted it with a smile.

"You haven't looked recently," Mandor said. "There have been more deaths."

"Really? So many?"

"To Chaos," Jasra said, raising her goblet. "Long may she wave."

"To Chaos," Mandor replied, raising his.

"Chaos," I echoed, and we touched the goblets together and drank.

A number of delightful aromas came to me suddenly. Turning, I saw that the table now bore serving dishes. Jasra had turned at the same moment, and Mandor stepped forward and gestured, causing the chairs to slide back to accommodate us.

"Be seated, please, and let me serve you," he said.

We did, and it was more than good. Several minutes passed, and apart from compliments on the soup nothing was said. I did not want to be the first with a conversational gambit, though it had occurred to me that the others might feel the same way.

Finally, Jasra cleared her throat, and we both looked at her. I was surprised that she suddenly seemed slightly nervous.

"So, how are things in Chaos?" she asked.

"At the moment, chaotic," Mandor replied, "not to be facetious." He thought a moment, then sighed and added, "Politics."

She nodded slowly, as if considering asking him for the details he did not seem to care to divulge, then deciding against it. She turned toward me.

"Unfortunately, I'd no opportunity to sight-see while I was in Amber," she said. "From what you told me, though, life seems a bit chaotic there also."

I nodded.

"It's good that Dalt's gone," I said, "if that's what you mean. But he was never a real threat, just a nuisance. Speaking of whom——"

"Let's not," she interrupted, smiling sweetly. "What I really had in mind was anything else."

I smiled back.

"I forgot. You're not a fan of his," I said.

"It's not that," she responded. "The man has his uses. It's just"——she sighed——"politics," she finished.

Mandor laughed, and we joined him. Too bad I hadn't thought to use that line about Amber. Too late now.

"I bought a painting awhile back," I said, "by a lady named Polly Jackson. It's of a red '57 Chevy. I like it a lot. It's in storage in San Francisco right now. Rinaldo liked it, too."

She nodded, stared out the window.

"You two were always stopping in some gallery or other," she said. "Yes, he dragged me to a lot of them, too. I always thought he had good taste. No talent, but good taste."

"What do you mean, 'no talent'?"

"He's a very good draftsman, but his own paintings were never that interesting."

I had raised the subject for a very special reason, and this wasn't it. But I was fascinated by a side of Luke I'd never known, and I decided to pursue the matter.

"Paintings? I never knew he painted."

"He's tried any number of times, but he never shows them to anyone because they're not good enough."

"Then how do you know about them?"

"I'd check out his apartment periodically."

"When he wasn't around?"

"Of course. A mother's privilege."

I shuddered. I thought again of the burning woman down the Rabbit Hole. But I didn't want to say what I felt and spoil the flow now that I had her talking. I decided to return to my original trail.

"Was it in connection with any of this that he met Victor Melman?" I asked.

She studied me for a moment through narrowed eyes, then nodded and finished her soup.

"Yes," she said then, laying her spoon aside. "He took a few lessons from the man. He'd liked some of his paintings and looked him up. Perhaps he bought something of his, too. I don't know. But at some point he mentioned his own work and Victor asked to see it. He told Rinaldo he liked it and said he thought he could teach him a few things that might be of help."

She raised her goblet and sniffed it, sipped her wine, and stared at the mountains.

I was about to prompt her, hoping she'd go on, when she began to laugh. I waited it out.

"A real asshole," she said then. "But talented. Give him that."

"Uh, what do you mean?" I asked.

"After a time he began speaking of the development of personal power, using all those circumlocutions the half-enlightened love to play with. He wanted Rinaldo to know he was an occultist with something pretty strong going for him. Then he began to hint that he might be willing to pass it along to the right person."

She began laughing again. I chuckled myself, at the thought of that trained seal addressing the genuine article in such a fashion.

"It was because he realized Rinaldo was rich, of course," she continued. "Victor was, as usual, broke himself at the time. Rinaldo showed no interest, though, and simply stopped taking painting lessons from him shortly after that—as he felt he'd learned all he could from him. When he told me about it later, however, I realized that the man could be made into a perfect cat's-paw. I was certain such a person would do anything for a taste of real power."

I nodded.

"Then you and Rinaldo began the visitation business? You took turns clouding his mind and teaching him a few real things?"

"Real enough," she said, "though I handled most of his training. Rinaldo was usually too busy studying for exams. His point average was generally a little higher than yours, wasn't it?"

"He usually had pretty good grades," I conceded. "When you talk of empowering Melman and turning him into a tool, I can't help thinking about the reason: You were priming him to kill me, in a particularly colorful fashion."

She smiled.

"Yes," she said, "though probably not as you think. He knew of you, and he had been trained to play a part in your sacrifice. But he acted on his own the day he tried it, the day you killed him. He had been warned against such a solo action, and he paid the price. He was anxious to possess all of the powers he thought would come of it, rather than share them with another. As I said—an asshole."

I wanted to appear nonchalant, to keep her going. Continuing my meal seemed the best measure to indicate such poise. When I glanced down, however, I discovered that my soup bowl had vanished. I picked up a roll, broke it, was about to butter it when I saw that my hand was shaking. A moment later I realized that this was because I wanted to strangle her.

So I took a deep breath and let it go, had another drink of wine. An appetizer plate appeared before me, and a faint aroma of garlic and various tantalizing herbs told me to be calm. I nodded thanks to Mandor, and Jasra did the same. A moment later I buttered the roll.

Several mouthfuls after that, I said, "I confess that I do not understand. You say that Melman was to play a part in my ritual slaying—but only a part?"

She continued eating for a half minute or so, then found another smile.

"It was too appropriate an opportunity to pass up," she told me then, "when you broke up with Julia and she grew interested in the occult. I saw that I would have to get her together with Victor, to have him train her, to teach her a few simple effects, to capitalize on her unhappiness at your parting, to turn it into a full-blown hatred so intense that she would be willing to cut your throat when the time came for the sacrifice."

I choked on something which otherwise tasted wonderful.

A frosty crystal goblet of water appeared beside my right hand. I raised it and washed everything down. I took another sip.

"Ah, that reaction is worth something, anyhow," Jasra remarked. "You must admit that having someone you once loved as executioner adds spice to vengeance."

Out of the corner of my eye I saw that Mandor was nodding. And I, also, had to agree that she was right.

"I must acknowledge it as a well-conceived bit of revenge," I said. "Was Rinaldo in on this part?"

"No, you two had grown too chummy by then. I was afraid he'd warn you."

I thought about it for another minute or so, then, "What went wrong?" I asked.

"The one thing I'd never have guessed," she said. "Julia really had talent. A few lessons from Victor, and she was better than he was at anything he could do—except painting. Hell! Maybe she paints, too. I don't know. I'd dealt myself a wild card, and it played itself."

I shuddered. I thought of my conversation with the *ty'iga* at Arbor House, back when it was possessing Vinta Bayle. "Did Julia develop the abilities she sought?" it had asked me. I'd told it that I didn't know. I'd said that she'd never shown any signs. . . . And shortly thereafter I'd remembered our meeting in the supermarket parking lot and the dog she told to sit that may never have moved again. . . . I'd recalled this, but—

"And you never noticed any indication of her talent?" Jasra ventured.

"I wouldn't say that," I replied as I began to realize why things were as they were. "No, I wouldn't say that."

. . . Like that time at Baskin-Robbins when she caused a change of flavors 'twixt cone and lip. Or the storm she'd stayed dry in without an umbrella . . .

She frowned a puzzled frown and narrowed her eyes as she stared. "I don't understand," she said. "If you knew, you could have trained her yourself. She was in love with you. You would have been a formidable team."

I writhed internally. She was right, and I *had* suspected, had probably even known, but I'd been suppressing it. I'd possibly even triggered its onset myself, with that shadow walk, with my body energies. . . .

"It's tricky," I said, "and very personal."

"Oh. Matters of the heart are either very simple or totally inscrutable to me," she said. "There doesn't seem to be a middle ground."

"Let's stipulate simple," I told her. "We were already breaking up when I noticed the signs, and I'd no desire to call up the power in an ex-lover who might one day want to practice on me."

"Understandable," Jasra said. "Very. And ironic in the extreme."

"Indeed," Mandor observed, and with a gesture he caused more steaming dishes to appear before us. "Before you get carried away with a narrative of intrigue and the underside of the psyche, I'd like you to try a little breast of quail drowned in Mouton Rothschild, with a bit of wild rice and a few amusing asparagus tips."

I had driven her to her studies by showing her another layer of reality, I realized. And I had driven her away from me because I had not really trusted her enough to tell her the truth about myself. I suppose this said something about my capacity for love as well as trust. But I had felt this all along. There was something else. There was more. . . .

"This is delicious," Jasra announced.

"Thank you." He rose, rounded the table, and refilled her glass manually rather than use a levitation trick. As he did, I noticed that the fingers of his left hand lightly brushed her bare shoulder. He sloshed a little into my glass as an afterthought then and went back and sat down.

"Yes, excellent," I observed as I continued my quick introspect through the dark glass suddenly cleared.

I had felt something, had suspected something from the beginning, I knew now. Our shadow walk was only the most spectacular of a series of small, off-the-cuff tests I had occasionally thrown her way, hoping to catch her off guard, hoping to expose her as——what? Well, a potential sorceress. So?

I set my utensils aside and rubbed my eyes. It was near, though I'd been hiding it from myself for a long while. . . .

"Is something the matter, Merlin?" I heard Jasra asking.

"No. Just realized I was a little tired," I said. "Everything's fine."

A sorceress. Not just a potential sorceress. There had been the buried fear, I now understood, that she was behind the April 30 attempts on my life——and I had suppressed this and kept on caring for her. Why? Because I knew and did not care? Because she was my Nimue? Because I had cherished my possible destroyer and hidden evidence from myself? Because I'd not only loved unwisely but had had one big death wish following me around, grinning, and any time now I might cooperate with it to the utmost?

"I'll be okay," I said. "It's really nothing."

Did it mean that I was, as they say, my own worst enemy? I hoped not. I didn't really have time to go through therapy, not when my life depended on so many external things as well.

"A penny for your thoughts," Jasra said sweetly.

II

"They're priceless," I answered. "Like your jokes. I must applaud you. Not only did I know nothing of this at the time, but I didn't make any correct guesses when I did have a few facts to rub together. Is that what you wanted to hear?"

"Yes," she said.

"I'm pleased there came a point where things went wrong for you," I added.

She sighed, nodded, took a drink of wine.

"Yes, it came," she acknowledged. "I was hardly expecting any recoil from such a simple bit of business. I still find it hard to believe that there's that much irony running around loose in the world."

"If you want me to appreciate the whole thing, you're going to have to be a little more explicit," I suggested.

"I know. In a way, I hate trading that vaguely puzzled expression you're wearing for one of delight at my own discomfort. On the other hand, there may still be material able to distress you in some fresh fashion on the other side of it."

"Win a few, lose a few," I said. "I'm willing to bet there are still features of those days that puzzle you."

"Such as?" she asked.

"Such as why none of those April thirtieth attempts on my life succeeded."

"I assume Rinaldo sabotaged me some way, tipped you off."

"Wrong."

"What, then?"

"The *ty'iga*. She's under a compulsion to protect me. You might recall her from those days, as she resided in the body of Gail Lampron."

"Gail? Rinaldo's girlfriend? My son was dating a demon?"

"Let's not be prejudiced. He'd done a lot worse his freshman year."

She thought a moment, then nodded slowly.

"You've got a point there," she admitted. "I'd forgotten Carol. And you still have no idea—beyond what the thing admitted back in Amber—as to why this was going on?"

"I still don't know," I said.

"It casts that entire period in an even stranger light," she mused, "especially since our paths have crossed again. I wonder . . . ?"

"What?"

"Whether she was there to protect you or to thwart me—your bodyguard or my curse?"

"Hard to say, since the results came to the same thing."

"But she's apparently been hanging around you most recently, which would seem to indicate the former."

"Unless, of course, she knows something we don't."

"Such as?"

"Such as the possibility of a conflict developing between us again."

She smiled.

"You should have gone to law school," she said. "You're as devious as your relatives back in Amber. I can be truthful, though, in saying I have nothing planned that could be taken that way."

I shrugged.

"Just a thought. Please continue with Julia's story."

She proceeded to eat several mouthfuls. I kept her company, then discovered I could not stop eating. I glanced at Mandor, but he remained inscrutable. He'll never admit to magically enhancing a flavor or laying a compulsion on diners to clean their plates. Either way, we did finish the course before she spoke again. And I could hardly complain, considering.

"Julia studied with a variety of teachers after you two broke up," she began. "Once I hit upon my plan, it was a simple matter to cause them to do or say things which would disillusion or discourage her and set her to looking for someone else. It was not long before she came to Victor, who was already under our tutelage. I ordered him to sweeten her stay and to skip many of the usual preliminaries and to proceed to teaching her about an initiation I had chosen for her——"

"That being?" I interrupted. "There are an awful lot of initiations around, with a variety of specialized ends."

She smiled and nodded, breaking a roll and buttering it.

"I led her myself through a version of my own—the Way of the Broken Pattern."

"Sounds like something dangerous from the Amber end of Shadow."

"I can't fault your geography," she said. "But it is

not all that dangerous if you know what you're doing."

"It is my understanding," I said, "that those Shadow worlds which contain shadows of the Pattern can only hold imperfect versions and that this always represents a hazard."

"It is a hazard only if one does not know how to deal with it."

"And you had Julia walk this—Broken Pattern?"

"My knowledge of what you refer to as walking the Pattern is restricted to what my late husband and Rinaldo have told me of it. I believe that you follow the lines from a definite external beginning to an interior point where the power comes to you?"

"Yes," I acknowledged.

"In the Way of the Broken Pattern," she explained, "you enter through the imperfection and make your way to the center."

"How can you follow the lines if they are broken or imperfect? The real Pattern would destroy you if you departed the design."

"You don't follow the lines. You follow the interstices," she said.

"And when you emerge . . . wherever?" I asked.

"You bear the image of the Broken Pattern within you."

"And how do you conjure with this?"

"Through the imperfection. You summon the image, and it is like a dark well from which you draw power."

"And how do you travel among shadows?"

"Much as you do—as I understand it," she said. "But the break is always with you."

"The break? I don't understand."

"The flaw in the Pattern. It follows you through Shadow. It is always there beside you as you travel, sometimes as a hair-fine crack, sometimes a great chasm. It shifts about; it may appear suddenly, anywhere——a lapse in reality. This is the hazard for those of the Broken Way. To fall into it is the final death."

"It must lie within all of your spells then also, like a booby trap."

"All occupations have their hazards," she said. "Avoiding them is a part of the art."

"And this is the initiation through which you took Julia?"

"Yes."

"And Victor?"

"Yes."

"I understand what you are saying," I replied, "but you must realize that the broken Patterns are drawing their power from the real one."

"Of course. What of it? The image is almost as good as the real thing, if you're careful."

"For the record, how many useful images are there?"

"Useful?"

"They must degenerate from shadow to shadow. Where do you draw the line and say, 'Beyond this broken image I will not risk breaking my neck'?"

"I see what you mean. You can work with perhaps the first nine. I've never gone farther out. The first three are best. The circle of the next three is still manageable. The next three are a lot riskier."

"A bigger chasm for each?"

"Exactly."

"Why are you giving me all this esoteric information?"

"You're a higher-level initiate, so it doesn't matter. Also, there is nothing you could do to affect the setup. And finally, you need to know this to appreciate the rest of the story."

"All right," I said.

Mandor tapped the table, and small crystal cups of lemon sherbet appeared before us. We took the hint and cleared our palates before resuming the conversation. Outside, the shadows of clouds slid across the mountain slopes. A faint music drifted into the room from somewhere far back along the corridor. Clinking and scraping noises, sounding like distant pick-and-shovel work, came to us from somewhere outside—most likely at the Keep.

"So you initiated Julia," I prompted.

"Yes," Jasra said.

"What happened then?"

"She learned to summon the image of the Broken Pattern and use it for magical sight and the hanging of spells. She learned to draw raw power through the break in it. She learned to find her way through Shadow—"

"While minding the chasm?" I suggested.

"Just so, and she had a definite knack for it. She'd a flair for everything, as a matter of fact."

"I'm amazed that a mortal can traverse even a broken image of the Pattern and live."

"Only a few of them do," Jasra said. "The others step on a line or die mysteriously in the broken area. Ten percent make it, maybe. That isn't bad. Keeps it somewhat exclusive. Of them, only a few can learn the proper mantic skills to amount to anything as an adept."

"And you say that she was actually better than Victor, once she knew what she was about?"

"Yes. I didn't appreciate just how good until it was too late."

I felt her gaze upon me, as if she were checking for a reaction. I glanced up from my food and cocked an eyebrow.

"Yes," she went on, apparently satisfied. "You didn't know that was Julia you were stabbing back at the Fount, did you?"

"No," I admitted. "I'd been puzzled by Mask all along. I couldn't figure any motive for whatever was going on. The flowers were an especially odd touch, and I never really understood whether it was you or Mask behind the bit with the blue stones."

She laughed.

"The blue stones, and the cave they come from, are something of a family secret. The material is a kind of magical insulator, but two pieces—once together—maintain a link, by which a sensitive person can hold one and track the other—"

"Through Shadow?"

"Yes."

"Even if the person doing the tracking otherwise has no special abilities along these lines?"

"Even so," she said. "It's similar to following a shadow shifter while she's shifting. Anyone can do it if she's quick enough, sensitive enough. This just extends the practice a little further. It's following the shifter's trail rather than the shifter herself."

"Herself, herself . . . You trying to tell me it's been pulled on you?"

"That's right."

I looked up in time to see her blush.

"Julia?" I said.

"You begin to understand."

"No," I said. "Well, maybe a little. She was more talented than you'd anticipated. You already told me that. I get the impression she suckered you on something. But I'm not sure where or how."

"I brought her here," Jasra said, "to pick up some equipment I wanted to take along to the first circle of shadows near Amber. She did have a look at my workroom in the Keep at that time. And perhaps I was overly communicative then. But how was I to know she was making mental notes and probably formulating a plan? I'd felt her too cowed to entertain such thoughts. I must admit she was a pretty good actress."

"I read Victor's diary," I said. "I take it you were masked or hooded and possibly using some sort of voice-distorting spell the whole time?"

"Yes, but rather than awe Julia into submission, I think I roused her cupidity for things magical. I believe she picked up one of my tragoliths—the blue stones—at that time. The rest is history."

"Not for me."

A bowl of totally unfamiliar but delicious-smelling vegetables appeared, steaming, before me.

"Think about it."

"You took her to the Broken Pattern and conducted her initiation . . ." I began.

"Yes."

"The first chance she had," I continued, "she used the . . . tragolith to return to the Keep and learn some of your other secrets."

Jasra applauded softly, sampled the veggies, quickly ate more. Mandor smiled.

"Beyond that I draw a blank," I admitted.

"Be a good boy and eat your vegetables," she said.

I obeyed.

"Basing my conclusions concerning this remarkable tale solely upon my experience of human nature," Mandor suddenly observed, "I would say that she wished to test her talons as well as her wings. I'd guess she went back and challenged her former master—this Victor Melman—and fought a sorcerous duel with him."

I heard Jasra's intake of breath.

"Is that truly only a guess?" she asked.

"Truly," he answered, swirling his wine in his goblet.

"And I would guess further that you had once done something similar with your own teacher."

"What devil told you that?" she asked.

"It is only a guess that Sharu was your teacher—and perhaps more than that," he said. "But it would explain both your acquisition of this place and your ability to catch its former lord off guard. He might even have had a stray moment before his defeat for a wishful curse that the same fate attend you one day. And even if not, these things do sometimes have a way of running full circle with people in our trade."

She chuckled.

"The devil called Reason, then," she said, a note of admiration in her voice. "Yet you summon him by intuition, which makes it an art."

"It is good to know he still comes when I call. I take it Julia was surprised, however, by Victor's ability to thwart her."

"True. She did not anticipate that we tend to wrap apprentices in a layer or two of protection."

"Yet her own defenses obviously proved adequate—at least."

"True. Though that, of course, was tantamount to defeat. For she knew that I would learn of her rebellion and come soon to discipline her."

"Oh," I observed.

"Yes," she stated. "That is why she faked her death, which I must admit had me completely fooled for a long while."

I recalled the day I had visited Julia's apartment, found the body, been attacked by the beast. The corpse's face had been partly destroyed, the remaining features gory. But the lady had been the right size, and general resemblances had jibed. And she had been in the right place.

And then I had become the object of the lurking doglike creature's attention, which had distracted me more than a little from the minutiae of identity. By the time my struggle for my life was concluded, to the accompaniment of approaching sirens, I was more interested in flight than in further investigation. Thereafter, whenever I had returned in memory to that scene, it was Julia dead whom I beheld.

"Incredible," I said. "Then whose body was it that I found?"

"I've no idea," she replied. "It could have been one of her own shadow selves or some stranger off the street. Or a corpse stolen from the morgue. I've no way of knowing."

"It was wearing one of your blue stones."

"Yes. And its mate was on the collar of the beast you slew—and she opened the way for it to come through."

"Why? And why all that business with the Dweller on the Threshold as well?"

"Red herring of the first water. Victor thought I'd killed her, and I thought he had. He assumed I'd opened a way from the Keep and sent the hunting beast after her. I guessed he'd done it, and I was irritated he'd hidden his rapid development from me. Such things seldom bode well."

I nodded.

"You breed those creatures around here?"

"Yes," she replied, "and I show them, too, in several adjacent shadows. I've a number who've taken blue ribbons."

"I'll stick with pit bulls," I said. "They're a lot cuter and better behaved. So, she left a body and a hidden corridor to this place, and you thought Victor had done her in and was setting things up for a raid on your sanctum sanctorum."

"More or less."

"And he thought she'd become sufficiently dangerous to you—as with the corridor—that you'd killed her?"

"I don't really *know* that he ever found the corridor. It was fairly well hidden, as you learned. Either way, neither of us was aware of what she'd really done."

"That being?"

"She'd also planted a piece of tragolith on me. Later, after the initiation, she used its mate to track me through Shadow to Begma."

"Begma? What the hell were you doing there?"

"Nothing important," she said. "I mention it only to show her subtlety. She did not approach me at that time. I know of it, in fact, only because she told me of it later. She trailed me then from the perimeter of the Golden Circle back here to the Citadel. The rest you know."

"I'm not sure that I do."

"She had designs on this place. When she surprised me, I was surprised indeed. It was how I became a coatrack."

"And she took over here, donning a goalie mask for public relations purposes. She dwelled here for a time, building her powers, increasing her skills, hanging umbrellas on you—"

Jasra growled softly, and I remembered that her bite was worse. I hastened into a fresh area of speculation. "I still don't understand why she spied on me on occasion and sometimes threw flowers."

"Men are exasperating," Jasra said, raising her wineglass and draining it. "You've managed to understand everything but her motive."

"She was on a power trip," I said. "What's to understand past that? I even recall a long discussion we once had concerning power."

I heard Mandor chuckle. When I glanced at him, he looked away, shaking his head.

"Obviously," Jasra said, "she still cared about you. Most likely, a great deal. She was playing games with you. She wanted to rouse your curiosity. She wanted you to come after her, to find her, and she probably wanted to try her power against your own. She wanted to show you that she was worthy of all those things you'd denied her when you denied her your confidence."

"So you know about that, too."

"There were times when she spoke freely to me."

"So she cared for me so well that she sent men with tragoliths to track me to Amber and try to slay me. They almost succeeded, too."

Jasra looked away, coughed. Mandor immediately rose, circled the table, and refilled her goblet, interposing himself between us. At that time, while she was wholly blocked from my sight, I heard her say softly, "Well, not exactly. The assassins were... mine. Rinaldo wasn't around to warn you, as I'd guessed he was doing, and I thought I'd have one more shot at you."

"Oh," I observed. "Any more wandering around out there?"

"They were the last," she said.

"That's a comfort."

"I'm not apologizing. I'm just explaining, to clear our differences. Are you willing to cancel this account, too? I've got to know."

"I already said I was willing to call things even. It still goes. Where does Jurt come into all this? I don't understand how they got together and what they are to each other."

Mandor added a touch of wine to my own glass before returning to his seat. Jasra met my eyes.

"I don't know," she said. "She had no allies when we

fought. It had to have happened while I was rigid."

"Have you any idea where she and Jurt might have fled?"

"No."

I glanced at Mandor, and he shook his head.

"Neither have I," he said. "However, a peculiar thought has occurred to me."

"Yes?"

"Besides the fact that he has negotiated the Logrus and come into his powers, is it necessary for me to point out that Jurt—apart from his scars and missing pieces—bears you a strong resemblance?"

"Jurt? Me? You've got to be kidding!"

He glanced at Jasra.

"He *is* right," she said. "It's obvious that the two of you are related."

I put down my fork and shook my head.

"Preposterous," I said, more in self-defense than as a matter of certainty. "I never noticed."

Mandor shrugged, very slightly.

"You want a lecture on the psychology of denial?" Jasra asked me.

"No," I said. "I want a little while in which to let this sink in."

"Time for another course anyway," Mandor announced, and he gestured widely and it was delivered.

"Will you be in trouble with your relatives for having released me?" Jasra asked after a while.

"By the time they realize you're gone, I hope to have a good story ready," I answered.

"In other words, you will be," she said.

"Maybe a little."

"I'll see what I can do."

"What do you mean?"

"I don't like to be obligated to anyone," she said, "and

you've done more for me than I have for you in this. If I come upon a means of turning their wrath away from you, I'll employ it."

"What could you possibly have in mind?"

"Let it go at that. Sometimes it's better not to know too much."

"I don't like the sound of this at all."

"An excellent reason for changing the subject," she said. "How great an enemy has Jurt become?"

"To me?" I asked. "Or are you wondering whether he'll be returning here for second helpings?"

"Both, when you put it that way."

"I believe he'll kill me if he can," I said, glancing at Mandor, who nodded.

"I fear that is so," he stated.

"As for whether he'll be back here for more of whatever it is that he got," I continued, "you're the best judge. How close did he seem to be to possessing the full powers one might gain from that ritual at the Fountain?"

"It's hard to say exactly," she said, "as he was testing them under very chaotic conditions. Fifty percent, maybe. Just a guess. Will that satisfy him?"

"Perhaps. How dangerous does that make him?"

"Very. When he gets the full hang of things. Still, he must realize that this place will be heavily guarded—even against someone such as himself—should he decide to return. I suspect he'll stay away. Just Sharu—in his present circumstances—would be a formidable obstacle."

I went on eating.

"Julia will probably advise him not to try it," she continued, "familiar as she is with the place."

I nodded my acceptance of the notion. We would meet when we met. Nothing much I could do now to forestall it.

"Now may I ask you a question?" she said.

"Go ahead."

"The *ty'iga* . . ."

"Yes?"

"Even in the body of the duke Orkuz's daughter, I am certain that she did not just walk into the palace and wander on up to your apartments."

"Hardly," I replied. "She's with an official party."

"May I ask when the party arrived?"

"Earlier in the day," I answered. "I'm afraid, though, that I can't go into any detail as to——"

She flipped her well-ringed hand in a gesture of denial.

"I'm not interested in state secrets," she said, "though I know Nayda usually accompanies her father in a secretarial capacity."

"So?"

"Did her sister come along or did she stay home?"

"That would be Coral, wouldn't it?" I asked.

"Yes."

"She did," I replied.

"Thank you," she said, and returned to her food.

Damn. What was that about? Did she know something concerning Coral that I didn't? Something that might bear on her present, indeterminate state? If so, what might it cost me to find out?

"Why?" I said then.

"Just curious," she replied. "I knew the family in . . . happier times."

Jasra sentimental? Never. What then?

"Supposing the family had a problem or two?" I asked.

"Apart from Nayda's possession by the *ty'iga?*"

"Yes," I said.

"I would be sorry to hear that," she said. "What problem?"

"Just a little captivity thing involving Coral."

43

There came a small clatter as she dropped her fork and it fell upon her plate.

"What *are* you talking about?" she asked.

"A misplacement," I said.

"Of Coral? How? Where?"

"It depends partly on how much you really know about her," I explained.

"I'm fond of the girl. Don't toy with me. What happened?"

More than a little puzzling. But not the answer I was after.

"You knew her mother pretty well?"

"Kinta. I'd met her, at diplomatic functions. Lovely lady."

"Tell me about her father."

"Well, he's a member of the royal house, but of a branch not in the line of succession. Before he was prime minister, Orkuz was the Begman ambassador to Kashfa. His family was in residence with him, so naturally I saw him at any number of affairs——"

She looked up when she realized I was staring at her—through the Sign of the Logrus, across her Broken Pattern. Our eyes met, and she smiled.

"Oh. You did ask about her *father*," she said. Then she paused, and I nodded. "So there's truth in that rumor," she observed at last.

"You didn't really know?"

"There are so many rumors in the world, most of them impossible to check. How am I to know which of them hold truth? And why should I care?"

"You're right, of course," I said. "Nevertheless . . ."

"Another of the old boy's by-blows," she said. "Does anyone keep score? It's a wonder he had any time for affairs of state."

"Anyone's guess," I said.

"To be frank then, in addition to knowing the rumor I'd heard, there was indeed a family resemblance. I couldn't judge on that count, though, not being personally acquainted with most of the family. You're saying there's truth in it?"

"Yes."

"Just because of the resemblance, or is there something more?"

"Something more."

She smiled sweetly and retrieved her fork.

"I've always enjoyed that fairy-tale revelation which sees one rise in the world."

"I also," I said, and I resumed eating.

Mandor cleared his throat.

"It seems hardly fair," he said, "to tell only part of a story."

"You're right," I agreed.

Jasra returned her gaze to me and sighed.

"All right," she said, "I'll ask. How did you know for cer—Oh. Of course. The Pattern."

I nodded.

"Well, well, well. Little Coral, Mistress of the Pattern. This was a fairly recent occurrence?"

"Yes."

"I suppose she is off somewhere in Shadow now—celebrating."

"I wish I knew."

"What do you mean?"

"She's gone, but I don't know where. And it's the Pattern that did it to her."

"How?"

"Good question. I don't know."

Mandor cleared his throat.

"Merlin," he said, "perhaps there are some matters"—
he rotated his left hand—"that on reflection you may
wish—"

"No," I said. "Ordinarily discretion would rule—
perhaps even with you, my brother, as a Lord of Chaos.
And certainly in the case of Your Highness"—I nodded
to Jasra—"save that you are acquainted and may even
have a touch of affection for the lady." I decided against
laying it on too thick and quickly added, "Or at least no
malice toward her."

"As I said, I'm very fond of the girl," Jasra stated,
leaning forward.

"Good," I replied, "for I feel at least partly responsible
for what happened, even though I was duped in the matter. So I feel obliged to try to set things right. Only I
don't now how."

"What happened?" she asked.

"I was entertaining her when she expressed a desire to
see the Pattern. So I obliged her. On the way she asked
me questions about it. It seemed harmless conversation,
and I satisfied her curiosity. I was not familiar with the
rumors concerning her parentage, or I would have suspected something. As it was, when we got there, she set
foot upon the Pattern and commenced walking it."

Jasra sucked in her breath.

"It would destroy one not of the blood," she said.
"Correct?"

I nodded.

"Or even one of us," I said then, "if any of a number of
mistakes be made."

Jasra chuckled.

"Supposing her mother'd really been carrying on with a
footman or the cook?" she remarked.

"She's a wise daughter," I said. "At any rate, once one
begins the Pattern, one may not turn back. I was

obliged to instruct her as she went along. That, or be a very poor host and doubtless damage Begman-Amber relations."

"And spoil all sorts of delicate negotiations?" she asked, half-seriously.

I'd a feeling just then that she'd welcome a digression concerning the exact nature of the Begman visit, but I wasn't biting.

"You might say that," I said. "At any rate, she completed the Pattern, and then it took her away."

"My late husband told me that from its center one can command the Pattern to deliver one anywhere."

"True," I said, "but it was the nature of her command that was a bit unusual. She told the Pattern to send her wherever it wanted."

"I'm afraid I don't understand."

"Neither do I, but she did, and it did."

"You mean she just said, 'Send me wherever you want to send me,' and she was instantly dispatched for points unknown?"

"You've got it."

"That would seem to imply some sort of intelligence on the part of the Pattern."

"Unless, of course, it was responding to an unconscious desire on her part to visit some particular locale."

"True. I suppose there is that possibility. But have you no means of tracing her?"

"I'd a Trump I'd done of her. When I tried it, I reached her. She seemed pent in a dark place. Then we lost touch, and that's it."

"How long ago was this?"

"A matter of hours by my subjective reckoning," I said. "Is this place on anything near Amber time?"

"Close enough, I believe. Why didn't you try again?"

"I've been somewhat occupied ever since . Also, I've

been casting about for some alternate way of approaching this."

There came a clinking, rattling sound, and I smelled coffee.

"If you're asking whether I'll help you," Jasra said, "the answer is yes. Only I don't really know how to go about it. Perhaps if you were to try her Trump again—with me backing you—we might reach her."

"All right," I said, lowering my cup and fumbling forth the cards. "Let's give it a try."

"I will assist you also," Mandor stated, rising to his feet and coming to stand to my right.

Jasra came over and stood to my left. I held the Trump so that we all had a clear view.

"Let us begin," I said, and I moved forward with my mind.

III

A patch of light I had taken to be a stray sunbeam drifted from its position on the floor to a spot beside my coffee cup. It was ring-shaped, and I decided not to remark upon it since neither of the others seemed to take note of it.

I reached after Coral and found nothing. I felt Jasra and Mandor reaching also, and I tried again, joining forces with them. Harder.

Something?

Something . . . I recalled wondering what Vialle felt when she used the Trumps. It had to be something other than the visual cues with which the rest of us were familiar. It might be something like this.

Something.

What I felt was a sense of Coral's presence. I regarded her form upon the card, but it would not come alive. The card itself had grown perceptibly cooler, but it was not the same ice-edged chill I normally felt on achieving communication with one of the others. I tried harder. I felt Mandor and Jasra increasing their efforts also.

Then Coral's image on the card faded, but nothing came to replace it. I sensed her presence, however, as I regarded the void. The feeling came closest to that of attempting to make contact with someone who was asleep.

"I cannot tell whether it's simply a difficult place to reach," Mandor began, "or——"

"I believe she is under a spell," Jasra announced.

"That could account for a part of it," Mandor said.

"But only part," came a soft, familiar voice from near at hand. "There are awesome powers holding her, Dad. I've never seen anything like this before."

"The Ghostwheel is right," Mandor said. "I'm beginning to feel it."

"Yes," Jasra began, "there is something. . . ."

And suddenly the veil was pierced, and I beheld the slumped form of Coral, apparently unconscious, lying upon a dark surface in a very dark place, the only illumination coming from what seemed a circle of fire drawn about her. She couldn't have brought me through if she wanted to, and——

"Ghost, can you take me to her?" I asked.

Her image faded before he could reply, and I felt a cold draft. It was several seconds before I realized that it seemed to be blowing upon me from the now-icy card.

"I don't think so, I wouldn't want to, and it may be that there is no need," he answered. "The force that holds her has become aware of your interest and even now is reaching toward you. Is there some way you can turn off that Trump?"

I passed my hand across its face, which is usually sufficient. Nothing happened. The cold breeze even seemed to increase in intensity. I repeated the gesture along with a mental order. I began to feel whatever it was, focusing upon me.

Then the Sign of the Logrus fell upon the Trump, and the card was torn from my hand as I was cast backward, striking my shoulder against the edge of the door. Mandor lurched to his right as this occurred, catching hold of the table to steady himself. In my Logrus vision I had seen wild lines of light flash outward from the card before it fell away.

"Did that do the trick?" I called out.

"It broke the connection," Ghost replied.

"Thanks, Mandor," I said.

"But the power that was reaching for you through the Trump knows where you are now," Ghost said.

"What makes you privy to its awareness?" I inquired.

"It is a surmise, based upon the fact that it's still reaching for you. It is coming the long way round— across space—though. It could take as long as a quarter of a minute before it reaches you."

"Your use of the pronoun is a little indefinite," Jasra said. "Is it just Merlin that it wants? Or is it coming for all of us?"

"Uncertain. Merlin is the focus. I've no idea what it will do to you."

I lurched forward during this exchange and retrieved Coral's Trump.

"Can you protect us?" she asked.

"I've already begun transferring Merlin to a distant place. Shall I do this for you also?"

As I looked up from pocketing the Trump, I noted that the chamber had become something less than substantial—translucent, as if everything were made of colored glass.

"Please," the cathedral-window form of Jasra said softly.

"Yes," came my fading brother's faint echo.

Then I was passed through a fiery hoop into a place of darkness. I stumbled against a stone wall, felt my way along it. A quarter turn, a lighter area before me dotted with bright points . . .

"Ghost?" I asked.

No answer.

"I don't appreciate these interrupted conversations," I continued.

I moved forward until I came to what was obviously a cave mouth. A clear night sky hung before me, and when I stepped outside a cold wind rubbed up against me. I retreated several paces, shivering.

I had no idea where I might be. Not that it really mattered if it brought me a breathing spell. I reached through the Logrus Sign for a great distance before I located a heavy blanket. Wrapping it about myself, I sank to a seated position upon the cave's floor. Then I reached again. It was easier to find a stack of wood and no trick at all to ignite a portion of it. I'd also been looking forward to one more cup of coffee. I wondered. . . .

Why not? I reached again, and the bright circle rolled into view before me.

"Dad! Please stop!" came the offended voice. "I've gone to a lot of trouble to tuck you away in this obscure corner of Shadow. Too many sendings, though, and you'll call attention to yourself."

"Come on!" I said. "All I want is a cup of coffee."

"I'll get one for you. Just don't use your own powers for a while."

"Why won't your action draw just as much attention?"

"I'm using a roundabout route. There!"

A steaming mug of some dark stoneware stood on the floor of the cave near my right hand.

"Thanks," I said, taking it up and sniffing it. "What did you do with Jasra and Mandor?"

"I sent each of you off in a different direction amidst a horde of fake images flitting hither and yon. All you have to do now is lie low for a while. Let its attention subside."

"Whose attention? What's attention?"

"The power that has Coral. We don't want it to find us."

"Why not? I seem to recall your wondering earlier whether you were a god. What's for you to fear?"

"The real thing. It seems to be stronger than I am. On the other hand, I seem to be faster."

"That's something, anyway."

"Get a good night's sleep. I'll let you know in the morning whether it's still hunting you."

"Maybe I'll find out for myself."

"Don't go manifesting unless it's a matter of life or death."

"That wasn't what I meant. Supposing it finds me?"

"Do whatever seems appropriate."

"Why do I have a feeling you're keeping things from me?"

"I guess you're just suspicious by nature, Dad. It seems to run in your family. I've got to go now."

"Where?" I asked.

"Check on the others. Run a few errands. See to my personal development. Check my experiments. Things like that. Bye."

"What about Coral?"

But the circle of light which had hovered before me spun from brightness to dimness and vanished. An unarguable end to the conversation. Ghost was getting more and more like the rest of us—sneaky and misleading.

I sipped the coffee. Not as good as Mandor's, but acceptable. I began wondering where Jasra and Mandor had been sent. I decided against trying to reach them. In fact, it might not be a bad idea, I decided, to fortify my own position against magical intrusion.

I resummoned the Sign of the Logrus, which I had let slip while Ghost was transporting me. I used it to set wards at the cave mouth and about my situation within. Then I released it and took another sip. As I did, I realized that this coffee could not possibly keep me awake. I was coming off a nervous jag, and the weight of all my activities was suddenly heavy upon me. Two more sips, and I could hardly hold the cup. Another, and I noticed that each time I blinked my eyelids were closing a lot more easily than they opened.

I set the cup aside, drew my blanket more tightly about me, and found a relatively comfortable position on the stone floor, having become something of an expert on the activity back in the crystal cave. The flickering flames mustered shadow armies behind my eyelids. The fire popped like a clash of arms; the air smelled of pitch.

I went away. Sleep is perhaps the only among life's great pleasures which need not be of short duration. It filled me, and I drifted. How far and for how long, I cannot say.

Nor can I say what it was that roused me. I know only that I was somewhere else and the next moment I had returned. My position had changed slightly, my toes were cold, and I felt that I was no longer alone. I kept my eyes closed, and did not alter my breathing pattern. It could be that Ghost had simply decided to look in on me. It could also be that something was testing my wards.

I raised my eyelids but the smallest distance, peering outward and upward through a screen of eyelashes. A small misshaped figure stood outside the cave mouth, the fire's remaining glow faintly illuminating his strangely familiar face. There was something of myself in those features and something of my father.

"Merlin," he said softly. "Come awake now. You've places to go and things to do."

I opened my eyes wide and stared. He fitted a certain description. . . . Frakir throbbed, and I stroked her still.

"Dworkin . . . ?" I said.

He chuckled.

"You've named me," he replied.

He paced, from one side of the cave mouth to the other, occasionally pausing to extend a hand partway toward me. Each time he hesitated and drew it back.

"What is it?" I asked. "What's the matter? Why are you here?"

"I've come to fetch you back to the journey you abandoned."

"And what journey might that be?"

"Your search for the lady somewhere astray who walked the Pattern t'other day."

"Coral? You know where she is?"

He raised his hand, lowered it, gnashed his teeth.

"Coral? Is that her name? Let me in. We must discuss her."

"We seem to be talking just fine the way we are."

"Have you no respect for an ancestor?"

"I do. But I also have a shapeshifting brother who'd like to mount my head and hang it on the wall of his den. And he might just be able to do it real quick if I give him half a chance." I sat up and rubbed my eyes, my wits finishing the job of reassembling themselves. "So where's Coral?"

"Come. I will show you the way," he said, reaching forward. This time his hand passed my ward and was immediately outlined in fire. He did not seem to notice. His eyes were a pair of dark stars, drawing me to my feet, pulling me toward him. His hand began to melt. The flesh ran and dripped away like wax. There were no bones within, but rather an odd geometry——as if someone had sketched a hand quickly in a three-dimensional medium, then molded some fleshlike cover for it. "Take my hand."

I found myself raising my hand against my will, reaching toward the fingerlike curves, the swirls of the knuckles. He chuckled again. I could feel the force that drew me. I wondered what would happen if I took hold of that strange hand in a special way.

So I summoned the Sign of the Logrus and sent it on ahead to do my handclasping for me.

This may not have been my best choice of actions. I was momentarily blinded by the brilliant, sizzling flash that followed. When my vision cleared, I saw that Dworkin was gone. A quick check showed that my wards still held. I perked up the fire with a short, simple spell, noted that my coffee cup was half full, and warmed its tepid contents with an abbreviated version of the same rendering. I reshrouded myself then, settled, and sipped. Analyze as I might, I couldn't figure what had just happened.

I knew of no one who had seen the half-mad demiurge in years, though according to my father's tale, Dworkin's mind should have been largely mended when Oberon repaired the Pattern. If it had really been Jurt, seeking to trick his way into my presence and finish me off, it was an odd choice of form for him to assume. Come to think of it, I wasn't at all certain that Jurt even knew what Dworkin looked like. I debated the wisdom of calling for Ghostwheel to solicit an inhuman opinion on the matter. Before I could decide, however, the stars beyond the cave mouth were occulted by another figure, much larger than Dworkin's—heroically proportioned even.

A single step brought it within range of the firelight, and I spilled coffee when I beheld that face. We had never met, but I had seen his likeness in many places in Castle Amber.

"I understand that Oberon died in redrawing the Pattern," I said.

"Were you present at the time?" he asked.

"No," I replied, "but coming as you do, on the heels of a rather bizarre apparition of Dworkin, you must excuse my suspicions as to your bona fides."

"Oh, that was a fake you encountered. I'm the real thing."

"What was it then that I saw?"

"It was the astral form of a practical joker—a sorcerer named Jolos from the fourth circle of Shadow."

"Oh," I responded. "And how am I to know you're not the projection of someone named Jalas from the fifth?"

"I can recite the entire genealogy of the royal House of Amber."

"So can any good scribe back home."

"I'll throw in the illegitimates."

"How many were there, anyway?"

"Forty-seven, that I know of."

"Aw, come on! How'd you manage?"

"Different time streams," he said, smiling.

"If you survived the reconstruction of the Pattern, how come you didn't return to Amber and continue your reign?" I asked. "Why'd you let Random get crowned and muddy the picture even further?"

He laughed.

"But I didn't survive it," he said. "I was destroyed in the process. I am a ghost, returned to solicit a living champion for Amber against the rising power of the Logrus."

"Granted, *arguendo*, that you are what you say you are," I replied, "you're still in the wrong neighborhood, sir. I am an initiate of the Logrus and a son of Chaos."

"You are also an initiate of the Pattern and a son of Amber," the magnificent figure answered.

"True," I said, "and all the more reason for me not to choose sides."

"There comes a time when a man must choose," he stated, "and that time is now. Which side are you on?"

"Even if I believed that you are what you say, I do not feel obliged to make such a choice," I said. "And there is a tradition in the Courts that Dworkin himself was an initiate of the Logrus. If that is true, I'm only following in the footsteps of a venerable ancestor."

"But he renounced Chaos when he founded Amber."

I shrugged.

"Good thing I haven't founded anything," I said. "If there is something specific that you want of me, tell me what it is, give me a good reason for doing it and maybe I'll cooperate."

He extended his hand.

"Come with me, and I will set your feet upon the new Pattern you must follow, in a game to be played out between the Powers."

"I still don't understand you, but I am certain that the real Oberon would not be stopped by these simple wards. You come to me and clasp my hand, and I will be glad to accompany you and take a look at whatever it is you want me to see."

He drew himself up to an even greater height.

"You would test me?" he asked.

"Yes."

"As a man, it would hardly have troubled me," he

stated. "But being formed out of this spiritual crap now, I don't know. I'd rather not take the chance."

"In that case, I must echo your sentiment with respect to your own proposal."

"Grandson," he said levelly, a ruddy light entering his eyes, "even dead, none of my spawn may address me so. I come for thee now in a less than friendly fashion. I come for thee now, and this journey shall I hale thee amid fires."

I took a step backward as he advanced.

"No need to take it personally. . ." I began.

I shaded my eyes as he hit my wards, and the flashbulb effect began. Squinting through it, I saw something of a repetition of the flensing of Dworkin's flesh by fire. Oberon became transparent in places; other places he melted. Within him, through him, as the outward semblance of the kind passed away, I saw the swirls and curves, the straits and channels—black-lined, geometrizing abstractly inside the general outline of a large and noble figure. Unlike Dworkin, however, the image did not fade. Having passed my wards, its movement slowed, it continued toward me nevertheless, reaching. Whatever its true nature, it was one of the most frightening things I had ever encountered. I continued to back away, raising my hands, and I called again upon the Logrus.

The Sign of the Logrus occurred between us. The abstract version of Oberon continued to reach, scribbled spirit hands encountering the writhing limbs of Chaos.

I was not reaching through the Logrus's image to manipulate it against that apparition. I felt an unusual dread of the thing, even at our distance. What I did was more on the order of thrusting the Sign against the image of the king. Then I dived past them both, out the cave mouth, and I rolled, scrabbling for handholds and toeholds when I struck a slope, coming up hard against a boulder and hugging it as the cave erupted with the noise and flash of an ammo dump that had taken a hit.

I lay there shuddering, my eyes squeezed shut, for perhaps half a minute. Any second, I felt, and something would be on my ass—unless, perhaps, I crouched perfectly still and tried hard to look like another rock. . . .

The silence was profound, and when I opened my eyes, the light had vanished and the shape of the cave mouth was unaltered. I rose slowly to my feet, advanced even more slowly. The Sign of the Logrus had departed, and for reasons I did not understand I was loath to call it back. When I looked within the cave, there were no signs that anything at all had occurred, save for the fact that my wards were blown.

I stepped inside. The blanket still lay where it had fallen. I put out a hand and touched the wall. Cold stone. That blast must have taken place at some other level than the immediate. My small fire was still flickering feebly. I recalled it yet again to life. But the only thing I saw in its glow which I had not seen previously was my coffee cup, broken where it had fallen.

I let my hand remain upon the wall. I leaned. After a time, there came an uncontrollable tightening of my diaphragm. I began laughing. I am not sure why. The weight of everything which had transpired since April 30 was upon me. It just happened that laughter had edged out the alternative of beating my breast and howling.

I thought I knew who all the players were in this complex game. Luke and Jasra seemed to be on my side now, along with my brother Mandor, who'd always looked out for me. My mad brother Jurt wanted me dead, and he was now allied with my old lover Julia, who didn't seem too kindly disposed toward me either. There was the *ty'iga*—an overprotective demon inhabiting the body of

Coral's sister, Nayda, whom I'd left sleeping in the midst of a spell back in Amber. There was the mercenary Dalt —who, now I thought of it, was also my uncle—who'd made off with Luke for points and purposes unknown after kicking Luke's ass in Arden with two armies watching. He had nasty designs on Amber but lacked the military muscle to provide more than occasional guerrilla-style annoyance. And then there was Ghostwheel, my cybernetic Trump dealer and minor-league mechanical demigod, who seemed to have evolved from rash and manic to rational and paranoid—and I wasn't at all sure where he was headed from here, but at least he was showing some filial respect mixed in with the current cowardice.

And that had been pretty much it.

But these latest manifestations seemed evidence that there was something else at play here also, something that wanted to drag me off in yet another direction. I had Ghost's testimony that it was strong. I had no idea what it really represented. And I had no desire to trust it. This made for an awkward relationship.

"Hey, kid!" came a familiar voice from down the slope. "You're a hard man to find. You don't stay put."

I turned quickly, moved forward, stared downward.

A lone figure was toiling up the slope. A big man. Something flashed in the vicinity of his throat. It was too dark to make out his features.

I retreated several paces, commencing the spell which would restore my blasted wards.

"Hey! Don't run off!" he called. "I've got to talk to you."

The wards fell into place, and I drew my blade and held it, point lowered, at my right, entirely out of sight from the cave mouth when I turned my body. I ordered Frakir to hang invisible from my left hand also. The

ROGER ZELAZNY

second figure had been stronger than the first, to make it past my wards. If this third one should prove stronger than the second, I was going to need everything I could muster.

"Yeah?" I called out. "Who are you and what do you want?"

"Hell!" I heard it say. "I'm no one in particular. Just your old man. I need some help, and I like to keep things in the family."

I had to admit, when it reached the area of firelight, that it was a very good imitation of Prince Corwin of Amber, my father, complete with black cloak, boots, and trousers, gray shirt, silver studs, and buckle—and even a silver rose—and he was smiling that same quirky sort of smile the real Corwin had sometimes worn on telling me his story, long ago. . . . I felt a kind of wrenching in my guts at the sight. I'd wanted to get to know him better, but he'd disappeared, and I'd never been able to find him again. Now, for this thing—whatever it was—to pull this impersonation . . . I was more than a little irritated at such a patent attempt to manipulate my feelings.

"The first fake was Dworkin," I said, "and the second was Oberon. You're climbing right down the family tree, aren't you?"

He squinted and cocked his head in puzzlement as he advanced, another realistic mannerism.

"I don't know what you're talking about, Merlin," he responded. "I—"

Then it entered the warded area and jerked as if touching a hot wire.

"Holy shit!" it said. "You don't trust anybody, do you?"

"Family tradition," I replied, "backed up by recent experience."

I was puzzled, though, that the encounter had not involved more pyrotechnics. Also, I wondered why the thing's transformation into scrollwork had not yet commenced.

With another oath, it swirled its cloak to the left, wrapping it about its arm; its right hand crossed toward an excellent facsimile of my father's scabbard. A silver-chased blade sighed as it arced upward, then fell toward the eye of the ward. When they met, the sparks rose in a foot-high splash and the blade hissed as if it had been heated and were now being quenched in water. The design on the blade flared, and the sparks leaped again—this time as high as a man—and in that instant I felt the ward break.

Then it entered, and I turned my body, swinging my blade. But the blade that looked like Grayswandir fell and rose again, in a tightening circle, drawing my own weapon's point to the right and sliding straight in toward my breast. I did a simple parry in quarte, but he slipped under it and was still coming in from the outside. I parried sixte, but he wasn't there. His movement had been only a feint. He was back inside and coming in low now. I reversed myself and parried again as he slid his entire body in to my right, dropping his blade's point, reversing his grip, fanning my face with his left hand.

Too late I saw the right hand rising as the left slid behind my head. Grayswandir's pommel was headed straight for my jaw.

"You're really. . ." I began, and then it connected.

The last thing I remember seeing was the silver rose.

That's life: Trust and you're betrayed; don't trust and you betray yourself. Like most moral paradoxes, it places you in an untenable position. And it was too late for my normal solution. I couldn't walk away from the game.

I woke in a place of darkness. I woke wondering and wary. As usual when wondering and wary, I lay perfectly still and let my breathing continue its natural rhythm. And I listened.

Not a sound.

I opened my eyes slightly.

Disconcerting patterns. I closed them again.

I felt with my body for vibrations within the rocky surface upon which I was sprawled.

No vibes.

I opened my eyes entirely, fought back an impulse to close them. I raised myself onto my elbows, then gathered my knees beneath me, straightened my back, turned my head. Fascinating. I hadn't been this disoriented since I'd gone drinking with Luke and the Cheshire Cat.

There was no color anywhere about me. Everything was black, white, or some shade of gray. It was as if I had entered a photographic negative. What I presumed to be a sun hung like a black hole several diameters above the horizon to my right. The sky was a very dark gray, and ebon clouds moved slowly within it. My skin was the color of ink. The rocky ground beneath me and about me shone an almost translucent bone-white, however. I rose slowly to my feet, turning. Yes. The ground seemed to glow, the sky was dark, and I was a shadow between them. I did not like the feeling at all.

The air was dry, cool. I stood in the foothills to an albino mountain range, so stark in appearance as to rouse comparison with the Antarctic. These stretched off and up to my left. To the right—low and rolling—toward what I guessed to be a morning sun, lay a black plain. Desert? I had to raise my hand and "shade" against its . . what? Antiglow?

"Shit!" I tried saying, and I noticed two things immediately.

The first was that my word remained unvoiced. The second was that my jaw hurt where my father or his simulacrum had slugged me.

I repeated my silent observation and withdrew my Trumps. All bets were off when it came to messing with sendings. I shuffled out the Trump for the Ghostwheel and focused my attention upon it.

Nothing. It was completely dead to me. But, then, it was Ghost who'd told me to lie low, and maybe he was simply refusing to entertain my call. I thumbed through the others. I paused at Flora's. She was usually willing to help me out of a tight spot. I studied that lovely face, sent out my call to it. . . .

Not a golden curl stirred. Not a degree's drop in temperature. The card remained a card. I tried harder, even muttering an enhancement spell. But there was nobody home.

Mandor, then. I spent several minutes on his card with the same result. I tried Random's. Ditto. Benedict's, Julian's. No and no. I tried for Fiona, Luke, and Bill Roth. Three more negatives. I even pulled a couple of the Trumps of Doom, but I couldn't reach the Sphinx either, or a building of bones atop a green glass mountain.

I squared them, cased them, and put them away. It was the first time I had encountered a phenomenon of this sort since the Crystal Cave. Trumps can be blocked in any of a number of ways, however, and so far as I was concerned, the matter was, at the moment, academic. I was more concerned about removing myself to a more congenial environment. I could save the research for some future bit of leisure.

I began walking. My footsteps were soundless. When I kicked a pebble and it bounced along before me, I could detect nothing of sound to its passage.

White to the left of me, black to the right. Mountains or desert. I turned left, walking. Nothing else in motion that I could see except for the black, black clouds. To the lee side of every outcrop a near-blinding area of enhanced brightness: crazy shadows across a crazy land.

Turn left again. Three paces, then round the boulder. Upward. Over the ridge. Turn downhill. Turn right. Soon a streak of red amid rocks to the left . . .

Nope. Next time then . . .

Brief twinge in the frontal sinus. No red. Move on.

Crevice to the right, next turn . . .

I massaged my temples when they began to ache as no crevice was delivered. My breath came heavy, and I felt moisture upon my brow.

Textures of gray to green and brittle flowers, slate-blue, low on the next talus slope . . .

A small pain in my neck. No flowers. No gray. No green.

Then let the clouds part and the darkness pour down from the sun . . .

Nothing.

. . . and a sound of running water from a small stream, next gully.

I had to halt. My head was throbbing; my hands were shaking. I reached out and touched the rock wall to my left. It felt solid enough. Rampant reality. Why was it treading all over me?

And how had I gotten here?

And where was here?

I relaxed. I slowed my breathing and adjusted my energies. The pains in my head subsided, ebbed, were gone.

Again I began walking.

Birdsong and gentle breeze . . . Flower in a crannied nook .

No. And the first twinge of returning resistance . . .

What sort of spell might I be under, that I had lost my power to walk in Shadow? I had never understood it to be something that could be taken away.

"It's not funny," I tried saying. "Whoever you are, whatever you are, how did you do it? What do you want? Where are you?"

Again I heard nothing; least of all an answer.

"I don't know how you did it. Or why," I mouthed, and thought. "I don't feel as if I'm under a spell. But I must be here for a reason. Get on with your business. Tell me what you want."

Nada.

I walked on, continuing in a halfhearted fashion my attempts to shift away through Shadow. As I did, I pondered my situation. I'd a feeling there was something elementary that I was overlooking in this entire business.

. . . And a small red flower behind a rock, next turn.

I made the turn, and there was the small red flower I had half-consciously conjured. I rushed toward it to touch it, to confirm that the universe was a benign, essentially Merlin-loving place.

I stumbled in my rush, kicking up a cloud of dust. I caught myself, raised myself, looked about. I must have searched for the next ten or fifteen minutes, but I could not locate the flower. Finally, I cursed and turned away. No one likes to be a butt of the universe's jokes.

On a sudden inspiration I sought through all my pockets, should I have even a chip of the blue stones upon my person. Its odd vibrational abilities might just somehow conduct me through Shadow back toward its source. But no. Not even a speck of blue dust remained. They all were in my father's tomb, and that was it. It would have been too easy an out for me, I guess.

What was I missing?

A fake Dworkin, a fake Oberon, and a man who'd claimed to be my father all had wanted to conduct me to some strange place——to compete in some sort of struggle between the Powers, the Oberon figure had indicated, whatever that meant. The Corwin figure had apparently succeeded, I reflected as I rubbed my jaw. Only what sort of game was it? And what were the Powers?

The Oberon thing had said something about my choosing between Amber and Chaos. But, then, it had lied about other things during the same conversation. The devil with both of them! I didn't ask to get involved in their power game. I had enough problems of my own. I didn't even care to learn the rules to whatever was going on.

I kicked a small white stone, watched it roll away. This didn't feel like something of Jurt's or Julia's doing. It seemed either a new factor or an old one which had transformed itself considerably. Where had it first seemed to enter the picture? I guessed it had something to do with the force which had come rushing after me on our attempt to reach Coral. I could only assume that it had located me and this was the result. But what might it be? It would first, I supposed, be necessary that I learn where Coral lay in her circle of fire. Something in that place, I presumed, was behind my current situation. Where then? She had asked the Pattern to send her where she ought to go. . . . I had no way now of asking the Pattern where that might be——and no way at the moment of walking it, to have it send me after her.

It was time, therefore, to resign the game and employ different means to solve the problem. My Trumps having blown a circuit and my ability to traverse Shadow having encountered a mysterious blockage, I decided it was time to up the power factor by an order of magnitude in my favor. I would summon the Sign of the Logrus and continue my shadow walk, backing every step that I took with the power of Chaos.

Frakir cut into my wrist. I sought about quickly after any approaching menaces, but I saw nothing. I remained wary for several minutes longer, exploring the vicinity. Nothing occurred, though, and Frakir grew still.

It was hardly the first time her alarm system had been improperly cued—whether by some stray astral current or some odd thought of my own. But in a place like this, one could not afford to take chances. The highest stand of stone in the vicinity stood at about fifteen to twenty meters, perhaps a hundred paces uphill, to my left. I made my way over to it and commenced climbing.

When I finally reached its chalky peak, I commanded a view over a great distance in every direction. I did not behold another living thing in this strange silent yin-yang universe.

So I decided that it had indeed been a false alarm, and I climbed back down. I reached once again to summon the Logrus and Frakir practically behanded me. Hell. I ignored her, and I sent out my call.

The Sign of the Logrus rose and rushed toward me. It danced like a butterfly, hit like a truck. My newsreel world went away, black and white to black.

IV

Recovering.

My head ached, and there was dirt in my mouth. I was sprawled face down. Memory made its way home through the traffic, and I opened my eyes. Still black and white and gray all about. I spit sand, rubbed my eyes, blinked. The Logrus Sign was not present, and I could not account for my recent experience with it.

I sat up and hugged my knees. I seemed to be stranded, all of my extramundane means of travel and communication blocked. I couldn't think of anything to do other than get up, pick a direction, and start walking.

I shuddered. Where would that take me? Just through more of the same—more of this monotonous landscape?

There came a soft sound, as of a throat being gently cleared.

I was on my feet in an instant, having inspected every direction on the way up.

Who's there? I inquired, having given up on articulation.

I seemed to hear it again, very near at hand.

Then, *I've a message for you*, something seemed to say within my head.

What? Where are you? Message? I tried asking.

Excuse me, came the muffled voice, *but I'm new at this business. To take things in order, I am where I've always been—on your wrist—and when the Logrus blasted through here, it enhanced me additionally, so that I could deliver the message.*

Frakir?

Yes. My first enhancement, that day you bore me through the Logrus, involved sensitivity to danger, mobility, combat reflexes, and a limited sentience. This time the Logrus added direct mental communication and expanded my awareness to the point where I could deliver messages.

Why?

It was in a hurry, could stay in this place for only an instant, and this was the only way for it to let you know what is going on.

I didn't realize the Logrus was sentient.

Something like a chuckle followed.

Then, *It is hard to classify an intelligence of that order, and I suppose it doesn't really have much to say most of the time*, came Frakir's reply. *Its energies are mainly expended in other areas.*

Well, why did it come through here and blitz me?

Unintentional. It was a by-product of my enhancement, once it saw that I was the only means of reaching you with more than a few words or images.

Why was its time here so limited? I asked.

It is the nature of this land, which lies between the shadows, that it be mainly inaccessible both to the Pattern and the Logrus.

A sort of demilitarized zone?

No, it is not a matter of truce. It is simply that it is extremely difficult for either of them to manifest here at all. This is why the place is pretty much unchanging.

This is a place they can't reach?

That's about the size of it.

How come I never heard of it before?

Probably because no one else can reach it too readily either.

So what's the message?

Basically, that you not try calling upon the Logrus again while you're here. The place represents such a distorting medium that there's no assurance how any projected energy might manifest outside some convenient vessel. It could be dangerous for you.

I massaged my throbbing temples. At least it got my mind off my sore jaw.

All right, I agreed. *Any hints as to what I'm supposed to be doing here?*

Yes, this is a trial. Of what, I can't say.

Do I have a choice?

What do you mean?

May I refuse to participate?

I suppose. But then I don't know how you get out of here.

So I do get released from this place at the end, if I play?

If you're still living, yes. Even if you're not, I'd imagine.

Then I really have no choice.

There will be a choice.

When?

Somewhere along the way. I don't know where.

Why don't you just repeat all of your instructions to me?

Can't. I don't know what all is here. It will surface only in response to a question or a situation.

Will any of this interfere with your strangling function?

It shouldn't.

That's something, anyway. Very well. Have you any idea what I'm supposed to do next?

Yes. You should begin climbing the highest hill to your left.

Which— Okay, I guess that's the one, I decided, my gaze settling upon a broken fang of blazing white stone.

And so I walked toward it, up a gradually steepening slope. The black sun mounted higher into the grayness. The eerie silence continued.

Uh, do you know exactly what we will find whenever we get to wherever we're going? I tried to say in Frakir's direction.

I am certain that the information is present, came the reply, *but I do not believe that it will be available until we reach the appropriate locale.*

I hope you're right.

Me, too.

The way continued to steepen. While I had no way to measure the time exactly, it seemed that more than an hour passed before I left the foothills and was climbing the white mountain itself. While I observed no footprints nor saw any other sign of life, I did, on several occasions, encounter long stretches of natural-seeming trail, shelflike, leading up that high bleached face. Several more hours must have passed as I negotiated this, the dark sun riding to mid-heaven and beginning its descent toward a west that lay beyond this peak. It was annoying not to be able to curse aloud.

How can I be sure we're on the proper side of the thing? Or heading for the right area? I asked.

You're still going in the proper direction, Frakir answered.

But you don't know how much farther it'll be?

Nope. I'll know when I see it, though.

The sun is going to slip behind the mountain fairly soon. Will you be able to see it to know it then?

I believe the sky actually brightens here when the sun goes

73

away. Negative space is funny that way. Whatever, something is always bright here and something is always dark. There'll be the wherewithal for detection.

Any idea what we're actually doing?

One of those damned quest-things, I think.

Vision? Or practical?

It was my understanding that they all partake of both, though I feel this one is heavily weighted toward the latter. On the other wrist, anything you encounter between shadows is likely to partake of the allegorical, the emblematic—all that crap people bury in the nonconscious parts of their beings.

In other words, you don't know either.

Not for sure, but I make my living as a sensitive guesser.

I reached high, grabbed handholds, drew myself up to another ledge. I followed it for a time, climbed again.

At length the sun went away, and it made no difference in my ability to see. Darkness and light changed places.

I scaled a five- or six-meter irregularity and halted when I finally got a look into the recessed area it rose to. There was an opening in the face of the mountain to its rear. I hesitated to label it a cave because it appeared artificial. It looked as if it had been carved in the form of an arch, and it was big enough to ride through on horseback.

What do you know, Frakir commented, twitching once upon my wrist. *This is it.*

What? I asked.

The first station, she replied. *You stop here and go through a bit of business before moving on.*

That being?

It's easier just to go and look.

I hauled myself up over the edge, got to my feet, and walked forward. The big entranceway was filled with that sourceless light. I hesitated on the threshold, peered within.

It looked to be a generic chapel. There was a small altar, a pair of candles upon it sporting flickering coronas of blackness. There were stone benches carved along the walls. I counted five doorways apart from the one by which I stood: three in the wall across from me; one in that to the right; another to the left. Two piles of battle gear lay in the middle of the room. There were no symbols of whatever religion might be represented.

I entered.

What am I supposed to do here? I asked.

You are supposed to sit vigil, guarding your armor overnight.

Aw, come on, I said, moving forward to inspect the stuff. *What's the point?*

That's not a part of the information I've been given.

I picked up a fancy white breastplate which would have made me look like Sir Galahad. Just my size, it seemed. I shook my head and lowered the piece. I moved over to the next pile and picked up a very odd-looking gray gauntlet. I dropped it immediately and rooted through the rest of the stuff. More of the same. Contoured to fit me, also. Only—

What is the matter, Merlin?

The white stuff, I said, *looks as if it would fit me right now. The other armor appears to be of a sort used in the Courts. It looks as if it would fit me just right when I'm shifted into my Chaos form. So either set would probably do for me, depending on circumstances. I can use only one outfit at a time, though. Which am I supposed to guard?*

I believe that's the crux of the matter. I think you're supposed to choose.

Of course! I snapped my fingers, heard nothing. *How slow of me, that I need to have things explained by my strangling cord!*

I dropped to my knees, swept both sets or armor and weapons together into one nasty-looking heap.

If I have to guard them, I said, *I'll guard both sets. I don't care to take sides.*

I've a feeling something isn' going to like that, Frakir answered.

I stepped back and regarded the pile.

Tell me about this vigil business again, I said. *What all's involved?*

You're supposed to sit up all night and guard it.

Against what?

Against anything that tries to misappropriate it, I guess. The powers of Order—

—or Chaos

Yeah, I see what you mean. Heaped up together that way, anything might come by to grab off a piece.

I seated myself on the bench along the rear wall, between two doorways. It was good to rest for a bit after my long climb. But something in my mind kept grinding away. Then, after a time, *What's in it for me?* I asked.

What do you mean?

Say I sit here all night and watch the stuff. Maybe something even comes along and makes a pass at it. Say I fight it off. Morning comes, the stuff is still here, I'm still here. Then what? What have I gained?

Then you get to don your armor, pick up your weapons, and move on to the next stage of affairs.

I stifled a yawn.

You know, I don't think I really want any of that stuff, I said then. *I don't like armor, and I'm happy with the sword I've got.* I clapped my hand to its hilt. It felt strange, but then so did I. *Why don't we just leave the whole pile where it is and move on to the next stage now? What is the next stage anyway?*

I'm not sure. The way the Logrus threw information at me it just seems to surface at the appropriate time. I didn't even know about this place till I saw the entrance.

I stretched and folded my arms. I leaned my back against the wall. I extended my legs and crossed them at the ankles.

Then we're stuck here till something happens or you get inspired again?

Right.

Wake me when it's over, I said, and I closed my eyes.

The wrist twitch that followed was almost painful.

Hey! You can't do that! Frakir said. *The whole idea is that you sit up all night and watch.*

And a very half-assed idea it is, I said. *I refuse to play such a stupid game. If anything wants the stuff, I'll give it a good price on it.*

Go ahead and sleep if you want. But what if something comes along and decides you had better be taken out of the picture first?

To begin with, I replied, *I don't believe that anything could care about that pile of medieval junk, let alone lust after it— and in closing, it's your job to warn me of danger.*

Aye, aye, Captain. But this is a weird place. What if it limits my sensitivity some way?

You're really reaching now, I said. *I guess you'll just have to improvise.*

I dozed. I dreamed that I stood within a magic circle and various things tried to get at me. When they touched the barrier, though, they were transformed into stick figures, cartoon characters which rapidly faded. Except for Corwin of Amber, who smiled faintly and shook his head.

"Sooner or later you'll have to step outside," he said.

"Then let it be later," I replied.

"And all your problems will still be there, right where you left them."

I nodded.

"But I'll be rested," I answered.

"Then it's a trade-off. Good luck."

"Thanks."

The dream fell apart into random images then. I seem to remember standing outside the circle a little later, trying to figure a way to get back in. . . .

I wasn't certain what woke me. It couldn't have been a noise. But suddenly I was alert and rising, and the first thing I beheld was a dwarf with a mottled complexion, his hands clasped at his throat, lying unmoving in a twisted position near the armor pile.

"What's going on?" I tried saying.

But there was no reply.

I crossed and knelt beside the short big-shouldered guy. With my fingertips, I felt after a carotid pulse but couldn't locate one. At that moment, however, I felt a tickling sensation about my wrist, and Frakir—phasing into and out of visibility—made her way back into touch with with me.

You took that guy out? I asked.

There came a soft pulsation then. *Suicides don't strangle themselves,* she replied.

Why didn't you alert me?

You needed your rest, and it wasn't anything I couldn't handle. Our empathy is too strong, though. Sorry I woke you.

I stretched.

How long was I asleep?

Several hours, I'd judge.

I feel kind of sorry about this, I said. *That scrap heap isn't worth somebody's life.*

It is now, Frakir answered.

True. Now that someone's died for the stuff have you gotten the word as to what we do next?

Things are a little clearer, but not enough to act on. We must remain until morning for me to be certain.

Does the information you have include anything on whether there's food or drink available in the neighborhood?

Yes. There's supposed to be a jug of water behind the altar. Also a loaf of bread. But that's for morning. You're supposed to be fasting throughout the night.

That's only if I take this whole business seriously, I said, turning toward the altar.

I took two steps, and the world started to come apart. The floor of the chapel trembled, and I heard my first sounds since my arrival; a deep growling, grating noise came from somewhere far beneath me. A horde of colors flashed through the air of this colorless place, half blinding me with their intensity. Then the colors fled, and the room divided itself. The whiteness grew intense in the vicinity of the archway by which I had entered. I had to raise my hand to shield my eyes against it. Across from this, a profound darkness occurred, masking the three doorways in that wall.

What . . . is it? I asked.

Something terrible, Frakir replied, *beyond my ability to assess.*

I clasped the hilt of the blade I wore and reviewed the spells I still had hanging. Before I could do any more than that, an awful sense of presence pervaded the place. So potent did it seem that I did not feel that drawing my blade or reciting a spell was the most politic action I might take.

Ordinarily I'd have summoned the Sign of the Logrus by then, but that way was barred to me also. I tried clearing my throat, but no sound came forth. Then there came a movement at the heart of the light, a coalescing. . . .

The shape of a Unicorn, like Blake's Tyger, burning bright, took form, so painful to behold that I had to look away.

I shifted my gaze to the deep, cool blackness, but there was no rest for my eyes in that place either. Something stirred within the darkness, and there came another sound—a grating, as of metal being scraped on stone. This was followed by a powerful hissing. The ground trembled again. Curved lines flowed forward. Even before the brightness of the Unicorn etched its lineaments within that mighty gloom, I realized it was the head of a one-eyed serpent which had come partway into the chapel. I shifted my gaze to a point between them, catching each within my peripheral vision. Far better than any attempt to behold either directly. I felt their gazes upon me, the Unicorn of Order and the Serpent of Chaos. It was not a pleasant feeling, and I retreated until the altar was at my back.

Both came slightly farther into the chapel. The Unicorn's head was lowered, horn pointed directly at me. The Serpent's tongue darted in my direction.

"Uh, if either of you want this armor and stuff," I ventured, "I certainly have no object——"

The Serpent hissed and the Unicorn raised a hoof and let it fall, cracking the floor of the chapel, the fracture line racing toward me like a streak of black lightning and halting just at my feet.

"On the other hand," I observed, "no insult is intended by the offer, Your Eminences——"

Wrong thing to say—again, Frakir interjected, weakly.

Tell me what's right, I said, trying for a mental sotto voce.

I don't—— Oh!

The Unicorn reared; the Serpent drew itself upward. I

dropped to my knees and looked away, their gazes having somehow become physically painful. I was trembling, and all of my muscles had begun to ache.

It is suggested, Frakir recited, *that you play the game the way it is set up.*

What metal entered my backbone I know not. But I raised my head and turned it, looking first to the Serpent, then to the Unicorn. Though my eyes watered and ached as if I were trying to stare down the sun, I managed the gesture.

"You can make me play," I said, "but you cannot make me choose. My will is my own. I will guard this armor all night, as is required of me. In the morning I will go on without it because I do not choose to wear it."

Without it you may die, Frakir stated, as if translating.

I shrugged.

"If it is my choice to make, I choose not to place one of you before the other."

A rush of wind blew hot and cold past me, seemed a cosmic sigh.

You will choose, Frakir relayed, *whether you become aware of it or not. Everyone does. You are simply being asked to formalize your choice.*

"What's so special about my case?" I asked.

Again that wind.

Yours is a dual heritage, combined with great power.

"I never wanted either of you for an enemy," I stated.

Not good enough, came the reply.

"Then destroy me now."

The game is already in progress.

"Then let's get on with it," I answered.

We are not pleased with your attitude.

"Vice versa," I answered.

The thunderclap that followed left me unconscious.

The reason I felt I could afford total honesty was a strong hunch that players for this game might be hard to come by.

I woke sprawled across the pile of greaves, cuirasses, gauntlets, helms, and other good things of a similar nature, all of them possessed of corners or protuberances, most of which were jabbing into me. I became aware of this only by degrees, for I had gone numb in lots of important places.

Hi, Merlin.

Frakir, I responded. *Have I been out for long?*

I don't know. I just came around myself.

I didn't know a piece of rope could be knocked out.

Neither did I. It never happened to me before.

Let me amend my question then: Any idea how long we've been out?

Fairly long, I feel. Get me a glimpse out the doorway, and I may be able to give you a better idea.

I pushed myself slowly to my feet, could not remain standing, dropped. I crawled to the entranceway, noting in passing that nothing on the heap seemed to be missing. The floor was indeed cracked. There really was a dead dwarf to the rear of the chamber.

I looked outside, beheld a bright sky, black points disposed within it.

Well? I asked after a time.

If I figure right, it should be morning soon.

Always brightest before the dawn, eh?

Something like that.

My legs burned as their circulation was restored. I pushed myself upright, stood leaning against the wall.

Any new instructions?

Not yet. I've a feeling they're due with the dawn.

I staggered to the nearest bench, collapsed upon it.

If anything comes in now, all I've got to hit it with is an odd assortment of spells. Sleeping on armor leaves a few kinks. Almost as bad as sleeping in it.

Throw me at the enemy and the least I can do is buy you time.

Thanks.

How far back does your memory go?

To when I was a little kid, I guess. Why?

I recall sensations from when I was first enhanced, back in the Logrus. But everything up until we got here is kind of dreamlike. I just sort of used to react to life.

A lot of people are that way, too.

Really? I couldn't think, or communicate this way before.

True.

Do you think it will last?

What do you mean?

Might this just be a temporary condition? Might I just have been enhanced to deal with the special circumstances in this place?

I don't know, Frakir, I answered, massaging my left calf. *I suppose it's possible. Are you getting attached to the state?*

Yes. Silly of me, I guess. How can I care about something I won't miss when it's gone?

Good question, and I don't know the answer. Maybe you would have achieved this state anyway eventually.

I don't think so. But I don't know for certain.

You afraid to regress?

Yes.

Tell you what. When we find a way out of here, you stay behind.

I couldn't do that.

Why not? You've come in handy on occasion, but I can take care of myself. Now you're sentient you should have a life of your own.

But I'm a freak.

Aren't we all? I just want you to know I understand, and it's okay with me.

She pulsed once and shut up.

I wished I weren't afraid to drink the water.

I sat there for perhaps the better part of an hour, going over everything that had happened to me recently, looking for patterns, clues.

I can sort of hear you thinking, Frakir said suddenly, *and I can offer you something in one area.*

Oh? What might that be?

The one who brought you here—

The thing that looked like my father?

Yes.

What of him?

He was different from your other two visitors. He was human. They weren't.

You mean it might actually have been Corwin?

I never met him, so I can't say. He wasn't one of those constructs, though.

Do you know what they were?

No. I only know one peculiar thing about them, and I don't understand it at all.

I leaned forward and rubbed my temples. I took several deep breaths. My throat was very dry, and my muscles ached.

Go ahead. I'm waiting.

I don't quite know how to explain it, Frakir said. *But back in my presentient days you inconsiderately wore me about your wrist when you walked the Pattern.*

I recall. I had a scar for a long time after, from your reaction to it.

Things of Chaos and things of Order do not mix well. But I survived. And the experience is recorded within me. Now the

Dworkin and the Oberon figures that visited you back at the cave—

Yes?

Beneath their apparent humanity they were pulsing energy fields within geometrical constructs.

Sounds sort of like computer animation.

Maybe it is something like that. I couldn't say.

And my father wasn't one of these?

Nope. But that wasn't what I was getting at. I recognized the source.

I was suddenly alert.

What do you mean?

The swirls—the geometrical constructs on which the figures were based—they reproduced sections of the Pattern at Amber.

You must be mistaken.

No. What I lacked in sentience I made up in memory. Both figures were three-dimensional twistings of Pattern segments.

Why would the Pattern be creating simulacra to bug me?

I'm just a humble killing aid. Reasoning is not one of my strong points yet.

If the Unicorn and the Serpent are involved, I suppose the Pattern might be also.

We know that the Logrus is.

And it seemed to me that the Pattern demonstrated sentience the day Coral walked it. Say that's true and add on the ability to manufacture constructs— Is this the place it wanted them to bring me? Or did Corwin transport me someplace else? And what does the Pattern want of me? And what does my father want of me?

I envy your ability to shrug, Frakir answered. *Those are what I take it you call rhetorical questions?*

I guess so.

Information of another sort is beginning to come to me, so I assume the night is ending.

I sprang to my feet.

85

Does that mean I can eat—and drink? I asked.

I believe so.

I moved quickly then.

While I am new to these things, I cannot help wondering whether it might be considered disrespectful to vault over an altar that way, Frakir commented.

The black flames flickered as I passed between them.

Hell, I don't even know what it's an altar to, I answered, *and I've always thought of disrespect as something that had to be identity-specific.*

The ground trembled slightly as I seized the jug and took a deep swallow.

Then, again, perhaps you have a point there, I said, choking.

I carried the jug and the loaf around the altar, past the stiffening dwarf and over to the bench which ran along the back wall. Seating myself, I commenced eating and drinking more slowly.

What comes next? I asked. *You said that the information was flowing again.*

You have kept vigil successfully, she said. *Now you must select what you need from among the armor and weapons you watched, then pass through one of the three doorways in this wall.*

Which one?

One is the door of Chaos, one the door of Order, and I know not the nature of the third.

Uh, how does one make an informed decision in these matters?

I think your way may be barred by all but the one you're supposed to pass.

Then one does not really have a choice, does one?

I believe that the matter of the doorways may be predicated upon the choice one makes in the hardware department.

I finished the bread, washed it down with the rest of the water. I got to my feet then.

Well, I said, *let's see what they'll do if I don't make a choice. Too bad about the dwarf.*

He knew what he was doing, what chances he was taking.

That's more than I can say.

I approached the right-hand door since it was the nearest. It let into a bright corridor which grew brighter and brighter as it receded until sight of it was lost to me beyond a few paces' distance. I kept walking. Damn near broke my nose, too. It was as if I'd encountered a wall of glass. It figures. I couldn't picture myself walking off into the light that way.

You're actually getting more cynical as I watch, Frakir observed. *I caught that thought.*

Good.

I approached the middle one more carefully. It wore gray and seemed to let into a long corridor also. I could see down it perhaps a little farther than the first, though no features other than walls, roof, and floor presented themselves. I extended my arm and discovered that my way was not barred.

Seems to be the one, Frakir observed.

Maybe.

I moved over to the left-hand doorway, its passage black as the inside of God's pocket. Again there was no resistance when I explored for hidden barriers.

Hm. It appears I do have a choice.

Odd. I haven't any instructions to cover this.

I returned to the middle one, took a step forward. Hearing a sound behind me, I turned. The dwarf had sat up. He was holding his sides and laughing. I tried to turn back then, but now something barred my return. Suddenly then the scene dwindled, as if I were accelerating to the rear.

I thought the little guy was dead, I said.

So did I. He gave every indication.

I turned away, back to the direction I'd been headed. There was no feeling of acceleration. Perhaps it was the chapel that was receding while I stood still.

I took a step forward, then another. Not a sound from my footfalls. I began walking. After a few paces I put out my hand to touch the left-hand wall. It encountered nothing. I tried again with the right. Again nothing. I took a step to the right and reached again. Nope. I still seemed approximately equidistant from two shadowy walls. Growling, I ignored them and strode forward.

What's the matter, Merle?

Do you or do you not sense walls to the right and left of us? I asked.

Nope, Frakir replied.

Any idea at all where we are?

We are walking between shadows.

Where are we headed?

Don't know yet. We're following the Way of Chaos, though.

What? How do you know that? I thought we had to pick something Chaosian for the pile to be admitted here.

At this I gave myself a quick search. I found the dagger tucked into my right boot sheath. Even in the dim light I could recognize the workmanship as something from back home.

We were set up somehow, I said. *Now I know why the dwarf was laughing. He planted this on me while we were passed out.*

But you still had a choice—between this and the dark corridor.

True.

So why'd you pick this one?

The light was better.

V

A half dozen steps later even the impression of walls had vanished. Ditto the roof, for that matter. Looking back, I saw no sign of the corridor or its entrance. There was only a vast dismal area. Fortunately the floor or ground remained firm underfoot. The only manner in which I could distinguish the way I traveled from the surrounding gloom had to do with visibility. I walked a pearl-gray trail through a valley of shadow, though, technically, I supposed, I walked between shadows. Picky-picky. Someone or something had grudgingly spilled a minimum of light to mark my way.

I trudged through the eerie silence, wondering how many shadows I passed among, then wondering whether that was too linear a way of considering the phenomenon. Probably.

At that moment, before I could invoke mathematics, I thought I saw something move off to my right. I halted. A tall ebon pillar had come into view, barely, at the edge of vision. But it was not moving. I concluded that it was my own movement which had given it the appearance of motion. Thick, still, smooth—I ran my gaze up that dark shaft until I lost sight of it. There seemed no way of telling how high the thing stood.

I turned away. I took a few more paces. I noted another pillar then—ahead of me, to the left. I gave this one only a glance as I continued. Shortly more came into view at either hand. The darkness into which they ascended held nothing resembling stars, positive or negative; my world's canopy was a simple, uniform blackness. A little later, the pillars occurred in odd groupings, some very near at hand, and their respective sizes no longer seemed uniform.

I halted, reached toward a stand of them to my left which seemed almost within touching range. It wasn't, though. I took a step in that direction.

There came a quick squeeze at my wrist.

I wouldn't do that if I were you, Frakir observed.

Why not? I inquired.

It might be easy to get lost and into a lot of trouble.

Maybe you're right.

I broke into a jog. Whatever was going on, my only real desire concerning it was to have it over with as soon as possible, so that I could get back to matters I considered important—like locating Coral, springing Luke, finding a way to deal with Jurt and Julia, looking for my father. . . .

The pillars, at varying distances, slid by, and items which were not pillars began occurring among them. Some were squat, asymmetrical; others were tall, tapered; some leaned upon neighbors, bridged them, or lay broken at their bases. It was something of a relief to see that monotonous regularity destroyed, in a way that showed that forces played upon forms.

The ground lost its flatness then, though it retained a stylized geometric quality in the stacked, step, and shelflike appearance of its various levels. My own way remained flat and vaguely lighted as I jogged amid the ruins of a thousand Stonehenges.

I increased my pace, and soon I was running past galleries, amphitheaters, forestlike stands of stone. I seemed to glimpse movement within several of these, but again it could easily have been a function of velocity and poor lighting.

Sense anything alive in the neighborhood? I asked Frakir.

No, came the answer.

Thought I saw something move.

Maybe you did. Doesn't mean it's there.

Talking for less than a day, and you've already learned sarcasm.

I hate to say it, boss, but anything I learn I pick up from your vibes. Ain't no one else around to teach me manners and like that.

Touché, I said. *Maybe I'd better warn you if there's trouble.*

Touché, boss. Hey, I like these combat metaphors.

Moments later I slowed my pace. Ahead something was flickering off to the right. There were moments of blue and red within the changing light intensities. I halted. These glimpses lasted only a few moments but were more than sufficient to make me wary. I regarded their apparent source for a long while.

Yes, Frakir said after a time. *Caution is in order. But don't ask me what to expect. It is only a general feeling of menace that I have.*

Perhaps there's some way I could just sneak by whatever it is.

You'd have to leave the trail to do that, Frakir replied, *and since the trail does run through the circle of stones where it's coming from, I'd say no.*

Nobody told me I couldn't leave the trail. Do you have any instructions to that effect?

I know you are supposed to follow the trail. I've nothing specific concerning the consequences of leaving it, though.

Hm.

The way curved to the right, and I followed it. It ran directly into the massive circle of stones, and though I slowed my pace, I did not deviate. I studied it as I drew near, however, and noted that while the trail entered there, it did not emerge again.

You're right, Frakir observed. *Like the den of the dragon.*

But we're supposed to go this way.

Yes.

Then we will.

I'd slowed to a walk by then, and I followed the shining way between two gray plinths.

The lighting was different within the circle from without. There was more of it, though the place was still a study in black and white, with a fairyland sparkle to it. For the first time here I saw something that appeared to be living. There was something like grass underfoot; it was silver and seemed to be studded with dewdrops.

I halted, and Frakir constricted in a very odd fashion —less a warning, it seemed, than a statement of interest. Off to my right was an altar—not at all like the one over which I had vaulted back in the chapel. This one was a rude slab of stone set atop a couple of boulders. No candles, linens, or other ecclesiastical niceties kept company with the lady who lay atop it, her wrists and ankles bound. Because I recalled a similar bothersome situation in which I had once found myself, my sympathies were all with the lady—white-haired, black-skinned, and somehow familiar—my animus with the peculiar individual who stood behind the altar, faced in my direction, blade upraised in his left hand. The right half of his body was totally black; the left, blindingly white. Immediately galvanized by the tableau, I moved forward. My Concerto for Cuisinart and Microwave spell would have minced him and parboiled him in an instant, but it was useless to me when I could not speak the guide words.

I seemed to feel his gaze upon me as I raced toward him, though one side of him was too dark and the other too bright for me to know for certain. And then the knife hand descended and the blade entered her breast beneath the sternum with an arcing movement. At that instant she screamed, and the blood spurted and it was red against all those blacks and whites, and I realized as it covered the man's hand that had I tried, I might have uttered my spell and saved her.

Then the altar collapsed, and a gray whirlwind obliterated my view of the entire tableau. The blood swirled through it to a barber pole-like effect, gradually spreading and attenuating to turn the funnel rosy, then pink, then faded to silver, then gone. When I reached the spot, the grasses sparkled, sans altar, sans priest, sans sacrifice.

I drew up short, staring.

"Are we dreaming?" I asked aloud.

I do not believe I am capable of dreaming, Frakir replied.

"Then tell me what you saw."

I saw a guy stab a lady who was tied up on a stone surface. Then the whole thing collapsed and blew away. The guy was black and white, the blood was red, the lady was Deirdre——

"What? By God, you're right! It did look like her——in negative. But she's already dead——"

I must remind you that I saw whatever you thought you saw. I don't know what the raw data were, just the mixing job your nervous system did on them. My own special perceptions told me that these were not normal people but were beings on the order of the Dworkin and Oberon figures that visited you back in the cave.

An absolutely terrifying thought occurred to me just then. The Dworkin and Oberon figures had had me thinking briefly of three-dimensional computer simulations. And the Ghostwheel's shadow-scanning ability was based on digitized abstractions of portions of the Pattern I believed to be particularly concerned with this quality. And Ghost had been wondering—almost wistfully, it now seemed—concerning the qualifications for godhood.

Could my own creation be playing games with me? Might Ghost have imprisoned me in a stark and distant shadow, blocked all my efforts at communication, and set about playing an elaborate game with me? If he could beat his own creator, for whom he seemed to feel something of awe, might he not feel he had achieved personal elevation—to a level beyond my status in his private cosmos? Maybe. If one keeps encountering computer simulations, *cherchez le deus ex machina*.

It made me wonder just how strong Ghost really was. Though his power was, in part, an analogue of the Pattern, I was certain it did not match that of the Pattern—or the Logrus. I couldn't see him blocking this place off from either.

On the other hand, all that would really be necessary would be to block me. I suppose he could have impersonated the Logrus in our flash encounter on my arrival. But that would have required Ghost's actually enhancing Frakir, and I didn't believe he could do it. And what about the Unicorn and the Serpent?

"Frakir," I asked, "are you sure it was really the Logrus that enhanced you this time and programmed you with all the instructions you're carrying?"

Yes.

"What makes you certain?"

It had the same feeling as our first encounter back within the Logrus, when I was enhanced initially.

"I see. Next question: Could the Unicorn and the Serpent we saw back in the chapel have been the same sort of things as the Oberon or Dworkin figures back at the cave?"

No. I'd have known. They weren't like them at all. They were terrible and powerful and very much what they seemed.

"Good," I said. "I was worried this might be some elaborate charade on the part of the Ghostwheel."

I see that in your mind. Though I fail to see why the reality of the Unicorn and the Serpent defeats the thesis. They could simply have entered the Ghost's construct to tell you to stop horsing around because they want to see this thing played out.

"I hadn't thought of that."

And maybe the Ghost was able to locate and penetrate a place that is pretty much inaccessible to the Pattern and the Logrus.

"I suppose you've a point there. Unfortunately this pretty much puts me back where I started."

No, because this place is not something Ghost put together. It's always been around. I learned that much from the Logrus.

"I suppose there's some small comfort in knowing that, but——"

I never completed the thought because a sudden movement called my attention to the opposite quadrant of the circle. There I beheld an altar I had not noted before, a female figure standing behind it, a man dappled in shadow and light lying, bound, upon it. They looked very similar to the first pair. .

"No!" I cried. "Let it end!"

But the blade descended even as I moved in that direction. The ritual was repeated, and the altar collapsed, and everything again swirled away. When I reached the site, there was no indication that anything unusual had occurred upon it.

"What do you make of that one?" I asked Frakir.

Same forces as before, but somehow reversed.

"Why? What's going on?"

It is a gathering of powers. The Pattern and the Logrus are both attempting to force their way into this place, for a little while. Sacrifices, such as those you just witnessed, help provide the openings they need.

"Why do they wish to manifest here?"

Neutral ground. Their ancient tension is shifting in subtle ways. You are expected in some fashion to tip the balance of power one way or another.

"I haven't the faintest idea how to go about such a thing."

When the time comes, you will.

I returned to the trail and walked on.

"Did I pass by just as the sacrifices were due?" I said. "Or were the sacrifices due because I was passing by?"

They were marked to occur in your vicinity. You are a nexus.

"Then do you think I can expect——"

A figure stepped out from behind a stone to my left and chuckled softly. My hand went to my sword, but his hands were empty, and he moved slowly.

"Talking to yourself. Not a good sign," he remarked.

The man was a study in black, white, and gray. In fact, from the cast of the darkness upon his right-hand side and the lay of the light on his left, he might have been the first wielder of the sacrificial dagger. I'd no real way of telling. Whoever or whatever he or it was, I'd no desire to become acquainted.

So I shrugged.

"The only sign I care about here has 'exit' written on it," I told him as I brushed past him.

His hand fell upon my shoulder and turned me back easily in his direction.

Again the chuckle.

"You must be careful what you wish for in this place," he told me in low and measured tones, "for wishes are sometimes granted here, and if the granter be depraved and read 'quietus' for your 'exit'—why, then, poof! You may cease to be. Up in smoke. Downward to the earth. Sideways to hell and gone."

"I've already been there," I answered, "and lots of points along the way."

"What ho! Look! Your wish *has* been granted," he remarked, his left eye catching a flash of light and reflecting it, tapetumlike, in my direction. No matter how I turned or squinted, however, could I find sight of his right eye. "Over there," he finished, pointing.

I turned my head in the direction he indicated, and there upon the top stone of a dolmen shone an exit sign exactly like the one above the emergency door at a theater I used to frequent near campus.

"You're right," I said.

"Will you go through it?"

"Will you?"

"No need," he replied. "I already know what's there."

"What?" I inquired.

"The other side."

"How droll," I answered.

"If one gets one's wish and spurns it, one might piss off the Powers," he said then.

"You have firsthand knowledge of this?"

I heard a grinding, clicking noise then, and it was several moments before I realized he was gnashing his teeth. I walked away then toward the exit sign, wanting to inspect whatever it represented at nearer range.

There were two standing stones with a flat slab across

the top. The gateway thus formed was large enough to walk through. It was shadowy, though. . . .

You going through it, boss?

"Why not? This is one of the few times in my life that I feel indispensable to whoever is running the show."

I wouldn't get too cocky . . . Frakir began, but I was already moving.

Three quick paces were all that it took, and I was looking outward across a circle of stones and sparkling grass past a black-and-white man toward another dolmen bearing an exit sign, a shadowy form within it. Halting, I took a step backward and turned. There was a black-and-white man regarding me, a dolmen to his rear, dark Form within it. I raised my right hand above my head. So did the shadowy figure. I turned back in the direction I had initially been headed. The shadowy figure across from me also had his hand upraised. I stepped on through.

"Small world," I observed, "but I'd hate to paint it."

The man laughed.

"Now you are reminded that your every exit is also an entrance," he said.

"Seeing you here, I am reminded even more of a play by Sartre," I responded.

"Unkind," he answered, "but philosophically cogent. I have always found that hell is other people. Only I have done nothing to rouse your distrust, have I?"

"Were you or were you not the person I saw sacrifice a woman in this vicinity?" I asked.

"Even if I were, what is that to you? You were not involved."

"I guess I have peculiar feelings about little things—like the value of life."

"Indignation is cheap. Even Albert Schweitzer's reverence for life didn't include the tapeworm, the tsetse fly, the cancer cell."

"You know what I mean. Did you or did you not sacrifice a woman on a stone altar a little while ago?"

"Show me the altar."

"I can't. It's gone."

"Show me the woman."

"She is, too."

"Then you haven't much of a case."

"This isn't a court, damn it! If you want to converse, answer my question. If you don't, let's stop making noises at each other."

"I have answered you."

I shrugged.

"All right," I said. "I don't know you, and I'm very happy that way. Good day."

I took a step away from him, back in the direction of the trail. As I did, he said, "Deirdre. Her name was Deirdre, and I did indeed kill her," and he stepped into the dolmen from which I had just emerged, and there he disappeared. Immediately I looked across the way, but he did not exit beneath the exit sign. I did an about-face and stepped into the dolmen myself. I did emerge from the other side, across the way, catching sight of myself entering the opposite one as I did so. I did not see the stranger anywhere along the way.

"What do you make of that?" I asked Frakir as I moved back toward the trail.

A spirit of place, perhaps? A nasty spirit for a nasty place? she ventured. *I don't know, but I think he was one of those damned constructs, too—and they're stronger here.*

I headed down to the trail, set foot upon it, and commenced following it once again.

"Your speech patterns have altered enormously since your enhancement," I remarked.

Your nervous system's a good teacher.

"Thanks. If that guy puts in an appearance again and

you sense him before I see him, give me the high sign."

Right. Actually, this entire place has the feeling of one of those constructs. Every stone here has a bit of Pattern scribble to it.

"When did you learn this?"

Back when we first tried the exit. I scanned it for dangers then.

As we came to the periphery of the outer circle, I slapped a stone. It felt solid enough.

He's here! Frakir warned suddenly.

"Hey!" came a voice from overhead, and I looked up. The black-and-white stranger was seated atop the stone, smoking a thin cigar. He held a chalice in his left hand. "You interest me, kid," he went on. "What's your name?"

"Merlin," I answered. "What's yours?"

Instead of replying, he pushed himself outward, fell in slow motion, landed on his feet beside me. His left eye squinted as he studied me. The shadows flowed like dark water down his right side. He blew silvery smoke into the air.

"You're a live one," he announced then, "with the mark of the Pattern and the mark of Chaos upon you. You bear the blood of Amber. What is your lineage, Merlin?"

The shadows parted for a moment, and I saw that his right eye was hidden by a patch.

"I am the son of Corwin," I told him, "and you are—somehow—the traitor Brand."

"You have named me," he said, "but I never betrayed what I believed in."

"That being your own ambition," I said. "Your home and your family and the forces of Order never mattered to you, did they?"

He snorted.

"I will not argue with a presumptuous puppy."

"I've no desire to argue with you either. For whatever it's worth, your son Rinaldo is probably my best friend."

I turned away and began walking. His hand fell upon my shoulder.

"Wait!" he said. "What is this talk? Rinaldo is but a lad."

"Wrong," I answered. "He's around my age."

His hand fell away, and I turned. He had dropped his cigar, which lay smoking upon the trail, and he'd transferred the chalice to his shadow-clad hand. He massaged his brow.

"That much time has passed in the mainlines . . ." he remarked.

On a whim, I withdrew my Trumps, shuffled out Luke's, held it up for him to see.

"That's Rinaldo," I said.

He reached for it, and for some obscure reason I let him take it. He stared at it for a long while.

"Trump contact doesn't seem to work from here," I said.

He looked up, shook his head, and handed the card back to me.

"No, it wouldn't," he stated. "How . . . is he?"

"You know that he killed Caine to avenge you?"

"No, I didn't know. But I'd expect no less of him."

"You're not exactly Brand, are you?"

He threw back his head and laughed.

"I am entirely Brand, and I am not Brand as you might have known him. Anything more than that will cost you."

"What will it cost me to learn what you really are?" I inquired as I cased my cards.

He raised the chalice, held it before him with both hands, like a begging bowl.

"Some of your blood," he said.

"You've become a vampire?"

"No, I'm a Pattern-ghost," he replied. "Bleed for me, and I'll explain."

"All right," I said. "It'd better be a good story, though," and I drew my dagger and pricked my wrist, which I'd extended to a position above his cup.

Like a spilled oil lamp, the flames came forth. I don't really have fire flowing around inside me, of course. But the blood of a Chaosite is highly volatile in certain places, and this, apparently, was such a place.

It spewed forth, half into and half past the cup, splashing over his hand, his forearm. He screamed and seemed to collapse in upon himself. I stepped backward as he was transformed into a vortex—not unlike those following the sacrifices I had witnessed, only this one of the fiery variety—which rose into the air with a roar and vanished a moment later, leaving me startled, staring upward and applying direct pressure to my smoking wrist.

Uh, colorful exit, Frakir remarked.

"Family specialty," I responded, "and speaking of exits . . ."

I stepped past the stone, departing the circle. The darkness moved in again, intensified. Reflexively my trail seemed to brighten. I released my wrist, saw that it had stopped smoking.

I broke into a jog then, anxious to be away from that place. When I looked back a little later, I no longer saw the standing stones. There was only a pale, fading vortex, drawing itself upward, upward, then gone.

I jogged on, and the trail began, gradually, to slope until I was running downhill with an easy, loping gait.

The trail ran like a bright ribbon downward and off into a great distance before it faded from view. I was puzzled, however, to see that it intersected another glowing line not too far below. These lines quickly faded off to my right and my left.

"Any special instructions pertaining to crossroads?" I inquired.

Not yet, Frakir answered. *Presumably, it's a decision point, with no way of knowing what to base one on till you get there.*

It seemed a vast, shadowy plain that was spread below, with here and there a few isolated dots of light, some of them constant, others appearing, then fading, all of them stationary. There were no other lines, however, than my trail and the one which intersected it. There were no sounds other than my breathing and that of my footfalls. There were no breezes, no peculiar odors, and the temperature was so clement that it claimed no notice. Again there were dark shapes at either hand, but I'd no desire to investigate them. All I wanted was to conclude whatever business was in progress and get the hell out and be about my own affairs as soon as possible.

Hazy patches of light then began occurring at irregular intervals, both sides of the trail, wavery, sourceless, blotchy, popping into and out of existence. These seemed like gauzy, dappled curtains hung beside the trail, and I did not pause to examine them at first, not till the obscure areas grew fewer and fewer, being replaced by shadings of greater and greater distinction. It was almost as if a tuning process were in operation, with increasing clarity of outline indicating familiar objects: chairs; tables; parked cars; store windows. Before long, faded colors began to occur within these tableaus.

I halted beside one and stared. It was a red '57 Chevy with some snow on it, parked in a familiar-looking driveway. I advanced and reached toward it.

My left hand and arm faded as they entered the dim light. I reached to touch the left fin. There followed a vague sensation of contact and a faint coolness. I swept my hand to the right then, brushing away some of the snow. When I withdrew my hand, there was snow upon it. Immediately the prospect faded to black.

"I intentionally used my left hand," I said, "with you on the wrist. What was there?"

Thanks a lot. It seemed a red car with snow on it.

"It was a construct of something picked from my mind. That's my Polly Jackson painting, upscaled to life size."

Then things are getting worse, Merle. I couldn't tell it was a construct.

"Conclusions?"

Whatever's doing it is getting better at it, or stronger. Or both.

"Shit," I observed, and I turned away and jogged on.

Perhaps something wants to show you that it can baffle you completely now.

"Then it's succeeded," I acknowledged. "Hey, Something!" I shouted. "You hear that? You win! You've baffled me completely. Can I go home now? If it's something else you're trying to do, though, you've failed! I'm missing the point completely!"

The dazzling flash which followed cast me down upon the trail and blinded me for several long moments. I lay there tense and twitching, but no thunderclap followed. When my vision cleared and my muscles stopped their spasms, I beheld a giant regal figure posed but a few paces before me: Oberon.

Only it was a statue, a duplicate of one which occupied the far end of the Main Concourse back in Amber, or possibly even the real thing, for on closer inspection I noted what appeared to be bird droppings upon the great man's shoulder.

"Real thing or construct?" I said aloud.

Real, I'd say, Frakir replied.

I rose slowly.

"I understand this to be an answer," I said. "I just don't understand what it means."

I reached out to touch it, and it felt like canvas rather than bronze. In that instant my perspective somehow shifted, and I felt myself touching a larger than life-size painting of the Father of His Country. Then its borders began to waver, it faded, and I saw that it was part of one of those hazy tableaux I had been passing. Then it rippled and was gone.

"I give up," I said, walking through the space it had occupied but moments before. "The answers are more confusing than the situations that cause the questions."

Since we are passing between shadows, could this not be a statement that all things are real—somewhere?

"I suppose. But I already knew that."

And that all things are real in different ways, at different times, in different places?

"Okay, what you are saying could well be the message. I doubt that something is going to these extremes, however, just to make philosophical points that may be new to you but are rather well worn elsewhere. There must be a special reason, one that I still don't grasp."

Up until now the scenes I'd passed had been still lifes. Now, however, a number occurred which contained people; some, other creatures. In these, there was action—some of it violent, some amorous, some simply domestic.

Yes, it seems to be a progression. It may be leading up to something.

"When they leap out and attack me, I'll know I've arrived."

Who knows? I gather that art criticism is a complex area.

But the sequences faded shortly thereafter, and I was left jogging on my bright trail through darkness once again. Down, down the still gentle slope toward the crossroads. Where was the Cheshire Cat when rabbit hole logic was what I really needed?

One moment I was watching the crossroads as I advanced upon it. An eye blink later I was still watching the crossroads, only now the scene was altered. There was now a lamppost on the near right-hand corner. A shadowy figure stood beneath it, smoking.

"Frakir, how'd they pull that one?" I asked.

Very quickly, she replied.

"What do the vibes read?"

Attention focused in your direction. No vicious intent, yet.

I slowed as I drew near. The trail became pavement, curbs at either hand, sidewalks beyond them. I stepped out of the street onto the right-hand walk. As I moved along it, a damp fog blew past me, hung between me and the light. I slowed my pace even more. Shortly I saw that the pavement had grown damp. My footsteps echoed as if I walked between buildings. By then the fog had grown too dense for me to discern whether buildings had actually occurred beside me. It felt as if they had, for there were darker areas here and there within the gloom. A cold wind began to blow against my back, and droplets of moisture fell upon me at random intervals. I halted. I turned up the collar of my cloak. From somewhere entirely out of sight, high overhead, came the faint buzzing sound of an airplane. I began walking again after it had gone by. Tinily then, and muffled, from across the street perhaps, came the sound of a piano playing a half-familiar tune. I drew my cloak about me. The fog swirled and thickened.

Three paces more, and then it cleared, and she was

standing before me, back against the lamppost. A head shorter than I was, she had on a trench coat and a black beret, her hair glossy, inky. She dropped her cigarette and slowly ground it out beneath the toe of a high-heeled black patent-leather shoe. I glimpsed something of her leg as she did so, and it was perfectly formed. She removed from within her coat then a flat silver case, the raised outline of a rose upon it, opened it, took out a cigarette, placed it between her lips, closed the case, and put it away. Then, without looking at me, she asked, "Have you a light?"

I hadn't any matches, but I wasn't about to let a little thing like that deter me.

"Of course," I said, extending my hand slowly toward those delicate features. I kept it turned slightly away from her so that she could not see that it was empty. As I whispered the guide word which caused the spark to leap from my fingertip to the tip of the cigarette, she raised her hand and touched my own, as if to steady it. And she raised her eyes—large, deep blue, long-lashed—and met mine as she drew upon it. Then she gasped, and the cigarette fell away.

"*Mon Dieu!*" she said, and she threw her arms about me, pressed herself against me, and began to sob. "Corwin!" she said. "You've found me! It has been forever!"

I held her tightly, not wanting to speak, not wanting to break her happiness with something as cloddish as truth. The hell with truth. I stroked her hair.

After a long while she pulled away, looked up at me. A moment or so more, and she would realize that it was only a resemblance and that she was seeing but what she wanted to see. So, "What's a girl like you doing in a place like this?" I asked.

She laughed softly.

"Have you found a way?" she said, and then her eyes narrowed. "You're not—"

I shook my head.

"I hadn't the heart," I told her.

"Who are you?" she asked, taking a half step backward.

"My name is Merlin, and I'm on a crazy quest I don't understand."

"Amber," she said softly, her hands still on my shoulders, and I nodded.

"I don't know you," she said then. "I feel that I should, but . . . I . . . don't. . . ."

Then she came to me again and rested her head on my chest. I started to say something, to try to explain, but she placed a finger across my lips.

"Not yet, not now, maybe never," she said. "Don't tell me. Please don't tell me more. But *you* ought to know whether you're a Pattern-ghost."

"Just what is a Pattern-ghost?" I said.

"An artifact created by the Pattern. It records everyone who walks it. It can call us back whenever it wants, as we were at one of the times we walked it. It can use us as it would, send us where it will with a task laid upon us—a *geas*, if you like. Destroy us, and it can create us over again."

"Does it do this sort of thing often?"

"I don't know. I'm not familiar with its will, let alone its operations with any other than myself." Then, "You're not a ghost! I can tell!" she announced suddenly, taking hold of my hand. "But there is something different about you—different from others of the blood of Amber. . . ."

"I suppose," I answered. "I trace my lineage to the Courts of Chaos as well as to Amber."

She raised my hand to her mouth as if she were about

to kiss it. But her lips moved by, to the place on my wrist where I had cut myself at Brand's request. Then it hit me: Something about the blood of Amber must hold a special attraction for Pattern-ghosts.

I tried to draw my hand away, but the strength of Amber was hers also.

"The fires of Chaos sometimes flow within me," I said. "They may do you harm."

She raised her head slowly and smiled. There was blood on her mouth. I glanced down and saw that my wrist was wet with it, too.

"The blood of Amber has power over the Pattern," she began, and the fog rolled, churned about her ankles. "No!" she cried then, and she bent forward once more.

The vortex rose to her knees, her calves. I felt her teeth upon my wrist, tearing. I knew of no spell to fight this thing, so I laid my arm across her shoulder and stroked her hair. Moments later she dissolved within my embrace, becoming a bloody whirlwind.

"Go right," I heard her wail as she spun away from me, her cigarette still smoldering upon the pavement, my blood dripping beside it.

I turned away. I walked away. Faintly, faintly, through the night and the fog I could still hear the piano playing some tune from before my time.

VI

I took the road to the right, and everywhere my blood fell reality melted a little. I heal fast, though, and I stopped bleeding soon. Even stopped throbbing before too long.

You got blood all over me, boss.

"Could have been fire," I observed.

I got singed a little, too, back at the stones.

"Sorry about that. Figure out what's going on yet?"

No new instructions, if that's what you mean. But I've been thinking, now I know how to do it, and this place gets more and more fascinating. This whole business of Pattern-ghosts, for instance. If the Pattern can't penetrate here directly, it can at least employ agents. Wouldn't you think the Logrus might have some way of doing the same?

"I suppose it's possible."

I get the impression there's some sort of duel going on between them here, on the underside of reality, between shadows. What if this place came first? Before Shadow, even? What if they've been fighting here since the very beginning, in some strange metaphysical way?

"What if they have?"

That could almost make Shadow an afterthought, a by-product of the tension between the poles.

"I'm afraid you've lost me, Frakir."

What if Amber and the Courts of Chaos were created only to provide agents for this conflict?

"And what if this idea were placed within you by the Logrus during your recent enhancement?"

Why?

"Another way to make me think that the conflict is more important than the people. Another pressure to make me choose a side."

I don't feel manipulated.

"As you pointed out, you're new to this thinking business. And that's a pretty damned abstract line of thought for you to be following this early in the game."

Is it?

"Take my word for it."

What does that leave us with?

"Unwelcome attention from On High."

Better watch your language if this is their war zone.

"A pox on both their houses. For some reason I don't understand, they need me for this game. They'll put up with it."

From somewhere up ahead I heard a roll of thunder.

See what I mean?

"It's a bluff," I replied.

Whose?

"The Pattern's, I believe. Its ghosts seem in charge of reality in this sector."

You know, we could be wrong on all of this. Just shooting in the dark.

"I also feel shot at out of the dark. That's why I refuse to play by anybody else's rules."

Have you got a plan?

"Hang loose. And if I say 'kill,' do it. Let's get to where we're going."

I began to run again, leaving the fog, leaving the ghosts to play at being ghosts in their ghost city. Bright road through dark country, me running, reverse shadow-shifting, as the land tried to change me. And there ahead a flare and more thunder, virtual street scene flashing into and out of existence beside me.

And then it was as if I raced myself, dark figure darting along a bright way—till I realized it was indeed, somehow, a mirror effect. The movements of the figure to my right which paralleled my own mimicked mine; fleeting scenes to my left were imaged to the other's right.

What's going on, Merle?

"Don't know," I said. "But I'm not in the mood for symbolism, allegory, and assorted metaphorical crap. If it's supposed to mean that life is a race with yourself, then it sucks——unless they're real platitudinizing Powers that are running this show. Then I guess it would be in character. What do you think?"

I think you might still be in danger of being struck by lightning.

The lightning did not follow, but my reflection did. The imaging effect continued for much longer than any of the previous beside-the-road sequences I'd witnessed. I was about to dismiss it, to ignore it completely, when my reflection put on a burst of speed and shot ahead of me.

Uh-oh.

"Yeah," I agreed, stepping up my own pace to close the gap with and match the stride of that dark other.

We were parallel for no more than a few meters after I caught up. Then it began to pull ahead again. I stepped up my pace and caught up once more. Then, on an impulse, I sucked air, bore down, and moved ahead.

My double noted it after a time, moved faster, began to gain. I pushed harder, held my lead. What the hell were we racing for anyway?

I looked ahead. In the distance I could see an area where the trail widened. There appeared to be a tape stretched across it at that point. Okay. Whatever the significance, I decided to go for it.

I held my lead for perhaps a hundred meters before my shadow began to gain on me again. I leaned into it and was able to hold that shortened distance for a time. Then it moved again, coming up on me at a pace I suspected might be hard to hold the rest of the way to the tape. Still, it was not the sort of thing one waited around to find out. I poured it on. I ran all out.

The son of a bitch gained on me, kept gaining, caught me, drew ahead, faltered for an instant. I was back beside it in that instant. But the thing did not flag again. It held the terrible pace at which we were now moving, and I had no intention of stopping unless my heart exploded.

We ran on, damn near side by side. I didn't know whether I had a finishing spurt in me or not. I couldn't tell whether I was slightly ahead, just abreast, or slightly to the rear of the other. We pounded our parallel gleaming trails toward the line of brightness when abruptly the sensation of a glass interface vanished. The two narrow-seeming trails became one wide one. The other's arms and legs were moving differently from my own.

We drew closer and closer together as we entered the final stretch—close enough, finally, for recognition. It was not an image of myself that I was running against, for its hair streamed back and I saw that its left ear was missing.

I found a final burst of speed. So did the other. We were awfully close together when we came to the tape. I think that I hit it first, but I could not be certain.

We went on through and collapsed, gasping. I rolled quickly, to keep him under surveillance, but he just lay there, panting. I rested my right hand on the hilt of my weapon and listened to the sound of my blood in my ears.

When I'd caught my breath somewhat, I remarked, "Didn't know you could run a race like that, Jurt."

He gave a brief laugh.

"There're a lot of things you don't know about me, brother."

"I'm sure," I said.

Then he wiped his brow with the back of his hand, and I noted that the finger he'd lost in the caves of Kolvir was back in place. Either this was the Jurt of a different time line or——

"So how's Julia?" I asked him. "Is she going to be all right?"

"Julia?" he said. "Who's that?"

"Sorry," I said. "You're the wrong Jurt."

"Now what else does that mean?" he asked, propping himself on an elbow and glaring at me with his good eye.

"The real Jurt was never anywhere near the Pattern of Amber——"

"I *am* the real Jurt!"

"You've got all your fingers. He lost one very recently. I was there."

He looked away suddenly.

"You must be a Logrus-ghost," I continued. "It must pull the same stunt the Pattern does——recording those who make it through it."

"Is that . . . what happened?" he asked. "I couldn't quite recall . . . why I was here—except to race with you."

"I'll bet your most recent memories before this place involve negotiating the Logrus."

He looked back. He nodded.

"You're right. What does it all mean?" he asked.

"I'm not sure," I said. "But I've got some ideas about it. This place is a kind of eternal underside to Shadow. It's damn near off limits for both the Pattern and the Logrus. But both can apparently penetrate here by means of their ghosts—artificial constructs from the recordings they made of us back when we passed through them—"

"You mean that all I am is some sort of recording?" He looked as if he were about to cry. "Everything seemed so glorious just a little while ago. I'd made it through the Logrus. All of Shadow lay at my feet." He massaged his temples. Then, "You!" he spat. "I was somehow brought here because of you—to compete with you, to show you up in this race."

"You did a pretty good job, too. I didn't know you could run like that."

"I started practicing when I learned you were doing it in college. Wanted to get good enough to take you on."

"You got good," I acknowledged.

"But I wouldn't be in this damned place if it weren't for you. Or—" He gnawed his lip. "That's not exactly right, is it?" he asked. "*I* wouldn't be anywhere. I'm just a recording. . . ." Then he stared directly at me. "How long do we last?" he said. "How long is a Logrus-ghost good for?"

"I've no idea," I said, "what goes into creating one or how it's maintained. But I've met a number of Pattern-ghosts, and they gave me the impression that my blood would somehow sustain them, give them some sort of autonomy, some independence of the Pattern. Only one of them—Brand—got the fire instead of the blood, and it dissolved. Deirdre got the blood but was taken away then. I don't know whether she got enough."

He shook his head.

"I've a feeling—I don't know where it comes from— that something like that would work for me, too, and that it's blood for the pattern, fire for the Logrus."

"I don't know how to tell in what regions my blood is volatile," I said.

"It'd flame here," he answered. "Depends on who's in control. I just seem to know it. I don't know how."

"Then why did Brand show up in Logrus territory?"

He grinned.

"Maybe the Pattern sought to use a traitor for some sort of subversion. Or maybe Brand was trying to pull something on his own—like double-crossing the Pattern."

"That would be in character," I agreed, my breath finally slowing.

I whipped the Chaos blade out of my boot, slashed my left forearm, saw that it spouted fire, and held it toward him.

"Quick! Take it if you can!" I cried. "Before the Logrus calls you back!"

He seized my arm and seemed almost to inhale the fire that fountained from me. Looking down, I saw his feet become transparent, then his legs. The Logrus seemed anxious to reclaim him, just as the Pattern had Deirdre. I saw the fiery swirls begin within the haze that had been his legs. Then, suddenly, they flickered out, and the outline of those limbs became visible once again. He continued to draw my volatile blood from me, though I could no longer see flames as he was drinking now as

Deirdre had, directly from the wound. His legs began to solidify.

"You seem to be stabilizing," I said. "Take more."

Something struck me in the right kidney, and I jerked away, turning as I fell. A tall dark man stood beside me, withdrawing his boot from having kicked me. He had on green trousers and a black shirt, a green bandanna tied about his head.

"Now what perverse carrying-on is this?" he asked. "And in a sacred spot?"

I rolled to my knees and continued on up to my feet, my right arm bending, its wrist turning over, coming in to hold the dagger beside my hip. I raised my left arm, extended it before me. Blood rather than fire now fell from my latest wound.

"None of your damn business," I said, then added his name, having grown certain on the way up, "Caine."

He smiled and bowed, and his hands crossed and came apart. They'd been empty going in, but the right one held a dagger coming out. It must have come from a sheath strapped to his left forearm, inside the billowy sleeve. He had to have practiced the move a lot, too, to be that fast at it. I tried to remember things I'd heard about Caine and knives, and then I did and wished I hadn't. He was supposed to have been a master knife fighter. Shit.

"You have the advantage of me," he stated. "You look very familiar, but I do not believe I know you."

"Merlin," I said. "Corwin's son."

He had begun circling me slowly, but he halted.

"Excuse me if I find that difficult to believe."

"Believe as you wish. It is true."

"And this other one——his name is Jurt, isn't it?"

He gestured toward my brother, who had just gotten to his feet.

"How do you know that?" I asked.

He halted, furrowing his brow, narrowing his eyes.

"I—I'm not certain," he said then.

"I am," I told him. "Try to remember where you are and how you got here."

He backed away, two paces. Then he cried, "He's the one!" just as I saw it coming and shouted, "Jurt! Watch out!"

Jurt turned and bolted. I threw the dagger—always a bad thing to do, save that I was wearing a sword with which I could reach Caine before Caine could reach me now.

Jurt's speed was still with him, and he was out of range in an instant. The dagger, surprisingly, struck at the side of Caine's right shoulder point first, penetrating perhaps an inch or so into muscle. Then, even before he could turn back toward me, his body erupted in a dozen directions, emitting a series of vortices which sucked away all semblance of humanity in an instant, producing high-pitched whistling sounds as they orbited one another, two of them merging into a larger entity, which quickly absorbed the others then, its sound falling lower with each such acquisition. Finally there was but the one. For a moment it swayed toward me, then shot skyward and blew apart. The dagger was blown back in my direction, landing a pace to my right. When I recovered it, I found it to be warm, and it hummed faintly for several seconds before I sheathed it in my boot.

"What happened?" Jurt asked, turning back, approaching.

"Apparently Pattern-ghosts react violently to weapons from the Courts," I said.

"Good thing you had it handy. But why did he turn on me like that?"

"I believe that the Pattern sent him to stop you from

gaining autonomy——or to destroy you if you already had. I've a feeling it doesn't want agents of the other side gaining strength and stability in this place."

"But I'm no threat. I'm not on anybody's side but my own. I just want to get the hell out of here and be about my own business."

"Perhaps that of itself constitutes a threat."

"How so?" he asked.

"Who knows what your unusual background may fit you for as an independent agent——in light of what's going on? You may disturb the balance of the Powers. You may possess or have access to information which the principals do not wish to see bruited about the streets. You may be like the gipsy moth. Nobody could see what its effect on the environment would be when it escaped from the lab. You may——"

"Enough!" He raised a hand to silence me. "I don't care about any of those things. If they let me go and leave me alone, I'll stay out of their way."

"I'm not the one you have to convince," I told him.

He stared at me for a moment, then turned, describing a full circle. Darkness was all that I could see beyond the light of the roadway, but he called out in a large voice to anything, I suppose, "Do you hear me? I don't want to be involved in all this. I just want to go away. Live and let live, you know? Is that okay with you?"

I reached forward, caught hold of his wrist, and jerked him toward me. I did this because I had seen a small, ghostly replica of the Sign of the Logrus begin to take form in the air above his head. An instant later it fell, flashing like a lightning stroke, to the accompaniment of a sound like the cracking of a whip, passing through the space he had been occupying, opening a gap in the trail as it vanished.

"I guess it's not that easy to resign," he said. He

glanced overhead. "It could be readying another of those right now. It could strike again anytime, when I least expect it."

"Just like real life," I agreed. "But I think you may take it as a warning shot and let it go at that. They have a hard time reaching here. More important, since I was led to believe that this is my quest, do you know offhand whether you're supposed to be helping me or hindering me?"

"Now that you mention it," he said, "I remember suddenly being where I was with a chance to race you and a feeling that we'd fight or something afterward."

"What're your feelings on that now?"

"We've never gotten along all that well. But I don't like the idea of being used like this either."

"You willing to call a truce till I can see my way through this game and out of here?"

"What's in it for me?" he asked.

"I *will* find a way out of this damned place, Jurt. Come along and give me a hand—or at least don't get in the way—and I'll take you with me when I go."

He laughed.

"I'm not sure there is a way out of here," he said, "unless the Powers release us."

"Then you've nothing to lose," I told him, "and you'll probably even get to see me die trying."

"Do you really know both kinds of magic—Pattern and Logrus?" he asked.

"Yeah. But I'm a lot better at Logrus."

"Can you use either against its source?"

"That's a very intriguing metaphysical point, and I don't know the answer," I said, "and I'm not sure I'll find out. It's dangerous to invoke the Powers here. So all I'm left with is a few hung spells. I don't think it's magic that'll get us out of here."

"What, then?"

"I'm not certain. I am sure that I won't see the full picture till I get to the end of this trail, though."

"Well, hell—I don't know. This doesn't seem the healthiest place for me to spend my time. On the other hand, what if it's the only place something like me can have an existence? What if you find me a door and I step through it and melt?"

"If the Pattern-ghosts can manifest in Shadow, I'd guess you can, too. Those of Dworkin and Oberon came to me on the outside before I came to this place."

"That's encouraging. Would you try it if it were you?"

"You bet your life," I said.

He snorted.

"I get the point. I'll go a ways with you and see what happens. I'm not promising to help, but I won't sabotage you."

I held out my hand, and he shook his head.

"Let's not get carried away," he told me. "If my word's no good without a handshake, it's no good with one, is it?"

"I guess not."

"And I've never had a great desire to shake hands with you."

"Sorry I asked," I said. "Would you mind telling me why, though? I've always wondered."

He shrugged.

"Why does there always have to be a reason?" he said.

"The alternative is irrationality," I replied.

"Or privacy," he responded, turning away.

I commenced walking the trail once more. Shortly Jurt fell into step beside me. We walked for a long while in silence. One day I may learn when to keep my mouth shut or to quit when I'm ahead. Same thing.

The trail ran straight for a time but seemed to vanish

not too far ahead. When we neared the point of vanishment, I saw why: The trail curved behind a low prominence. We followed this turning and met with another shortly thereafter. Soon we had entered upon a regular series of switchbacks, realizing quickly that they were mitigating a fairly steep descent. As we proceeded down this turning way, I suddenly became aware of a bright squiggle, hanging in the middle distance. Jurt raised his hand, pointing at it, and began, "What ...?" just as it became apparent that it was the continuation of our trail, rising. At this, an instant reorientation occurred, and I realized that we were descending into what seemed a massive pit. And the air seemed to have grown somewhat cooler.

We continued our descent, and after a time something cold and moist touched the back of my right hand. I looked down in time to see a snowflake melting in the twilight glow which surrounded us. Moments later several more breezed by. A little after that we became aware of a larger brightness, far below.

I don't know what it is either, Frakir pulsed into my mind.

Thanks, I thought strongly back at her, having decided against advising Jurt of her presence.

Down. Down and around. Back. Back and forth. The temperature continued to decline. Snowflakes flitted. Arrays of rocks in the wall we now descended took on a bit of glitter.

Oddly, I didn't realize what it was until the first time I slipped.

"Ice!" Jurt announced suddenly, half toppling and catching himself up against the stone.

A distant sighing sound occurred, and it grew and grew, nearing us. It was not until it arrived, with a great buffeting gust, that we knew it to be a wind. And cold. It fled past like the breath of an ice age, and I raised my cloak against it. It followed us, softer thereafter, yet persistent, as we continued our descent.

By the time we reached the bottom it was damn cold, and the steps were either fully frosted over or carved of ice. The wind blew a steady, mournful note, and flakes of snow or pellets of ice came and went.

"Miserable climate!" Jurt growled, teeth chattering.

"I didn't think ghosts were susceptible to the mundane," I said.

"Ghost, hell!" he observed. "I feel the same as I always did. You'd think whatever sent me fully dressed to cross your trail might at least have provided for this eventuality.

"And this place isn't that mundane," he added. "They want us somewhere, you'd think they might have provided a shortcut. As it is, we'll be damaged merchandise by the time we get there."

"I don't really believe that either the Pattern or the Logrus has that much power in this place," I told him. "I'd just as soon they stayed out of our way entirely."

Our trail led outward across a gleaming plain——so flat and so gleaming that I feared it to consist entirely of ice. Nor was I incorrect.

"Looks slippery," Jurt said. "I'm going to shapeshift my feet, make them broader."

"It'll destroy your boots and leave you with cold feet," I said. "Why not just shift some of your weight downward, lower your center of gravity?"

"Always got an answer," he began sullenly. Then, "But this time you're right," he finished.

We stood there for several minutes as he grew shorter, more squat.

"Aren't you going to shift yourself?" he asked.

"I'll take my chances holding my center. I can move faster this way," I said.

"You can fall on your ass that way, too."

"We'll see."

We started out. We held our balance. The winds were stronger away from the wall we had descended. The surface of our icy trail, however, was not so slick as it had appeared on distant inspection. There were small ripples and ridges to it, adequate to provide some traction. The air burned its way into my lungs; flakes were beaten into swirling snow devil towers which fled like eccentric tops across our way. It was a bluish glow which emanated from the trail, tinting those flakes which came within its ambit. We hiked for perhaps a quarter mile before a new series of ghostly images began. The first appeared to be myself, sprawled across a heap of armor back at the chapel; the second was Deirdre beneath a lamppost, looking at her watch.

"What?" Jurt asked, as they came and went in a matter of instants.

"I didn't know the first time I saw them, and I still don't know," I answered, "though I thought you might be one of them when we first began our race. They come and go—at random, it would seem—with no special reason that I can figure."

The next was what appeared to be a dining room, a bowl of flowers on the table. There were no people in the room. There and gone—

No. Not entirely. It went away, but the flowers remained, there on the surface of the ice. I halted, then walked out toward them.

Merle, I don't know about leaving the trail. . . .

Oh, shit, I responded, moving toward a slab of ice which reminded me of the Stonehenge-like area back where I'd come aboard, incongruous flashes of color near its base.

There were a number of them—roses of many sorts. I stooped and picked one up. Its color was almost silver. . . .

"What *are* you doing here, dear boy?" I heard a familiar voice say.

I straightened immediately, to see that the tall dark figure which had emerged from behind the block of ice was not addressing me. He was nodding to Jurt, smiling.

"A fool's errand, I'm sure," Jurt replied.

"And this must be the fool," the other responded, "plucking that damnable flower. Silver rose of Amber— Lord Corwin's, I believe. Hello, Merlin. Looking for your father?"

I removed one of the spare clasp pins I keep pinned to the inside of my cloak. I used it to fasten the rose at my left breast. The speaker was Lord Borel, a duke of the royal House of Swayvill and reputedly one of my mother's lovers of long ago. He was also deemed to be one of the deadliest swordsmen in the Courts. Killing my father or Benedict or Eric had been an obsession with him for years. Unfortunately it had been Corwin whom he'd met, at a time when Dad was in a hurry—and they'd never crossed blades. Dad had suckered him instead and killed him in what I supposed was technically a somewhat less than fair fight. Which is okay. I'd never much liked the guy.

"You're dead, Borel. You know that?" I told him. "You're just a ghost of the man you were the day you took the Logrus. Out in the real world there is no Lord Borel anymore. You want to know why? Because Corwin killed you the day of the Patternfall War."

"You lie, you little shit!" he told me.

"Uh, no," Jurt offered. "You're dead all right. Run through, I heard. Didn't know it was Corwin did it, though."

"It was," I said.

He looked away, and I saw his jaw muscles bunching and relaxing, bunching and relaxing.

"And this place is some sort of afterlife?" he asked a little later, still not looking back at us.

"I suppose you could call it that," I said.

"Can we die yet again here?"

"I think so," I told him.

"What is that?"

His gaze had suddenly dropped, and I followed it. Something lay upon the ice nearby, and I took a step toward it.

"An arm," I replied. "It appears to be a human arm."

"What's it doing there?" Jurt asked, walking over and kicking it.

It moved in a fashion which showed us that it was not simply lying there but rather was extended up out of the ice. In fact, it twitched and continued to flex spasmodically for several seconds after Jurt kicked it. Then I noted another, some distance away, and what appeared to be a leg. Farther on, a shoulder, arm attached, a hand . . .

"Some cannibal's deep freeze," I suggested.

Jurt chuckled.

"Then you're dead, too," Borel stated.

"Nope," I replied. "I'm the real thing. Just passing through, on my way to a far, far better place."

"What of Jurt?"

"Jurt's an interesting problem, both physically and theologically," I explained. "He's enjoying a peculiar kind of bilocation."

"I'd hardly say I'm enjoying it," Jurt observed. "But considering the alternative, I suppose I'm glad I'm here."

"That's the sort of positive thinking that's worked so many wonders for the Courts over the years," I said.

Jurt chuckled again.

I heard that metallic sighing sound one does not easily forget. I knew that I could not possibly draw my blade, turn, and parry in time if Borel wished to run me through from the rear. On the other hand, he took great pride in observing every punctilio when it came to killing people. He always played fair because he was so damned good that he never lost anyway. Might as well go for the reputation, too. I immediately raised both hands, to irritate him by acting as if he had just threatened me from the rear.

Stay invisible, Frakir. When I turn and snap my wrist, let go. Stick to him when you hit, find your way to his throat. You know what to do when you get there.

Right, boss, she replied.

"Draw your blade and turn, Merle."

"Doesn't sound too sporting to me, Borel," I replied.

"You dare to accuse me of anything less than propriety?" he said.

"Hard to tell when I can't see what you're up to," I answered.

"Then draw your weapon and turn around."

"I'm turning," I said. "But I'm not touching the thing."

I turned quickly, snapping my left wrist, feeling Frakir depart. As I did, my feet went out from under me. I'd moved too fast on a very smooth patch of ice. Catching myself, I felt a shadow drift into place before me. When I looked up, I beheld the point of Borel's blade, about six inches from my right eye.

"Rise slowly," he said, and I did.

"Draw your weapon now," he ordered.

"And if I refuse?" I inquired, trying to buy time.

"You will prove yourself unworthy to be considered a gentleman, and I will act accordingly."

"By attacking me anyway?" I asked.

"The rules permit this," he said.

"Shove your rules," I replied, crossing my right foot behind my left and springing backward as I drew my blade and let it fall into a guard position.

He was on me in an instant. I continued my retreat, backing past the big slab of ice from behind which he had appeared. I had no desire to stand and trade techniques with him, especially now that I could see the speed of those attacks. Parrying them took a lot less effort while I was backing off. My blade did not feel quite right, however, and as I scanned it quickly I saw why. It was *not* my weapon.

In the glittering light from the trail, bounced off the ice, I saw the swirling inlay along part of the blade. There was only one weapon like this that I knew of, and I had only just seen it recently, in what might have been my father's hand. It was Grayswandir that moved before me. I felt myself smile at the irony. This was the weapon which had slain the real Lord Borel.

"You smile at your own cowardice?" he asked. "Stand and fight, bastard!"

As if in answer to his suggestion, I felt my rearward movement arrested. I was not run through when I ventured a quick downward glance, however, for I realized from his expression that something similar had happened to my attacker.

Our ankles had been seized by several of those hands which extended up through the ice, holding us firmly in place. And this made it Borel's turn to smile, for though he could not lunge, I could no longer retreat. Which meant—

His blade flashed forward, and I parried in quarte,

attacked in sixte. He parried and feinted. Then quarte again, and the next attack. Riposte. Parry sixte— No, that was a feint. Catch him in four. Feint. Feint again. Hit—

Something white and hard passed over his shoulder and struck my forehead. I fell back, though the grasping hands kept me from collapsing completely. Good thing I sagged, actually, or his thrust might have punctured my liver. My reflexes or some touch of the magic I've heard may dwell in Grayswandir threw my arm forward as my knees buckled. I felt the blade strike something, though I was not even looking in that direction, and I heard Borel grunt surprisedly, then utter an oath. I heard Jurt mouthing an oath of his own about then, too. He was out of my line of sight.

Then came a bright flash, even as I flexed my legs, stabilizing, parried a head cut, and began rising. I saw then that I had succeeded in cutting Borel's forearm, and fire spurted fountainlike from the wound. His body began to glow, his lower outline to blur.

"It was by no skill you bested me!" he cried.

I shrugged.

"It isn't the Winter Olympics either," I told him.

He changed his grip on his blade, drew back his arm, and hurled the weapon at me—right before he dissolved into a tower of sparks and was drawn upward and vanished above.

I parried the blade, and it passed me to the left, buried itself partway in the ice and stood vibrating there, like something in a Scandinavian's version of Arthurian legend. Jurt rushed toward me, kicked at the hands which held my ankles until they released me, and squinted at my brow.

I felt something fall upon me.

Sorry, boss. I hit around his knee. By the time I reached his throat he was already on fire, Frakir said.

All's well that ends well, I replied. *You weren't singed, were you?*

Didn't even feel the heat.

"Sorry I hit you with that piece of ice," Jurt said. "I was aiming at Borel."

I moved away from the plain of hands, heading back toward the trail.

"Indirectly it helped," I said, but I didn't feel like thanking him. How could I know where he'd really been aiming? I glanced back once, and several of the hands Jurt had kicked were giving us the finger.

Why had I been wearing Grayswandir? Would another weapon have affected a Logrus-ghost as strongly? Had it really been my father, then, who had brought me here? And had he felt I might need the extra edge his weapon could provide? I wanted to think so, to believe that he had been more than a Pattern-ghost. And if he was, I wondered at his part in the entire affair. What might he know about all this? And which side might he be on?

The winds died down as we moved along the trail, and the only arms we saw extended above the ice bore torches which brightened our way for a great distance—to the foot of the far escarpment, actually. Nothing untoward occurred as we crossed that frozen place.

"From what you've told me and what I've seen," Jurt said, "I get the impression it's the Pattern that's sponsoring this trip and the Logrus that's trying to punch your ticket."

Just then the ice cracked in a number of places. Fracture lines rushed toward us from several directions, both sides. They slowed, however, as they neared our trail, causing me to notice for the first time that it had risen

above the general level of the plain. We now occupied
something of a causeway, and the ice shattered itself
harmlessly along its sides.

"Like that," Jurt observed with a gesture. "How'd you
get into this mess anyway?"

"It all started on April thirtieth," I began.

VII

Some of the arms seemed to be waving good-bye to us as we commenced our climb after reaching the wall. Jurt thumbed his nose at them.

"Can you blame me for wanting to escape this place?" he asked.

"Not in the least," I replied.

"If that transfusion you gave me really placed me beyond control of the Logrus, then I might dwell here for some indefinite period of time."

"Sounds possible."

"That's why you must realize I threw the ice at Borel, not you. Besides the fact that you're smarter than he was and might be able to find a way out of here, he was a creature of the Logrus, too, and wouldn't have had enough fire if the need arose."

"That had occurred to me also," I said, withholding a possible out I'd guessed at, to keep myself indispensable. "But what are you getting at?"

"I'm trying to say that I'll give you any kind of help you need, just so you don't leave me behind when you go. I know we never got along before, but I'm willing to put that aside if you are."

"I always was," I said. "You were the one who started all our fights and kept me in trouble."

He smiled.

"I never did, and I won't do it again," he said. "Yeah, okay, you're right. I didn't like you, and maybe I still don't. But I won't mess you up when we need each other this way."

"The way I see it, you need me a hell of a lot more than I need you."

"I can't argue with that, and I can't make you trust me," he said. "Wish I could." We climbed a little more before he continued, and I fancied the air had already grown a trifle warmer. Then, "But look at it this way," he finally continued, "I resemble your brother Jurt, and I come close to representing something he once was—close, but not a perfect fit. I began diverging from his model beginning with our race. My circumstances are uniquely my own, and I've been thinking steadily since I gained my autonomy. The real Jurt knows things I do not and has powers I don't possess. But I have his memories up through his taking the Logrus, and I'm the second greatest authority there is on the way he thinks. Now, if he's become such a threat as you've indicated, you might find me more than a little useful when it comes to second-guessing him."

"You have a point," I acknowledged. "Unless, of course, the two of you were to throw in together."

He shook his head.

"He wouldn't trust me," he said, "and I wouldn't trust him. We'd both know better. A matter of introspection. See what I mean?"

"It means neither one of you is trustworthy."

His brow furrowed; then he nodded.

"Yeah, I guess so," he said.

"So why should I trust you?"

"Right now because you've got me by the balls. Later on because I'll be so damn useful."

After several more minutes' ascending, I told him, "The thing that bothers me the most about you is that it was not all that long ago that Jurt took the Logrus. You are not an older, milder version of my least favorite relative. You are a very recent model. As for your divergence from the original, I can't see this short while as making that much difference."

He shrugged.

"What can I say that I haven't said already?" he asked. "Let's just deal in terms of power and self-interest then."

I smiled. We both knew that that was the way it was anyway. The conversation helped pass the time, though.

A thought came to me as we climbed.

"Do you think you could walk through Shadow?" I asked him.

"I don't know," he answered after a time. "My last memory from before I came to this place was of completing the Logrus. I guess the recording was completed at that time, too. So I have no recollection of Suhuy instructing me in shadow-walking, no memory of trying it. I'd guess I could do it, wouldn't you think?"

I paused to catch my breath.

"It's such an arcane matter that I don't even feel qualified to speculate on it. I thought maybe you'd come equipped with ready-made answers for things like that—some sort of preternatural awareness of your limits and abilities."

"Afraid not. Unless you'd call a hunch preternatural."

"I suppose I would if you were right often enough."

"Shit. It's too soon to tell."

"Shit. You're right."

Soon we'd climbed above the line of haze from which the flakes seemed to fall. A little farther, and the winds died to breezes. Farther still, and these subsided to nothing. The rim was in sight by then, and shortly thereafter we achieved it.

I turned and looked back down. All I could see was a bit of glitter through the mist. In the other direction our trail ran on in a zigzag fashion, here and there looking like a series of Morse dashes—regular interruptions, possibly rock formations. We followed it to the right until it turned left.

I reserved some attention for Jurt, looking for signs of recognition at any feature of the terrain. A talk is only words, and he was still some version of the Jurt I'd grown up with. And if he became responsible for my falling into any sort of trap, I was going to pass Grayswandir through his personal space as soon as I became aware of it.

Flicker . . .

Formation to the left, cavelike, as if the hole in the rock opened into another reality. An oddly shaped car driving up a steep city street . . .

"What . . . ?" Jurt began.

"I still don't know their significance. A whole mess of sequences like this were with me earlier, though. In fact, at first I thought you were one of them."

"Looks real enough to walk into."

"Maybe it is."

"It might be our way out of here."

"Somehow that just seems a little too easy."

"Well, let's give it a try."

"Go ahead," I told him.

We departed the trail, advanced upon the reality window, and kept going. In a moment he was on the side-walk next to the street up which the car was passing. He turned and waved. I saw his mouth working, but no words came to me.

If I could brush snow off the red Chevy, why couldn't I enter entirely into one of these sequences? And if I could do that, mightn't it be possible that I could shadow-walk from there, wending my way to some more congenial spot, leaving this dark world behind? I moved forward.

Suddenly I was there, and the sound had been turned on for me. I looked about at the buildings, at the sharply inclined street. I listened to the traffic sounds, and I sniffed the air. This place could almost be one of San Francisco's shadows. I hurried to catch up with Jurt, who was moving toward the corner.

I reached him quickly, fell into step beside him. We came to the corner. We turned. We froze.

There was nothing there. We faced a wall of black-ness. That is, not just darkness but an absolute empti-ness, from which we immediately drew back.

I put my hand forth slowly. A tingling began as it neared the blackness, then a chill, followed by a fear. I drew back. Jurt reached for it, did the same. Abruptly he stopped, picked up the bottom of a broken bottle from the gutter, turned, and hurled it through a nearby window. Immediately he began running in that direc-tion.

I followed. I joined him before the broken pane, stared within.

Again the blackness. There was nothing at all on the other side of the window.

"Kind of spooky," I remarked.

"Uh-huh," Jurt said. "It's as if we're being granted extremely limited access to various shadows. What do you make of it?"

"I'm beginning to wonder whether there isn't something we're supposed to be looking for in one of these places," I said.

Suddenly the blackness beyond the window was gone, and a candle flickered on a small table beyond it. I began to reach through the broken glass toward it. Immediately it vanished. Again there was only blackness.

"I'd take that as an affirmative response to your question," Jurt said.

"I believe you're right. But we can't be looking for something in every one of these things we pass."

"I think maybe something's just been trying to get your attention, to get you to realize that you should be watching what appears, that something probably will be presented once you begin noticing."

Brightness. A whole tableful of candles now blazed beyond the window.

"Okay," I hollered. "If that's all you want, I'll do it. Is there anything else I should be looking for here?"

The darkness came. It crept around the corner and moved slowly toward us. The candles vanished, and it flowed from the window. The buildings across the street disappeared behind an ebon wall.

"I take it the answer is no," I cried. Then I turned and beat it back along our narrowing black tunnel toward the trail. Jurt was right behind me.

"Good thinking," I told him when we stood back on the glowing way, watching that rising street get squeezed out of existence beside us. "Do you think it was just pulling these sequences at random till I finally entered one?"

"Yes."

"Why?"

"I think it has more control in those places and could respond to your questions more readily in one of them."

"'It' being the Pattern?"

"Probably."

"Okay. The next one it opens to me, I'm going in. I'll do whatever it wants there if it means I get out of here sooner."

"We, brother. We."

"Of course," I answered.

We commenced walking again. Nothing new and intriguing appeared beside us, though. The road zigged and zagged, and we walked along it, and I got to wondering whom we might meet next. If I were indeed on the Pattern's turf and on the verge of doing something it wanted, then it seemed that the Logrus might send along someone I knew to attempt to dissuade me. No one appeared at all, though, and we took the final turn, followed a trail suddenly grown straight for some time, then saw it end abruptly within a dark mass far ahead.

Continuing, I saw that it plunged on into a great, dark, mountainous mass. I felt vaguely claustrophobic, just considering the implications, and I heard Jurt mutter an obscenity as we trudged toward it. Before we reached it, there came a flickering to my right. Turning, I beheld Random and Vialle's bedroom, back in Amber. I was looking from the southern side of the room, between the sofa and a bedside table, past a chair, across the rug and the cushions toward the fireplace, the windows which flanked it admitting a soft daylight. No one was present in the bed or occupying any other piece of furniture, and the logs on the grate had burned themselves down to red embers, smoking fitfully.

"What now?" Jurt asked.

"This is it," I replied. "It has to be, don't you see? Once I got the message as to what was going on, it presented the real thing. I've got to act fast, too, I think—as soon as I figure just what—"

One of the stones beside the fireplace began to glow redly. It increased in intensity as I watched. There was no way that those embers could be doing it. Therefore . . .

I rushed forward under the influence of a powerful imperative. I heard Jurt shout something behind me, but his voice was cut off as I entered the room. I caught a whiff of Vialle's favorite perfume as I passed beside the bed. This was really Amber, I was certain, not just some shadowy facsimile thereof. I moved quickly to the right of the fireplace.

Jurt burst into the room behind me.

"Better come out fighting!" he cried.

I whirled to face him, shouted, "Shut up!" then raised a finger to my lips.

He crossed to my side, caught hold of my arm, and whispered hoarsely, "Borel's trying to materialize again! He might be solid and waiting by the time you leave!"

From the sitting room I heard Vialle's voice.

"Is someone there?" she called.

I jerked my arm free of Jurt's grasp, knelt upon the hearth, and seized hold of the glowing stone. It appeared to be mortared in place but came loose easily when I drew upon it.

"How'd you know that one came free?" Jurt whispered.

"The glow," I replied.

"What glow?" he asked.

I did not answer him but thrust my right hand into the opened area, hoping offhandedly there were no booby traps. The opening extended back for a good distance beyond the length of the stone. And there I felt it, suspended from peg or hook: a length of chain. I caught hold of it and drew it forth. I heard Jurt catch his breath beside me.

The last time I had seen it was when Random had worn it at Caine's funeral. It was the Jewel of Judgment that I held in my hand. I raised it quickly and slipped the chain over my head, letting that red stone fall upon my breast, just as the door to the sitting room was opened.

Placing my finger to my lips, once more I reached forward, caught hold of Jurt's shoulders, and turned him back toward the opened wall which let upon our trail. He began to protest, but I propelled him with a sharp push, and he moved off in that direction.

"Who's there?" I heard Vialle ask, and Jurt glanced back at me, looking puzzled.

I did not feel we could afford the time for my explaining by sign language or whisper that she was blind. So I gave him another push. Only this time he stepped to the side, extended his leg, slipped a hand behind my back, and pushed me forward. A brief expletive escaped my lips, and then I was falling. From behind me, I heard Vialle's "Who—" before her voice was cut off.

I tumbled onto the trail, managing to draw the dagger from my right boot as I fell. I rolled and came up with the point extended toward the figure of Borel, which seemed to have found its form once more.

He was smiling, his weapon yet undrawn, as he regarded me.

"There is no field of arms here," he stated, "to provide you with a lucky accident such as you enjoyed when last we met."

"Too bad," I said.

"If I but gain that bauble you wear about your neck and deliver it to the place of the Logrus, I will be granted a normal existence, to replace my living counterpart—he who was treacherously slain by your father, as you pointed out."

The vision of Amber's royal apartments had vanished. Jurt stood off the trail, near what had been its interface with this odd realm. "I knew I couldn't beat him," he called out when he felt my glance, "but you took him once."

I shrugged.

At this Borel turned toward Jurt.

"You would betray the Courts and the Logrus?" he asked him.

"On the contrary," Jurt responded. "I may be saving them from a serious mistake."

"What mistake might that be?"

"Tell him, Merlin. Tell him what you told me while we were climbing out of the deep freeze," he said.

Borel glanced back at me.

"There's something funny about this entire setup," I said. "I've a feeling it's all a duel between the Powers—the Logrus and the Pattern. Amber and the Courts may be secondary to the entire affair. You see—"

"Ridiculous!" he interrupted, drawing his weapon. "This is just made-up nonsense to avoid *our* duel."

I tossed the dagger into my left hand and drew Grayswandir with my right.

"The hell with you then!" I said. "Come and get it!"

A hand fell upon my shoulder. And it kept right on falling with a sort of twist to it, spinning me into a downward spiral which threw me off to the left of the trail. From the corner of my eye, I saw that Borel had taken a step backward.

"You've a resemblance to Eric or to Corwin," came a soft, familiar voice, "though I know you not. But you wear the Jewel, which makes your person too important to risk in a petty squabble."

I came to a stop and turned my head. It was Benedict whom I beheld—a Benedict with two normal hands.

"My name is Merlin and I'm Corwin's son," I said, "and this is a master duelist from the Courts of Chaos."

"You appear to be on a mission, Merlin. Be about it then," Benedict said.

The point of Borel's blade flicked into a position about ten inches from my throat. "You are going nowhere," he stated, "not with that jewel."

There was no sound as Benedict's blade was drawn and moved to beat Borel's off its line.

"As I said, be on your way, Merlin," Benedict told me.

I got to my feet, moved quickly out of range, passed them both cautiously.

"If you kill him," Jurt said, "he can rematerialize after a period of time."

"How interesting," Benedict remarked, flicking off an attack and retreating slightly. "How long a time?"

"Several hours."

"And how much time will you need to complete whatever you're about?"

Jurt looked at me.

"I'm not certain," I answered.

Benedict executed an odd little parry, followed by a strange shuffling step and a brief slashing attack. A button flew from Borel's shirt front.

"In that case I'll make this last for a time," Benedict said. "Good luck, lad."

He gave me a quick salute with the weapon, at which moment Borel attacked. Benedict used an Italianate sixte which threw both their points off to the side, advancing as he did so. He reached forward quickly then with his left hand and pulled the other's nose. Then he pushed him away, stepped back a pace, and smiled.

"What do you usually charge for lessons?" I overheard him asking as Jurt and I hurried down the path.

* * *

"I wonder how long it does take for one of the Powers to materialize a ghost," Jurt said as we jogged toward the mountainous mass the trail entered.

"Several hours for Borel alone," I said, "and if the Logrus wants the Jewel as badly as I'd guess, I'd think it would have summoned an army of ghosts if it could. I'm certain now that this place is very difficult for both Powers to reach. I get the feeling they can only manifest via the barest trickles of energy. If that weren't the case, I'd never have gotten this far."

Jurt reached out as if to touch the Jewel, apparently thought better of it, withdrew his hand.

"It seems you've definitely aligned yourself with the Pattern now," he observed.

"Looks as if you have, too. Unless you're planning on stabbing me in the back at the last moment," I said.

He chuckled. Then, "Not funny," he said. "I've got to be on your side. I can see that the Logrus just created me as a disposable tool. I'd wind up on the scrap heap when the job's done. I've a feeling I might have dissipated already had it not been for the transfusion. So I'm with you, like it or not, and your back is safe."

We ran on along the now-straight way, its terminus finally grown near. Jurt finally asked, "What is the significance of that pendant? The Logrus seems to want it badly."

"It's called the Jewel of Judgment," I answered. "It is said to be older than the Pattern itself and to have been instrumental in its creation."

"Why do you think you were led to it and obtained it with such ease?"

"I have no idea whatsoever," I said. "If you get one before I do, I'll be glad to hear it."

Soon we reached the place where the trail plunged into the greater darkness. We halted and regarded it.

"No signs posted," I said, checking above and to either side of that entranceway.

Jurt gave me an odd look.

"You've always had a weird sense of humor, Merlin" he said. "Who'd put up a sign in a place like this?"

"Someone else with a weird sense of humor," I replied.

"Might as well go on," he said, turning back toward the entrance.

A bright red exit sign had appeared above the opening. Jurt stared for a moment, then shook his head slowly. We entered.

We took our way down a wandering tunnel—a thing which puzzled me a bit. The artificial quality of most of the rest of this place had led me to expect a ruler-straight trail through a smooth-walled shaft, geometrically precise in all its features. Instead, it seemed as if we were traversing a series of natural caverns—stalactites, stalagmites, pillars, and pools displayed at either hand.

The Jewel cast a baleful light over any features I turned to scrutinize.

"Do you know how to use that stone?" Jurt asked me.

I thought back over my father's story.

"When the time comes, I believe that I will," I said, raising the Jewel and studying it for a moment, then letting it fall again. I was less concerned with it than with the route we were following.

I kept turning my head as we made our way from damp grotto to high cathedral chamber, along narrow passages, down stony waterfalls. There was something familiar here, though I couldn't put my finger on it.

"Anything about this place bring back memories?" I asked him.

"Not for me," Jurt replied.

We kept going, at one point passing a side cave containing three human skeletons. These being, in their fashion, the first real signs of life I had seen since the onset of this journey, I remarked on it.

Jurt nodded slowly.

"I am beginning to wonder whether we are still walking between shadows," he said, "or whether we might actually have departed that place and entered Shadow— perhaps when we came into these caves."

"I could find out by trying to summon the Logrus," I said, causing Frakir immediately to pulse sharply upon my wrist. "But considering the metaphysical politics of the situation, I'd rather not."

"I was just going by the colors of all the minerals in the walls," he said. "The place we left behind kind of favored monochrome. Not that I give a shit about the scenery. What I'm saying is that if we have, it's a kind of victory."

I pointed at the ground.

"So long as that glowing trail is there, we're not off the hook."

"What if we simply walked away from it now?" he asked, turning to the right and taking a single step in that direction.

A stalactite vibrated and crashed to the ground before him. It missed him by about a foot. He was back beside me in an instant.

"Of course, it would be a real shame not to find out where we're headed," he said.

"Quests are that way. It'd be bad form to miss the fun."

We hiked on. Nothing allegorical happened around us. Our voices and our footfalls echoed. Water dripped in some of the danker grots. Minerals flashed. Our way seemed a gradual descent.

For how long we walked I could not tell. After a time stony chambers took on a generic appearance—as if we passed regularly through a teleportation device which rerouted us back through the same caves and corridors. This had the effect of blurring my sense of time. Repetitious actions have a lulling effect and—

Suddenly our trail debouched into a larger passage, turned left. Finally, some variation. Only this way, too, looked familiar. We followed our line of light through the darkness. After a time we went by a side passage to the left. Jurt glanced up it and hurried past.

"Any damned thing might be lurking around here," he observed.

"True," I acknowledged. "But I wouldn't worry about it."

"Why not?"

"I think I'm beginning to understand."

"Mind telling me what's going on?"

"It'd take too long. Just wait. We'll be finding out pretty soon."

We went by another side passage. Similar, yet different. Of course.

I increased my pace, anxious to learn the truth. Another sideway. I broke into a run . . .

Another . . .

Jurt pounded along beside me, the echoes falling about us. Up ahead. Soon.

Another turning.

And then I slowed, for the passage continued ahead but our trail didn't. It curved to the left, vanishing beneath a big metal-bound door. I reached out to my right to where the hook was supposed to be, located it, removed the key that hung there. I inserted it, turned it, withdrew it, rehung it.

I don't like this place, boss, Frakir noted.

I know.

"Seems as if you know what you're doing," Jurt remarked.

"Yep," I said, then added, "Up to a point," as I realized that this door opened outward rather than inward.

I caught hold of the large handle to the left and began to pull upon it.

"Mind telling me where we've wound up?" he asked.

The big door creaked, commenced a slow movement as I walked backward.

"These are amazingly like a section of caverns in Kolvir beneath Amber Castle," I replied.

"Great," he said. "And what's behind the door?"

"This is much like the entrance to the chamber which houses the Pattern in Amber."

"Wonderful," he said. "I'll probably go up in a puff of smoke if I set foot inside."

"But it is not quite the same," I continued. "We had Suhuy come and look at the Pattern itself before I walked it. He didn't suffer any ill effects from the proximity."

"Our mother walked the Pattern."

"Yes, that's true."

"Frankly, I think anyone of proper consanguinity in the Courts could walk the Pattern—and vice versa for my relatives in Amber with the Logrus. Tradition has it we're all related from back somewhere in the dim and misty."

"Okay. I'll go in with you. There's room to move around inside without touching the thing, isn't there?"

"Yes."

I drew the door the rest of the way open, braced my shoulder against it, and stared. This was it. I saw that our glowing trail ended a few inches beyond the threshold.

I drew a deep breath and muttered some expletive as I let it go.

"What is it?" Jurt asked, trying to see past me.

"Not what I expected," I told him.

I moved aside and let him have a look.

He stared for several seconds, then said, "I don't understand."

"I am not certain that I do either," I said, "but I intend to find out."

I entered the chamber, and he followed me. This was not the Pattern that I knew. Or rather, it was and it wasn't. It conformed to the same general configuration as the Pattern in Amber, only it was broken. There were several places where the lines had been erased, destroyed, removed in some fashion—or perhaps never properly executed in the first place. The ordinarily dark interlinear areas were bright, blue-white, the lines themselves black. It was as if some essence had drained from the diagram to permeate the field. The lighted area seemed to ripple slowly as I viewed it.

And beyond all of this was the big difference: The Pattern in Amber did not contain a circle of fire at its center, a woman dead, unconscious, or under a spell within it.

And the woman, of course, had to be Coral. I knew that immediately, though I had to wait for more than a minute before I got a glimpse of her face beyond the flames.

The big door shut itself behind us while I stood staring. Jurt stood unmoving for a long time also before he said, "That Jewel is certainly busy at something. You should see your face in its light right now."

I glanced downward and observed its ruddy pulsations. Between the blue-white flux in which the Pattern was grounded and the flickering of that circle of flame I had not noted the sudden activity on the part of the stone.

I moved a step nearer, feeling a wave of coldness similar to that of an activated Trump. This had to be one of the Broken Patterns of which Jasra had been speaking—representative of one of the Ways in which she and Julia were initiates. This placed me in one of the early shadows, near Amber herself. Thoughts began to race through my mind at a ferocious pace.

I had only recently become aware of the possibility that the Pattern might actually be sentient. Its corollary, that the Logrus was sentient, seemed likely also. The notion of its sentiency had been presented to me when Coral had succeeded in negotiating the Pattern and then had asked it to send her where she should go. It had done so, and this was the place to which she had been transported, and her condition was obviously the reason I couldn't reach her by means of her Trump. When I had addressed the Pattern following her disappearance, it had—almost playfully, it seemed at the time—shifted me from one end of its chamber to the other, apparently to satisfy me on the matter of its sentience.

And it wasn't merely sentient, I decided, as I raised the Jewel of Judgment and stared into its depths. It was clever. For the images that I saw within the stone, showing me what it was that was desired of me, represented something I would not have been willing to do under other circumstances. Having come away from that strange realm through which I had been led on this quest, I would have shuffled out a Trump and called someone for a fast exit—or even summoned the image of the Logrus and let the two of them slug it out while I slipped away through Shadow. But Coral slept in a circle of flame at the heart of the Broken Pattern. . . . She was the authentic Pattern's hold over me. It had to have understood something back when she was walking it, laid its plan, and set me up at that time.

It wanted me to repair this particular image of itself, to mend this Broken Pattern, by walking it, bearing the

Jewel of Judgment with me. This was how Oberon had repaired the damage to the original. Of course, the act had been sufficiently traumatic to kill him . . .

On the other hand, the King had been dealing with the real thing, and this was only one of its images. Also, my father had survived the creation of his own ersatz Pattern from scratch.

Why me? I wondered then. Was it because I was the son of the man who had succeeded in creating another Pattern? Did it involve the fact that I bore the image of the Logrus within me as well as that of the Pattern? Was it simply because I was handy and coercible? All of the above? None of them?

"How about it?" I called out. "Have you got an answer for me?"

There was a quick pang in my stomach and a wave of dizziness as the chamber spun, faded, stood still, and I regarded Jurt across the expanse of the Pattern, the big door at his back.

"How'd you do that?" he hollered.

"I didn't," I replied.

"Oh."

He edged his way to his right till he came to the wall. Maintaining contact with it, he began moving about the Pattern's periphery, as if afraid to approach any nearer to it than he had to or to remove his gaze from it.

From this side I could see Coral a bit more clearly, within the fiery hedge. Funny. It was not as if there were a large emotional investment here. We were not lovers, not even terrifically close friends. We had become acquainted only the other day, shared a long walk about, around, and under the town and palace, had a meal together, a couple of drinks, a few laughs. If we became better acquainted, perhaps we would discover that we couldn't stand each other. Still, I had enjoyed her company, and I realized that I did want to take the time to get to know her better. And in some ways I felt responsible for her present condition, through a kind of contributory negligence. In other words, the Pattern had me by the balls. If I wanted to free her, I had to repair it.

The flames nodded in my direction.

"It's a dirty trick," I said aloud.

The flames nodded again.

I continued to study the Broken Pattern. Almost everything I knew about the phenomenon had come to me by way of my conversation with Jasra. But I recalled her telling me that initiates of the Broken Pattern walked it in the areas between the lines, whereas the image in the Jewel was instructing me to walk the lines, as one normally would the Pattern itself. Which made sense, as I recalled my father's story. It should serve to inscribe the proper path across the breaks. I wasn't looking for any half-assed between-the-lines initiation.

Jurt made his way about the far end of the Pattern, turned, and began to move toward me. When he came abreast of a break in the outer line, the light flowed from it across the floor. The look on his face was ghastly as it touched his foot. He screamed and began to melt.

"Stop!" I cried. "Or you can find another Pattern repairman! Restore him and leave him alone or I won't do it! I mean it!"

Jurt's collapsing legs lengthened again. The rush of blue-white incandescence which had fled upward through his body was withdrawn as the light retreated from him. The expression of pain left his face.

"I know he's a Logrus-ghost," I said, "and he's patterned on my least favorite relative, but you leave him alone, you son of a bitch, or I won't walk you! You can keep Coral and you can stay broken!"

The light flowed back through the imperfection, and things stood as they had moments before.

"I want a promise," I said.

A gigantic sheet of flame rose from the Broken Pattern to the top of the chamber, then fell again.

"I take it that is an affirmative," I said.

The flames nodded.

"Thanks," I heard Jurt whisper.

VIII

And so I commenced my walk. The black line did not have the same feeling to it as the blazing ones back under Amber. My feet came down as if on dead ground, though there was a tug and a crackle when I raised them.

"Merlin!" Jurt called out. "What should I do?"

"What do you mean?" I shouted back.

"How do I get out of here?"

"Go out the door and start shadow-shifting," I said, "or follow me through this Pattern and have it send you wherever you want."

"I don't believe you can shadow-shift this close to Amber, can you?"

"Maybe we are too close. So get away physically and then do it."

I kept moving. There came small crackling sounds whenever I raised my feet now.

"I'd get lost in the caves if I tried that."

"Then follow me."

"The Pattern will destroy me."

"It's promised not to."

He laughed harshly.

"And you believe it?"

"If it wants this job done properly, it has no choice."

I came to the first break in the Pattern. A quick consultation of the Jewel showed me where the line should lie. With some trepidation I took my first step beyond the visible marking. Then another. And another. I wanted to look back when I finally crossed the gap. Instead, I waited until the natural curving of my route granted me that view. I saw then that the entire line I had walked thus far had begun to glow, just like the real thing. The spilled luminescence seemed to have been absorbed within it, darkening the interstitial ground area. Jurt had moved to a position near that beginning.

He caught my gaze.

"I don't know, Merlin," he said. "I just don't know."

"The Jurt I knew wouldn't have had guts enough to try it," I told him.

"Neither do I."

"As you pointed out, our mother did it. Odds are you've got the genes. What the hell. If I'm wrong, it'll be over before you know it."

I took another step. He gave a mirthless laugh.

Then, "What the hell," he said, and he set his foot upon it.

"Hey, I'm still alive," he called out. "What now?"

"Keep coming," I said. "Follow me. Don't stop. And don't leave the line or all bets are off."

There followed another turning of the way, and I followed it and lost sight of him. As I continued along, I became aware of a pain in my right ankle—product of all the hiking and climbing I had done, I supposed. It began increasing with each step. It was hot and soon grew to be quite terrible. Had I somehow torn a ligament? Had I——

Of course. I could smell the burning leather now.

I plunged my hand into the sheath area of my boot and withdrew the Chaos dagger. It was radiating heat. This proximity to the Pattern was affecting it. I couldn't keep it about me any longer.

I drew my arm back and cast the weapon across the Pattern in the direction I was facing, toward the end of the room where the doorway was situated. Automatically my gaze followed its passage. There was a small movement in the shadows toward which it flew. A man was standing there, watching me. The dagger struck the wall and fell to the floor. He leaned over and picked it up. I heard a chuckle. He made a sudden movement, and the dagger came arcing back across the Pattern in my direction.

It landed ahead and to the right of me. As soon as it made contact with the Pattern, a fountain of blue flame engulfed it, rising well above the level of my head, splattering, sizzling. I flinched and I slowed, though I knew it would do me no permanent harm, and I kept walking. I had reached the long frontal arc where the going was slow.

"Stay on the line," I yelled to Jurt. "Don't worry about things like that."

"I understand," he said. "Who's that guy?"

"Damned if I know."

I pushed ahead. I was nearer to the circle of flame now. I wondered what the *ty'iga* would think of my present predicament. I made my way around another turn and was able to see back over a considerable section of my trail. It was glowing evenly, and Jurt was coming on strongly, moving as I had, the flames rising above his ankles now. They were almost up to my knees. From the corner of my eye I saw a movement from that area of the chamber where the stranger stood.

The man moved forth from his shadowy alcove, slowly, carefully, flowing along the far wall. At least he did not seem interested in walking the Pattern. He moved to a point almost directly opposite its beginning.

I had no choice but to continue my course, which took me through curves and turns that removed him from my sight. I came to another break in the Pattern and felt it knit as I crossed it. A barely audible music seemed to occur as I did so. The tempo of the flux within the lighted area seemed to increase also, as it flowed into the lines, etching a sharp, bright trail behind me. I called an occasional piece of advice to Jurt, who was several laps back, though his course sometimes brought him abreast of me and close enough to touch had there been any reason to.

The blue fires were higher now, reaching up to mid-thigh, and my hair was rising. I began a slow series of turns. Above the crackling and the music, I asked, *How're you doing, Frakir?* There was no reply.

I turned, kept moving through an area of high impedance, emerged from it, beholding the fiery wall of Coral's prison there at the Pattern's center. As I took my way around it, the opposite side of the Pattern slowly came into view.

The stranger stood waiting, the collar of his cloak turned high. Within the shadows which lay upon his face, I could see that his teeth were bared in a grin. I was startled by the fact that he stood in the midst of the Pattern itself—watching my advance, apparently waiting for me—until I realized that he had entered by way of a break in the design which I was headed to repair.

"You are going to have to get out of my way," I called out. "I can't stop, and I can't let you stop me!"

He didn't stir, and I recalled my father's telling me of a fight which had occurred on the primal Pattern. I slapped the hilt of Grayswandir.

"I'm coming through," I said.

The blue-white fires came up even higher with my next step, and in their light I saw his face. It was my own.

"No," I said.

"Yes," he said.

"You are the last of the Logrus-ghosts to confront me."

"Indeed," he replied.

I took another step.

"Yet," I observed, "if you are a reconstruction of myself from the time I made it through the Logrus, why should you oppose me here? The self I recall being in those days wouldn't have taken a job like this."

His grin went away.

"I am not you in that sense," he stated. "The only way to make this happen as it must, as I understand it, was to synthesize my personality in some fashion."

"So you're me with a lobotomy and orders to kill."

"Don't say that," he replied. "It makes it sound wrong, and what I'm doing is right. We even have many of the same memories."

"Let me through and I'll talk to you afterward. I think the Logrus may have screwed itself by trying this stunt. You don't want to kill yourself, and neither do I. Together we could win this game, and there's room in Shadow for more than one Merlin."

I'd slowed, but I had to take another step then. I couldn't afford to lose momentum at this point.

His lips tightened to a thin line, and he shook his head.

"Sorry," he said. "I was born to live one hour—unless I kill you. If I do, your life will be given to me."

He drew his blade.

"I know you better than you think I do," I said, "whether you've been restructured or not. I don't think you'll do it. Furthermore, I might be able to lift that death sentence. I've learned some things about how it works for you ghosts."

He extended his blade, which resembled one I'd had years ago, and its point almost reached me.

"Sorry," he repeated.

I drew Grayswandir for purposes of parrying it. I'd have been a fool not to. I didn't know what sort of job the Logrus had done on his head. I racked my memories for fencing techniques I'd studied since I'd become an initiate of the Logrus.

Yes. Benedict's game with Borel had reminded me. I'd taken some lessons in Italian-style fencing since then. It gave one wider, more careless-seeming parries, compensated by greater extension. Grayswandir went forth, beat his blade to the outside, and extended. His wrist bent into a French four, but I was already under it, arm still extended, wrist straight, sliding my right foot forward along the line as the forte of my blade beat heavily against the forte of his from the outside, and I immediately stepped forward with my left foot, driving the weapon across his body till the guards locked and continuing its drop in that direction.

And then my left hand fell upon the inside of his right elbow, in a maneuver a martial artist friend had taught me back in college—*zenponage*, I think he called it. I lowered my hips as I pressed downward. I turned my hips then, counterclockwise. His balance broke, and he fell toward my left. Only I could not permit that. If he landed on the Pattern proper, I'd a funny feeling he'd go off like a fireworks display. So I continued the drop for several more inches, shifted my hand to his shoulder, and pushed him, so that he fell back into the broken area.

Then I heard a scream, and a blazing form passed on my left side.

"No!" I cried, reaching for it.

But I was too late. Jurt had stepped off the line, springing past me, driving his blade into my double even as his own body swirled and blazed. Fire also poured from my double's wound. He tried unsuccessfully to rise and fell back.

"Don't say that I never served you, brother," Jurt stated, before he was transformed into a whirlwind, which rose to the chamber's roof, where it dissipated.

I could not reach far enough to touch my doppelgänger, and moments later I did not wish to, for he was quickly transformed into a human torch.

His gaze was directed upward, following Jurt's spectacular passing. He looked at me then and smiled crookedly.

"He was right, you know," he said, and then he, too, was engulfed.

It took awhile to overcome my inertia, but after a time I did, continuing my ritual dance about the fire. The next time around there was no trace of either of their persons, though their blades remained where they had fallen, crossed, across my path. I kicked them off the Pattern as I went by. The flames were up to my waist by then.

Around, back, over. I glanced into the Jewel periodically, to avoid missteps, and piece by piece I stitched the Pattern together. The light was drawn into the lines, and save for the central blaze, it came more and more to resemble the thing we kept in the basement back home.

The First Veil brought painful memories of the Courts and of Amber. I stayed aloof, shivering, and these things passed. The Second Veil mixed memory and desire in

San Francisco. I controlled my breathing and pretended I was only a spectator. The flames danced about my shoulders, and I thought of a series of half-moons as I traversed arc after arc, curve upon reverse curve. The resistance grew till I was drenched with sweat as I struggled against it. But I had been this way before. The Pattern was not just around me but inside me as well.

I moved, and I reached the point of diminishing returns, of less and less distance gained for the effort expended. I kept seeing dissolving Jurt and my own dying face amid flames, and it didn't matter a bit that I knew the memory rush was Pattern-induced. It still bothered me as I drove myself forward.

I swept my gaze around me once as I neared the Grand Curve, and I saw that this Pattern had now been fully repaired. I had bridged all of the breaks with connecting lines, and it burned now like a frozen Catherine wheel against a black and starless sky. Another step . . .

I patted the warm Jewel that I wore. Its ruddy glow came up to me even more strongly now than it had earlier. I wondered whether there was an easy way to get it back where it belonged. Another step . . .

I raised the Jewel and stared into it. There was an image of me completing the walking of the Grand Curve and continuing right on through the wall of flames as if this represented no problem whatsoever. While I took the vision as a piece of advice, I was reminded of a David Steinberg routine which Droppa had once appropriated. I hoped that the Pattern was not into practical jokes.

The flames enveloped me fully as I commenced the Curve. I continued to slow as my efforts mounted. Step after painful step I drew nearer to the Final Veil. I could feel myself being transformed into an expression of pure will, as everything that I was became focused upon a single end   Another step . . . It felt as if I were weighted down with heavy armor. It was the final three steps that pushed one near despair's edge.

Again . . .

Then came the point where even movement became less important than the effort. It was no longer the results but the attempt that mattered. My will was the flame; my body, smoke or shadow. . . .

And again . . .

Seen through my risen blue light, the orange flames which surrounded Coral became silver-gray spikes of incandescence. Within the crackling and the popping I heard something like music once again—low, adagio, a deep, vibrant thing, like Michael Moore playing bass. I tried to accept the rhythm, to move with it. Somehow, then, it seemed that I succeeded—that, or my time sense became distorted—as I moved with a feeling of something like fluidity through the next steps.

Or maybe the Pattern felt it owed me a favor and had eased up for a few beats. I'll never know.

I passed through the Final Veil, faced the wall of flame, suddenly orange again, and kept going. I drew my next breath in the heart of fire.

Coral lay there at the Pattern's center, looking pretty much as she had when last I had seen her—in a copper shirt and dark green breeches—save that she appeared to be sleeping, sprawled there upon her heavy brown cloak. I dropped to my right knee beside her and laid my hand upon her shoulder. She did not stir. I brushed a strand of her reddish hair off her cheek, stroked that cheek a few times.

"Coral?" I said.

No response.

I returned my hand to her shoulder, shook her gently.

"Coral?"

She drew a deep breath and sighed it out, but she did not awaken.

I shook her a bit harder. "Wake up, Coral."

I slipped my arm beneath her shoulders, raised her partway. Her eyes did not open. Obviously she was under some sort of spell. The middle of the Pattern was hardly the place to summon the Sign of the Logrus if one wished to remain unincinerated. So I tried the storybook remedy. I leaned forward and kissed her. She made a small, deep noise, and her eyelids fluttered. But she did not come around. I tried again. Same result.

"Shit!" I remarked. I wanted a little elbowroom for working on a spell like this, a place where I had access to some of the tools of my trade and could call upon the source of my powers with impunity.

I raised her higher and commanded the Pattern to transport us back to my apartment in Amber, where her *ty'iga*-possessed sister lay in a trance of her own— one of my brother's doing, for purposes of protecting me from her.

"Take us home," I said aloud, for emphasis.

Nothing happened.

I employed a strong visualization then and backed it once more with the mental command.

We didn't stir.

I lowered Coral gently, rose, and looked out across the Pattern through the faintest area of the flames.

"Look," I said, "I just did you a big favor, involving a lot of exertion and considerable risk. Now I want to get the hell out of here and take the lady with me. Will you please oblige?"

The flames died down, were gone, for several beats. In the diminished light which followed I became aware that the Jewel was pulsing, like the message light on a hotel phone. I raised it and stared into it.

I hardly expected an X-rated short feature, but that's what was playing.

"I believe I'm receiving the wrong channel," I said. "If you've got a message, let's have it. Otherwise, I just want to go home."

Nothing changed, save that I became aware of a strong resemblance between the two figures in the Jewel and Coral and myself. They were going at it on a cloak at what appeared to be the center of a Pattern, flagrante ad infinitum—rather like a spicier version of the old salt box label, it seemed, if they could be seeing into the Jewel the guy was wearing and watching. . . .

"Enough!" I cried. "This is fucking ridiculous! You want a Tantric ritual I'll send you some professionals! The lady isn't even awake——"

The Jewel pulsed again, with such intensity that it hurt my eyes. I let it fall. I knelt then, scooped Coral up, and stood.

"I don't know whether anyone's ever walked you backwards before," I said, "but I don't see why it shouldn't work."

I took a step in the direction of the Final Veil. Immediately the wall of flame sprang up before me. I stumbled in drawing away from it, fell back upon the outspread cloak. I held Coral to me that she not be cast into the fire. She came down on top of me. She seemed almost awake. . . .

Her arms went around my neck, and she sort of nuzzled my cheek. She seemed more drowsy than comatose now. I held her tightly and thought about it.

"Coral?" I tried again.

"Mm," she said.

"Seems the only way we can get out of here is by making love."

"Thought you'd never ask," she mumbled, eyes still closed.

That made it seem somewhat less like necrophilia, I told myself as I turned us onto our sides so I could get at those coppery buttons. She muttered a little more while I was about things, but it didn't exactly turn into a conversation. Still, her body was not unresponsive to my attentions, and the encounter quickly took on all the usual features, too commonplace to be of much concern to the sophisticated. It seemed an interesting way to break a spell. Maybe the Pattern did have a sense of humor. I don't know.

The fires died down at about the same time that the fires died down, so to speak. Coral's eyes finally opened.

"That seems to have taken care of the circle of flames," I said.

"When did this cease being a dream?" she asked.

"Good question," I replied, "and only you can answer it."

"Did you just rescue me from something?"

"That seems the easiest way to put it," I answered as she drew away somewhat and cast her gaze about the chamber. "See where it got you when you asked the Pattern to send you where you should go?" I said.

"Screwed," she replied.

"Precisely."

We drew apart. We adjusted our apparel.

"It's a good way to get to know each other better . . ." I had begun when the cavern was shaken by a powerful earth tremor.

"The timing is really off here," I observed as we were rocked together and clung to each other for comfort, if not support.

It was over in an instant, and the Pattern was suddenly blazing more brilliantly than I'd ever seen it before. I shook my head. I rubbed my eyes. Something was wrong, even though it felt very right. Then the great metal-bound door opened—inward!—and I realized that we had come back to Amber, the real Amber. My glowing trail still led up to the threshold, though it was fading fast, and a small figure stood upon it. Before I could even squint against the corridor's gloom, I felt a familiar disorientation, and we were in my bedroom.

"Nayda!" Coral exclaimed when she viewed the figure reclined upon my bed.

"Not exactly," I said. "I mean, it's her body. But the spirit that moves it is of a different order."

"I don't understand."

I was busy thinking of the person who had been about to invade the precincts of the Pattern. I was also a mass of aching muscles, screaming nerves, and assorted fatigue poisons. I crossed to the table where the wine bottle I'd opened for Jasra—how long ago?—still stood. I found us two clean glasses. I filled them. I passed one to Coral.

"Your sister was very ill awhile back, wasn't she?"

"Yes," she replied.

I took a big swallow.

"She was near death. At that time her body was possessed by a *ty'iga* spirit—a kind of demon—as Nayda no longer had any use for it."

"What do you mean by that?"

"I understand that she actually died."

Coral stared into my eyes. She didn't find whatever she sought, and she took a drink instead.

"I'd known something was wrong," she said. "She hasn't really been herself since the illness."

"She became nasty? Sneaky?"

"No, a lot nicer. Nayda was always a bitch."

"You didn't get along?"

"Not till recently. She's not in any pain, is she?"

"No, she's just sleeping. She's under a spell."

"Why don't you release her? She doesn't look like much of a danger."

"I don't think she is now. Just the opposite, in fact," I said. "And we will release her, soon. My brother Mandor will have to undo it, though. It's his spell."

"Mandor? I don't really know much about you—or your family—do I?"

"Nope," I said, "and vice versa. Listen, I don't even know what day it is." I crossed the room and peered out the window. There was daylight. It was cloudy, though, and I couldn't guess the time. "There's something you should do right away. Go see your father and let him know you're all right. Tell him you got lost in the caverns or took a wrong turn into the Corridor of Mirrors and wound up on some other plane of existence or something. Anything. To avoid a diplomatic incident. Okay?"

She finished her drink and nodded. Then she looked at me and blushed and looked away.

"We'll get together again before I leave, won't we?"

I reached out and patted her shoulder, not really knowing what my feelings were. Then I realized that wouldn't do, and I stepped forward and embraced her.

"You know it," I said as I stroked her hair.

"Thanks for showing me around town."

"We'll have to do it again," I told her, "as soon as the pace slackens."

"Uh-huh."

We walked to the door.

"I want to see you soon," she said.

"I'm fading fast," I told her, as I opened it. "I've been through hell and back."

She touched my cheek.

"Poor Merlin," she said. "Sleep tight."

I gulped the rest of my wine and withdrew my Trumps. I wanted to do just what she said, but certain unavoidables came first. I riffled my way to the Ghostwheel's card, removed it, and regarded it.

Almost immediately, following the faintest drop in temperature and the barest formation of desire on my part, Ghostwheel appeared before me—a red circle turning in the middle of the air.

"Uh, hello, Dad," it stated. "I was wondering where you'd gotten to. When I checked back at the cave, you were gone, and none of my shadow-indexing procedures could turn you up. It never even occurred to me that you might simply have come home. I—"

"Later," I said. "I'm in a hurry. Get me down to the chamber of the Pattern fast."

"There's something I'd better tell you first."

"What?"

"That force that followed you to the Keep—the one I hid you from in the cave . . . ?"

"Yes?"

"It was the Pattern itself that was seeking you."

"I guessed that," I said, "later. We've had our encounter and sort of come to terms for now. Get me down there right away. It's important."

"Sir, I am afraid of that thing."

"Then take me as close as you dare and step aside. I have to check something out."

"Very well. Come this way."

I took a step forward. Ghost rose into the air, rotated ninety degrees toward me, and dropped quickly, passing my head, shoulders, torso and vanishing beneath my feet. The lights went out as he did so, and I called up my Logrus vision immediately. It showed me that I stood in the passageway outside the big door to the chamber of the Pattern.

"Ghost?" I said softly.

There was no reply.

I moved forward, turned the corner, advanced to the door, and leaned upon it. It was still unlocked, and it yielded to my pushing. Frakir pulsed once upon my wrist.

Frakir? I inquired.

There came no answer from that quarter either.

Lose your voice, lady?

She pulsed twice. I stroked her.

As the door opened before me, I was certain that the Pattern had grown brighter. The observation was quickly pushed aside, however. A dark-haired woman stood at the Pattern's center, her back to me, her arms upraised. I almost shouted the name I thought she might answer to, but she was gone before my vocal mechanism responded. I slumped against the wall.

"I really feel used," I said aloud. "You've run my ass ragged, you placed my life in jeopardy more than once, you got me to perform to satisfy your metaphysical voyeurism, then you kicked me out after you got the last thing you wanted—a slightly brighter glow. I guess that gods or powers or whatever the hell you are don't have to say 'Thank you' or 'I'm sorry' or 'Go to hell' when they've finished using someone. And obviously you feel no need to justify yourself to me. Well, I'm not a baby carriage. I resent being pushed around by you and the Logrus in whatever game you're playing. How'd you like it if I opened a vein and bled all over you?"

Immediately there was a great coalescence of energies at my side of the Pattern. With a heavy whooshing sound a tower of blue flame built itself before me, widened, assumed genderless features of an enormous inhuman beauty. I had to shade my eyes against it.

"You do not understand," came a voice modulated of the roaring of flames.

"I know. That's why I'm here."

"Your efforts are not unappreciated."

"Glad to hear it."

"There was no other way to conduct matters."

"Well, were they conducted to your satisfaction?"

"They were."

"Then you are welcome, I guess."

"You are insolent, Merlin."

"The way I feel right now I've nothing to lose. I'm just too damned tired to care what you do to me. So I came down here to tell you that I think you owe me a big one. That's all."

I turned my back on it then.

"Not even Oberon dared address me so," it said.

I shrugged and took a step toward the door. When I set my foot down, I was back in my apartment.

I shrugged again, then went and splashed water in my face.

"You still okay, Dad?"

There was a ring around the bowl. It rose into the air and followed me about the room."

"I'm all right," I acknowledged. "How about yourself?"

"Fine. It ignored me completely."

"Do you know what it's up to?" I asked.

"It seems to be dueling with the Logrus for control of Shadow. And it just won a round. Whatever happened seems to have strengthened it. You were involved, right?"

"Right."

"Where were you after you left the cave I'd put you in?"

"You know of a land that lies between the shadows?"

"*Between?* No. That doesn't make sense."

"Well, that's where I was."

"How'd you get there?"

"I don't know. With considerable difficulty, I'd guess. Are Mandor and Jasra all right?"

"The last time I looked they were."

"How about Luke?"

"I'd no reason to seek him out. Do you want me to?"

"Not just now. Right now I want you to go upstairs and look in on the royal suite. I want to know whether it is, at the moment, occupied. And if so, by whom. I also want you to check the fireplace in the bedroom. See whether a loose stone which was removed from an area to the right of it has been replaced or is still lying upon the hearth."

He vanished, and I paced. I was afraid to sit down or to lie down. I'd a feeling that I'd go to sleep instantly if I did and that I'd be difficult to awaken. But Ghost spun back into existence before I chalked up much mileage.

"The Queen, Vialle, is present," he said, "in her studio, the loose stone has been replaced, and there is a dwarf in the hall knocking on doors."

"Damn," I said. "Then they know it's missing. A dwarf?"

"A dwarf."

I sighed.

"I guess I'd better walk on upstairs, return the Jewel, and try to explain what happened. If Vialle likes my story, she might just forget to mention it to Random."

"I'll transfer you up there."

"No, that would not be too politic. Or polite either.

I'd better go knock on the door and get admitted properly this time."

"How do people know when to knock and when to go on in?"

"In general, if it's closed, you knock on it."

"As the dwarf is doing?"

I heard a faint knocking from somewhere outside.

"He's just going along, indiscriminately banging on doors?" I asked.

"Well, he's trying them in sequence, so I don't know that you could say it's indiscriminate. So far all of the doors he's tried have been to rooms which are empty. He should reach yours in another minute or so."

I crossed to my door, unlocked it, opened it, and stepped out into the hallway.

Sure enough, there was a short guy moving along the hallway. He looked in my direction at the opening of my door, and his teeth showed within his beard as he smiled and headed toward me.

It quickly became apparent that he was a hunchback.

"My God!" I said. "You're Dworkin, aren't you? The real Dworkin!"

"I believe so," he replied in a not unpleasant voice. "And I do hope that you are Corwin's son, Merlin."

"I am," I said. "This is an unusual pleasure, coming at an unusual time."

"It is not a social call," he stated, drawing near and clasping my hand and shoulder. "Ah! These are your quarters!"

"Yes. Won't you come in?"

"Thank you."

I led him in. Ghost did a fly-on-the-wall imitation, became about a half inch in diameter, and took up residence on the armoire as if the result of a stray sunbeam. Dworkin did a quick turn about the sitting room, glanced into the bedroom, stared at Nayda for a time, muttered, "Always let sleeping demons lie," touched the Jewel as he passed me on his return, shook his head forebodingly, and sank into the chair I'd been afraid I'd go to sleep in.

"Would you care for a glass of wine?" I asked him.

He shook his head.

"No, thank you," he replied. "It was you who repaired the nearest Broken Pattern in Shadow, was it not?"

"Yes, it was."

"Why did you do it?"

"I didn't have much choice in the matter."

"You had better tell me all about it," the old man said, tugging at his grisly, irregular beard. His hair was long and could have used a trim also. Still, there seemed nothing of madness in his gaze or his words.

"It is not a simple story, and if I am to stay awake long enough to tell it, I am going to need some coffee," I said.

He spread his hands, and a small, white-clothed table appeared between us, bearing service for two and a steaming silvery carafe set above a squat candle. There was also a tray of biscuits. I couldn't have summoned it all that fast. I wondered whether Mandor could.

"In that case, I will join you," Dworkin said.

I sighed and poured. I raised the Jewel of Judgment.

"Perhaps I'd better return this thing before I start," I told him. "It may save me a lot of trouble later."

He shook his head as I began to rise.

"I think not," he stated. "If you take it off now, you will probably die."

I sat down again.

"Cream and sugar?" I asked him.

IX

I came around slowly. That familiar blueness was a lake of prebeing in which I drifted. Oh, yes, I was here because... I was here, as the song said. I turned over onto my other side within my sleeping bag, drew my knees up to my chest, and went back to sleep.

The next time I came around and gave it a quick glance the world was still a blue place. Fine. There is much to be said for the tried, the true. Then I recalled that Luke might be by at any time to kill me, and my fingers wrapped themselves around the hilt of the weapon beside me, and I strained my hearing after signs of anything's approach.

Would I spend the day chipping at the wall of my crystal cave? I wondered. Or would Jasra come and try again to kill me?

Again?

Something was wrong. There'd been an awful lot of

business involving Jurt and Coral and Luke and Mandor, even Julia. Had it all been a dream?

The moment of panic came and went, and then my wandering spirit returned, bringing along the rest of my memories, and I yawned and everything was all right again.

I stretched. I sat up. I knuckled my eyes.

Yes, I was back in the crystal cave. No, everything that had happened since Luke imprisoned me had not been a dream. I had returned here by choice (a) because a good night's sleep in this time line amounted to only a brief span back in Amber, (b) because nobody could bother me here with a Trump contact, and (c) because it was possible that even the Pattern and the Logrus couldn't track me down here.

I brushed my hair out of my eyes, rose, and headed back to the john. It had been a good idea, having Ghost transport me here following my colloquy with Dworkin. I was certain I had slept for something like twelve hours —deep, undisturbed stuff, the best kind. I drained a quart water bottle. I washed my face with more of the stuff.

Later, after I had dressed and stowed the bedclothes in the storeroom, I walked to the entrance chamber and stood in the light beneath the overhead adit. What I could see of the sky through it was clear. I could still hear Luke's words the day he had imprisoned me here and I'd learned we were related.

I drew the Jewel of Judgment up from within my shirt, removed it, held it high so that the light shone from behind it, stared into its depths. No messages this time.

Just as well. I wasn't in the mood for two-way traffic.

I lowered myself into a comfortable cross-legged position, still regarding the stone. Time to do it and be done with it, now that I felt rested and somewhat alert. As Dworkin had suggested, I sought the Pattern within that red pool.

After a time it began to take shape. It did not appear as I had been visualizing it, but this was not an exercise in visualization. I watched the structure come clear. It was not as if it were suddenly coming into existence, however, but rather as if it had been there all along and my eyes were just now adjusting to perceive it properly. Likely this was actually the case, too.

I took a deep breath and released it. I repeated the process. Then I began a careful survey of the design. I couldn't recall everything my father had said about attuning oneself to the Jewel. When I had mentioned this to Dworkin, he had told me not to worry about it, that I needed but to locate the three-dimensional edition of the Pattern within the stone, find its point of entry, and traverse it. When I pressed him for details, he had simply chuckled and told me not to worry.

All right.

Slowly I turned it, drawing it nearer. A small break appeared, high, to the right. As I focused upon it, it seemed to rush toward me.

I went to that place, and I went in there. It was a strange roller coaster of an experience, moving along Pattern-like lines within the gemstone. I went where it drew me, sometimes with a near-eviscerating feeling of vertigo, other times pushing with my will against the ruby barriers till they yielded and I climbed, fell, slid, or pushed my way onward. I lost most of the awareness of my body, hand holding the chain high, save that I knew I was sweating profusely, as it stung my eyes with some regularity.

I've no idea how much time passed in my attunement to the Jewel of Judgment, the higher octave of the Pattern. Dworkin felt that there were reasons other than my having pissed off the Pattern for its wanting me dead immediately following my completion of my bizarre quest and repairing of the nearest of the Broken Patterns. But Dworkin refused to elaborate, feeling that my knowing the reason could influence a possible future choice which should be made freely. All of which sounded like gibberish to me, save that everything else he said struck me as eminently sane, in contrast with the Dworkin I knew of from legend and hearsay.

My mind plunged and reared through the pool of blood that was the Jewel's interior. The Pattern segments I had traversed and those I had yet to travel moved about me, flashing like lightning. I'd a feeling my mind was going to crash against some invisible Veil and shatter. My movement was out of control now, accelerating. There was no way, I knew, for me to withdraw from this thing until I had run its course.

Dworkin felt that I had been protected from the Pattern during our confrontation, when I had gone back to check on the figure I had seen, because I was wearing the Jewel. I could not keep wearing it for too long, though, because this also had a tendency to prove fatal. He decided that I must become attuned to the Jewel—as were my father and Random—before I let it out of my possession. I would thereafter bear the higher-order image within me, which should function as well as the Jewel in defending me against the Pattern. I could hardly argue with the man who had supposedly created the Pattern, using the Jewel. So I agreed with him. Only I was too tired to do what he suggested. That was why I had had Ghost return me to my crystal cave, my sanctuary, to rest first.

Now, now...I flowed. I spun. Occasionally I stalled. The Jewel's equivalents of the Veils were no less formidable because I had left my body behind. Each such passage left me as wrung out as running a mile in Olympic time. Though I knew at one level that I stood holding the Jewel through which I took my initiatory way, at another I could feel my heart pounding, and at another I recalled parts of a guest lecture by Joan Halifax for an anthropology course I was taking, years before. The medium swirled like Geyser Peak Merlot 1985 in a goblet—and whom was I looking across the table at that night? No matter. Onward, down and around. The blood-brightened tide was loosed. A message was being inscribed upon my spirit. In the beginning was a word I cannot spell . . . Brighter, brighter. Faster, faster. Collision with a ruby wall, I a smear upon it. Come now, Schopenhauer, to the final game of will. An age or two came and went; then, suddenly, the way was opened. I was spilled forth into the light of an exploding star. Red, red, red, shifting me onward, away, like my little boat *Starburst,* driven, expanding, coming home . . .

I collapsed. Though I did not lose consciousness, my state of mind was not normal either. There was a hypnagogia I could have passed through at any time I chose, in either direction. But why? I am seldom the recipient of such a delivery of euphoria. I felt I'd earned it, so I drifted, right there, for a long, long time.

When it finally subsided below the level that made indulgence worthwhile, I climbed to my feet, swayed, leaned against the wall, made my way to the storeroom for another drink of water. I was also ravenous, but none of the tinned or freeze-dried foods appealed to me that greatly. Especially when fresher things were not that hard to come by.

I walked back through those familiar chambers. So I had followed Dworkin's advice. It was a pity I'd turned my back before I recalled a long list of questions I wished to ask him. When I turned back again, he was gone.

I climbed. Coming up out of my cave, I stood atop the blue prominence which held the only entranceway I knew of. It was a breezy, balmy, springlike morning with only a few small puffs of cloud to the east. I drew a deep breath for pleasure and expelled it. Then I stooped and moved the blue boulder to block the opening. I'd hate to be surprised by a predator should I come this way again in need of sanctuary.

I took off the Jewel of Judgment and hung it on a spur of the boulder. Then I moved off about ten paces.

"Hi, Dad."

The Ghostwheel was a golden Frisbee, come sailing out of the west.

"Good morning, Ghost."

"Why are you abandoning that device? It's one of the most powerful tools I've ever seen."

"I'm not abandoning it, but I'm about to summon the Sign of the Logrus, and I don't think they'd get on too well. I'm even a little leery over how the Logrus will take to me with this higher-order Pattern attunement I'm wearing."

"Perhaps I'd better move along and check back with you later."

"Stick around," I said. "Maybe you can bail me out if this turns into a problem."

I summoned the Sign of the Logrus then, and it came and hovered before me, and nothing happened. I shifted a part of my awareness into the Jewel, there on the side of the boulder, and through it I was able to perceive the Logrus from another perspective. Eerie. Also painless.

I centered myself within my own skull once again, extended my arms into the Logrus limbs, reached. . . .

In less than a minute I had a plate of buttermilk pancakes, a side order of sausages, a cup of coffee, and a glass of orange juice.

"I could have gotten them for you faster than that," Ghost remarked.

"I'm sure you could have," I said. "I was just testing systems."

As I ate, I tried to sort my priorities. When I finished, I sent the dishes back where they had come from, retrieved the Jewel, hung it about my neck, and stood.

"Okay, Ghost. Time to head back to Amber," I said.

He expanded and opened and sank, so that I stood before a golden arch. I stepped forward—

—and back into my apartment.

"Thanks," I said.

"*De nada,* Dad. Listen, I've a question: When you summoned breakfast, did you notice anything at all unusual in the way the Logrus Sign behaved?"

"How do you mean that?" I asked as I moved to wash my hands.

"Let's start with physical sensations. Did it seem . . . sticky?"

"That's an odd way to put it," I said. "But as a matter of fact, it did seem to take slightly longer than usual to disengage. Why do you ask?"

"A peculiar notion has just occurred to me. Can you do Pattern magic?"

"Yeah, but I'm better at the Logrus variety."

"You might want to try them both and compare them if you get a chance."

"Why?"

"I'm actually starting to get hunches. I'll tell you as soon as I've checked this one out."

Ghostwheel was gone.

"Shit," I said, and I washed my face.

I looked out the window, and a handful of snowflakes blew by. I fetched a key from my desk drawer. There were a couple of things I wanted to get out of the way immediately.

I stepped into the corridor. I had not gone more than a few paces before I heard the sound. I halted and listened. Then I continued, past the stairway, the sound growing steadily in volume as I advanced. By the time I reached the long corridor which ran past the library I knew that Random was back because I didn't know of anyone else around here who could drum like that—or would dare to use the King's drums if he could.

I continued on past the half-opened door to the corner, where I turned right. My first impulse had been to enter, give him back the Jewel of Judgment, and try to explain what had happened. Then I recalled Flora's advice that anything honest, straightforward, and aboveboard would always get you in trouble here. While I hated to give her credit for having enunciated a general rule, I could see that in this particular instance it would certainly tie me up with a lot of explaining when there were other things I wanted to be about—and, for that matter, it might also get me ordered not to do some of them.

I continued to the far entrance to the dining room, where I checked quickly and determined the place to be deserted. Good. Inside and to the right, as I recalled, there was a sliding panel which would get me into a hollow section of wall beside the library, furnished with pegs or a ladder that would take me up to a hidden entrance to the library's balcony. It could also take me down through the spiral stair's shaft and into the caverns below, if memory served. I hoped I never had reason to check that part out, but I was sufficiently into family tradition these days that I wanted to do a little spying, as several muttered exchanges as I'd passed the opened door led me to believe that Random was not alone in there. If knowledge really is power, then I needed all I could get my hands on, as I'd felt especially vulnerable for some time now.

Yes, the panel slid, and I was through it in a trice, sending my spirit-light on ahead. I hand-over-handed my way quickly to the top and opened the panel there slowly and quietly, feeling grateful to whoever had thought to conceal its space with a wide chair. I was able to see around the chair's right arm with comparative safety from detection——a good view of the room's north end.

And there was Random, drumming, and Martin, all chains and leather, was seated before him, listening. Random was doing something I'd never seen done before. He was playing with five sticks. He had one in each hand, one under each arm, and he held one in his teeth. And he was revolving them as he played, moving the one in his mouth to replace the one under his right arm, which replaced the one in his right hand, which he had switched over to his left hand, the left-hand one going up beneath his left arm, the left arm one going to his teeth, all without missing a beat. It was hypnotic. I stared until he wound out the number. His old set of traps was hardly the fusion drummer's dreamworld of translucent plastic with tipped cymbals the size of battle shields set around the snares, a mess of tomtoms, and a couple of basses, all lit up like Coral's circle of fire. Random's set went back to a time before snares grew thin and nervous, basses shrank, and cymbals caught acromegaly and began to hum.

"Never saw that done before," I heard Martin say.

Random shrugged.

"Bit of horsing around," he said. "Learned it from

Freddie Moore, in the thirties, either at the Victoria or the Village Vanguard, when he was with Art Hodes and Max Kaminsky. I forget which place. It goes back to vaudeville, when they didn't have any mikes and the lighting was bad. Had to do show-off things like that, or dress funny, he told me, to keep the audience paying attention."

"Shame they had to cater to the crowd that way."

"Yeah, none of you guys would dream of dressing funny or throwing your instruments around."

There followed a silence, and there was no way I could see the expression on Martin's face. Then, "I meant it different from that," Martin said.

"Yeah, me, too," Random replied. Then he tossed three of the sticks down and began to play again.

I leaned back and listened. A moment later I was startled to hear an alto sax come in. When I looked again, Martin was standing, his back still to me, and playing the thing. It must have been on the floor on the other side of his chair. There was a Richie Cole flavor to it that I rather liked, and it kind of surprised me. As much as I enjoyed it, I felt that I did not belong in this room right now, and I edged back, opened the panel, passed through, and closed it. After I'd climbed down and let myself out, I decided to cut through the dining room rather than pass the library entrance again. The music carried for some distance thereafter, and I wished I'd learned a spell of Mandor's for capturing sounds in precious stones, though I'm not sure how the Jewel of Judgment would have taken to containing "Wild Man Blues."

I was planning on walking up the east corridor to the point where it intersected with the north one in the vicinity of my apartment, turning left there, and taking the stairs up to the royal suite, knocking on the door, and returning the Jewel to Vialle, whom I hoped I could get to take a rain check on explanations. And if not, I'd rather explain to her than to Random anyway. I could leave out a lot that she wouldn't know to ask me. Of course, Random would catch up with me with questions eventually. But the later, the better.

But then I was going right past my father's rooms. I'd brought along the key so that I could stop in later, for what I considered obvious reasons. Still, since I was already on the spot, it would be more time-effective. I unlocked the door, opened it, and stepped inside.

The silver rose was gone from the bud vase on the dresser. Odd. I took a step toward it. There came a sound of voices from the other room, too soft for me to distinguish words. I froze. He might well be in there. But you don't just go bursting into someone's bedroom, especially when it's likely there's company present — particularly when it's your father's room and you had to unlock an outer door to get where you were. Suddenly I was extremely self-conscious. I wanted to get out of there, fast. I unbuckled my sword belt, from which Grayswandir depended in its not-quite-perfect fit of a sheath. I did not dare bear it any farther but hung it from one of the garment pegs on the wall near the door next to a short trench coat I hadn't noticed before. I slipped out then and locked the door as quietly as I could.

Awkward. Was he really coming and going with some regularity, somehow managing to avoid notice? Or was some sort of phenomenon of an entirely different order in progress within his quarters? I'd heard an occasional rumor that some of the older chambers had *sub specie spatium* doorways, if one could but figure how to activate them, providing considerable extra closet space as well as private means of entry and egress. Something else I should have asked Dworkin about. Maybe I've got a pocket universe under my bed. I'd never looked.

I turned and walked quickly away. As I neared the corner, I slowed. Dworkin had felt that the presence of the Jewel of Judgment on my person was the thing that had protected me from the Pattern, had it really been tempted to harm me earlier. On the other hand, the Jewel, worn too long, could itself do damage to the wearer. Therefore, he had counseled me to get some rest and then pass my mind through the stone's matrix, in effect creating a recording of a higher power of the Pattern within me along with some measure of immunity to assaults by the Pattern itself. Interesting conjecture. And that's all it was, of course: conjecture.

When I reached the cross corridor where a left would take me to the stairway or a right back to my rooms, I hesitated. There was a sitting room diagonally across the way, to the left, across from Benedict's seldom used rooms. I headed for it, entered, sank into a heavy chair in the corner. All I wanted to do was deal with my enemies, help my friends, get my name off any shit lists it currently occupied, locate my father, and come to some sort of terms with the sleeping *ty'iga*. Then I could see about the continuance of my interrupted *Wanderjahr*. All of which, I realized, required that I now reask myself the now near-rhetorical question, How much of my business did I want Random to know?

I thought of him in the library, playing a duet with his near-estranged son. I understood that he had once been pretty wild and footloose and nasty, that he hadn't really wanted the job of ruling this archetypal world. But parenthood, marriage, and the Unicorn's choice seemed to have laid a lot on him—deepening his character, I suppose, at the price of a lot of the fun things in his life. Right now he seemed to have a lot of problems with this

Kashfa-Begma business, possibly having just resorted to an assassination and agreed to a less than favorable treaty to maintain the complex political forces of the Golden Circle at an even level. And who knew what might be going on elsewhere to add to his troubles? Did I really want to draw this man into something I might well be able to handle myself with his never being any the wiser, or ever even bothered, concerning it? Conversely, if I did draw him into my affairs, it seemed likely that he might well lay restrictions on me which could hamper my ability to respond to what seemed the daily exigencies of my life. It could also raise another matter which had been shunted aside years ago.

I had never sworn allegiance to Amber. Nobody had ever asked me to. After all, I was Corwin's son, and I had come to Amber willingly and made my home here for some time before going off to the shadow Earth, where so many of the Amberites had gone to school. I returned often, and I seemed to be on good terms with everyone. I didn't really see why the concept of dual citizenship shouldn't apply.

I'd rather the matter did not come up at all, though. I did not like the thought of being forced to choose between Amber and the Courts. I wouldn't do it for the Unicorn and the Serpent, the Pattern and the Logrus, and I didn't care to do it for the royalty of either court.

All of which indicated that Vialle should not have even a sketchy edition of my story. Any version at all would require an eventual accounting. However, if the Jewel were returned without an explanation of where it had been, then no one would know to come after me on the matter, and things would still be set right. How could I lie if I were not even asked questions?

I mulled that along a little further. What I would actually be doing would be to save a tired, troubled man the burden of additional problems. There was nothing he could or should do about most of my affairs. Whatever was going on between the Pattern and the Logrus seemed mainly important as a metaphysical affair. I couldn't see where much good or bad might come out of it on a practical level. And if I saw something coming, I could always tell Random then.

Okay. That's one nice thing about reasoning abilities. You can use them to make yourself feel virtuous rather than, say, guilty. I stretched and cracked my knuckles.

"Ghost?" I said softly.

No response.

I reached for my Trumps, but even as I touched them, a wheel of light flashed on across the room.

"You did hear me," I said.

"I felt your need," came the reply.

"Whatever," I said, drawing the Jewel's chain up over my head and holding the stone out before me. "Do you think you could return this to its secret compartment beside the fireplace in the royal suite without anyone's being any wiser?" I asked.

"I'm leery about touching that thing," Ghost responded. "I don't know what its structure might do to my structure."

"Okay," I said. "I guess I'll find a way to do it myself then. But the time has come to test a hypothesis. If the Pattern attacks me, try to whisk me to safety, please."

"Very well."

I set the Jewel on a nearby table.

After about a half minute I realized that I had braced myself against the Pattern's death stroke. I relaxed my shoulders. I drew a deep breath. I remained intact. Could be that Dworkin was right and the Pattern would leave me alone. Also, I should be able to summon the Pattern in the Jewel now, he told me, as I do the Sign of the Logrus. There were Pattern-magics which could only be wrought via this route, though Dworkin hadn't taken the time to instruct me in their employment. He'd suggested that a sorcerer should be able to figure the system out. I decided that this could wait. I was in no mood just now for commerce of any sort with the Pattern in any of its incarnations.

"Hey, Pattern," I said. "Want to call it even?"

There came no reply.

"I believe it is aware of you here and what you just did," Ghost said. "I feel its presence. Could be you're off the hook."

"Could be," I responded, taking out my Trumps and sorting through them.

"Whom would you like to get in touch with?" Ghost asked.

"I'm curious about Luke," I said. "I want to see whether he's okay. And I'm wondering about Mandor. I assume you sent him to a safe place."

"Oh, nothing but the best," Ghost replied. "Same for Queen Jasra. Did you want her, too?"

"Not really. In fact, I don't *want* any of them. I just wanted to see——"

Ghost winked out while I was still talking. I wasn't at all certain that his eagerness to please was an improvement over his earlier belligerence.

I withdrew Luke's card and went inside it.

I heard someone passing along the corridor. The footsteps went on by.

I felt Luke's awareness, though no vision of his circumstances reached me.

"Luke, you hear me?" I inquired.

"Yep," he answered. "You okay, Merle?"

"I'm all right," I said. "How about yourself? That was quite a fight you——"

"I'm fine."

"I hear your voice, but I can't see a thing."

"Got a blackout on the Trumps. You don't know how to do that?"

"Never looked into the matter. Have to get you to teach me sometime. Uh, why are they blacked out anyway?"

"Somebody might get in touch and figure what I'm up to."

"If you're about to lead a commando raid on Amber, I'm going to be highly pissed."

"Come on! You know I swore off! This is something entirely different."

"Thought you were a prisoner of Dalt's."

"My status is unchanged."

"Well, he damn near killed you once and he just beat the shit out of you the other day."

"The first time he'd stumbled into an old berserker spell Sharu'd left behind for a trap; the second time was business. I'll be okay. But right now everything I'm up to is hush-hush, and I've got to run. G'bye."

Gone Luke, the presence.

The footsteps had halted, and I'd heard a knocking on a nearby door. After a time I heard a door being opened, then closed. I had not overheard any exchange of words. In that it had been nearby and that the two nearest apartments were Benedict's and my own, I began to wonder. I was fairly certain that Benedict was not in his, and I recalled not having locked my own door when I had stepped out. Therefore . . .

Picking up the Jewel of Judgment, I crossed the room and stepped out into the hall. I checked Benedict's door. Locked. I looked down the north-south hallway and walked back to the stairway and checked around in that area. There was no one in sight. I strode up to my own place then and stood listening for a time outside each of my doors. No sounds from within. The only alternatives I could think of were Gérard's rooms, back down the side corridor, and Brand's, which lay behind my own. I had thought of knocking out a wall—in keeping with the recent spirit of remodeling and redecorating Random had gotten into—adding Brand's rooms to my own, for a very good-size apartment. The rumor that his were haunted, though, and the wailings I sometimes heard through the walls late at night dissuaded me.

I took a quick walk then, knocking on and finally trying both Brand's and Gérard's doors. No response, and both were locked. Odder and odder.

Frakir had given a quick pulse when I'd touched Brand's door, and while I'd gone on alert for several moments, nothing untoward had approached. I was about to dismiss it as a disturbing reaction to the remnants of eldritch spells I had occasionally seen drifting about the vicinity when I noticed that the Jewel of Judgment was pulsing.

I raised the chain and stared into the gem. Yes, an image had taken form. I beheld the hallway around the corner, my two doors, and intervening artwork on the wall in plain view. The doorway to the left—the one that let upon my bedroom—seemed to be outlined in red and pulsing. Did that mean I was supposed to avoid it or rush in there? That's the trouble with mystical advice

I walked back and turned the corner again. This time the gem—perhaps having felt my query and decided some editing was in order—showed me approaching and opening the door it was indicating. Of course, of the two, that door was locked. . . .

I fumbled for my key, reflecting that I could not even rush in with a drawn blade, having just disposed of Grayswandir. I did have a couple of tricky spells hung, though. Maybe one of them would save me if the going got too rough. Maybe not, too.

I turned the key and flung the door open.

"Merle!" she shrieked, and I saw that it was Coral. She stood beside my bed, where her putative sister the *ty'iga* was reclined. She quickly moved one hand behind her back. "You, uh, surprised me."

"Vice versa," I replied, for which there *is* an equivalent in Thari. "What's up, lady?"

"I came back to tell you that I located my father and gave him a soothing story about that Corridor of Mirrors you told me about. Is there really such a place here?"

"Yes. You won't find it in any guides, though. It comes and goes. So, he's mollified?"

"Uh-huh. But now he's wondering where Nayda is."

"This gets trickier."

"Yes."

She was blushing, and she did not meet my eyes readily. She seemed aware, too, that I was noting her discomfort.

"I told him that perhaps Nayda was exploring, as I'd been," she went on, "and that I'd ask after her."

"Mm-hm."

I shifted my gaze to Nayda. Coral immediately moved forward and brushed against me. She placed a hand on my shoulder, drew me toward her.

"I thought you were going to sleep," she said.

"Yes, I was. Did, too. I was running some errands just now."

"I don't understand," she said.

"Time lines," I explained. "I economized. I'm rested."

"Fascinating," she said, brushing my lips with her own. "I'm glad that you're rested."

"Coral," I said, embracing her briefly, "you don't have to bullshit me. You know I was dead tired when you left. You had no reason to believe that I'd be anything but comatose if you returned this soon."

I caught hold of her left wrist behind her back and drew her hand around to the front, raising it between us. She was surprisingly strong. And I made no effort to pry open her hand, for I could see between the fingers what it was that she held. It was one of the metal balls Mandor often used to create impromptu spells. I released her hand. She did not draw away from me, but rather, "I can explain," she said, finally meeting my gaze and holding it.

"I wish you would," I said. "In fact, I wish you'd done it a bit sooner."

"Maybe the story you heard about her being dead and her body the host for a demon is true," she said. "But she's been good to me recently. She's finally become the sister I'd always wished she'd been. Then you brought me back here and I saw her like that, not knowing what you really planned to do with her—"

"I want you to know that I wouldn't hurt her, Coral," I interrupted. "I owe her—it—for favors past. When I was young and naive on the shadow Earth, she probably saved my neck, several times. You have no reason to fear for her here."

She cocked her head to the right and narrowed one eye.

"I'd no way of knowing that," she said, "from what you told me I came back, hoping to get in, hoping you were deeply asleep, hoping I could break the spell or at least lift it enough to talk with her. I wanted to find out for myself whether she was really my sister—or something else."

I sighed. I reached out to squeeze her shoulder and realized I was still clutching the Jewel of Judgment in my left hand. I squeezed her arm with my right hand instead and said, "Look, I understand. It was boorish of me to show you your sister laid out that way and not to have gone into a little more detail. I can only plead industrial fatigue and apologize. I promise you she's in no pain. But I really don't want to mess with this spell right now because it's not one of mine——"

Just then Nayda moaned softly. I studied her for several minutes, but nothing more followed.

"Did you pluck that metal ball out of the air?" I asked. "I don't recall seeing one for the final spell."

Coral shook her head.

"It was lying on her breast. One of her hands was over it," she said.

"What prompted you to check there?"

"The position looked unnatural, that's all. Here."

She handed me the ball. I took it and weighed it in the palm of my right hand. I had no idea how the things functioned. The metal balls were to Mandor what Frakir was to me—a piece of idiosyncratic personal magic, forged out of his unconscious in the heart of the Logrus.

"Are you going to put it back?" she asked.

"No," I told her. "Like I said, it wasn't one of my spells. I don't know how it works, and I don't want to fool around with it."

"Merlin . . . ?"—whispered, from Nayda, her eyes still closed.

"We'd better go talk in the next room," I said to Coral. "I'll lay a spell of my own on her first, though. Just a simple soporific——"

The air sparkled and spun behind Coral, and she must have guessed from my stare that something was going on, for she turned.

"Merle, what is it?" she asked, retreating toward me as a golden archway took form.

"Ghost?" I said.

"Right," came the reply. "Jasra was not where I left her. But I brought your brother."

Mandor, still clad mainly in black, his hair a great mass of silver-white, appeared suddenly, glancing at Coral and Nayda, focusing on me, beginning to smile, stepping forward. Then his gaze shifted, and he halted. He stared. I had never seen that frightened expression on his face before.

"Bloody Eye of Chaos!" he exclaimed, summoning up a protective screen with a gesture. "How did you come by it?"

He took a step backward. The arch immediately collapsed into a gold-leaf calligraphed letter *O*, and Ghost slid around the room to hover at my right side.

Suddenly Nayda sat up on my bed, darting wild glances.

"Merlin!" she cried. "Are you all right?"

"So far so good," I answered. "Not to worry. Take it easy. All's well."

"Who's been tampering with my spell?" Mandor asked as Nayda swung her legs over the side of the bed and Coral cringed.

"It was a sort of accident," I said.

I opened my right hand. The metal sphere immediately levitated and shot off in his direction, narrowly missing Coral, whose hands were now extended in a general martial arts defense pattern, though she seemed uncertain what or whom she should be defending against. So she kept turning—Mandor, Nayda, Ghost, repeat. . . .

"Cool it, Coral," I said. "You're in no danger."

"The left eye of the Serpent!" Nayda cried. "Free me,

oh, Formless One, and I will pledge with mine!"

Frakir in the meantime was warning me that all was not well, in case I hadn't noticed.

"Just what the hell is going on?" I yelled.

Nayda sprang to her feet, lunged forward, and with that unnatural demon strength snatched the Jewel of Judgment from my hand, pushed me aside, and tore out into the hallway.

I stumbled, recovered.

"Hold that *ty'iga!*" I cried, and the Ghostwheel flashed past me followed by Mandor's balls.

X

I was the next thing out into the hallway. I turned left and started running. A *ty'iga* may be fast, but so am I.

"I thought you were supposed to be protecting me!" I shouted after her.

"This takes precedence," she answered, "over your mother's binding."

"What?" I said. "My mother?"

"She placed me under a *geas* to take care of you when you went off to school," she replied. "This breaks it! Free at last!"

"Damn!" I observed.

Then, as she neared the stairway, the Sign of the Logrus appeared before her, larger than any I'd ever summoned, filling the corridor from wall to wall, roiling, sprawling, fire-shot, tentacular, a reddish haze of menace drifting about it. It took a certain measure of chutzpah for it to manifest like that here in Amber on the Pattern's turf, so I knew the stakes were high.

"Receive me, oh, Logrus," she cried, "for I bear the Eye of the Serpent," and the Logrus opened, creating a fiery tunnel at its center. I could somehow tell that its other end was not a place farther along my hallway.

But then Nayda was halted, as if she had suddenly encountered a glass partition, and she stiffened into a position of attention. Three of Mandor's gleaming spheres were suddenly orbiting her cataleptic form.

I was thrown from my feet and pressed back against the wall. I raised my right arm to block whatever might be coming down on me, as I looked backward.

An image of the Pattern itself, as large as the Logrus Sign, had just put in an appearance only a few feet behind me, manifesting about as far in that direction from Nayda as the Logrus was before her, parenthesizing the lady or the *ty'iga* between the poles of existence, so to speak, and incidentally enclosing me along with her. The area about me near the Pattern grew bright as a sunny morning while that at the other end took on the aspect of a baleful twilight. Were they about to reenact the Big Bang/Crunch, I wondered, with me as an unwilling momentary witness?

"Uh, Your Honors," I began, feeling obliged to try talking them out of it and wishing I were Luke, who just might be able to swing such a feat. "This is a perfect time to employ an impartial arbitrator, and I just happen to be uniquely qualified if you will but reflect—"

The golden circlet that I knew to be Ghostwheel suddenly dropped over Nayda's head, lengthening itself downward into a tube. Ghost had fitted himself within the orbits of Mandor's spheres and must somehow have insulated himself against whatever forces they were exerting, for they slowed, wobbled, and finally dropped to the floor, two striking the wall ahead of me and one rolling down the stairway ahead and to the right.

The Signs of the Pattern and the Logrus began to advance then, and I crawled quickly to keep ahead of the Pattern.

"Don't come any closer, fellows," Ghostwheel suddenly announced. "There's no telling what I might do if you make me even more nervous than I already am."

Both Power Signs halted in their advances. From around the corner to the left, up ahead, I heard Droppa's drunken voice, raised in some bawdy ballad, coming this way. Then it grew silent. Several moments passed, and he began singing "Rock of Ages" in a far, far weaker voice Then this, too, was cut off, followed by a heavy thud and the sound of breaking glass.

It occurred to me that I should be able, from a distance such as this, to extend my awareness into the Jewel. But I was uncertain what effects I might then be able to produce with the thing, considering the fact that none of the four principals involved in the confrontation was human.

I felt the beginnings of a Trump contact.

"Yes?" I whispered.

Dworkin's voice came to me then.

"Whatever control you may have over the thing," he said, "use it to keep the Jewel away from the Logrus."

Just then a crackly voice, shifting in pitch and gender from syllable to syllable, emerged from the red tunnel.

"Return the Eye of Chaos," it said. "The Unicorn took it from the Serpent when they fought, in the beginning. It was stolen. Return it. Return it."

The blue face I had seen above the Pattern did not materialize, but the voice I'd heard at that time responded, "It was paid for with blood and pain. Title passed."

"The Jewel of Judgment and the Eye of Chaos or Eye of

the Serpent are different names for the same stone?" I said.

"Yes," Dworkin replied.

"What happens if the Serpent gets its eye back?" I inquired.

"The universe will probably come to an end."

"Oh," I observed.

"What am I bid for the thing?" Ghost asked.

"Impetuous construct," the voice of the Pattern intoned.

"Rash artifact," wailed the Logrus.

"Save the compliments," Ghost said, "and give me something I want."

"I could tear it from you," the Pattern responded.

"I could have you apart and it away in an instant," stated the Logrus.

"But neither of you will do it," Ghost answered, "because such a focusing of your attention and energies would leave either of you vulnerable to the other."

In my mind, I heard Dworkin chuckle.

"Tell me why this confrontation need take place at all," Ghost went on, "after all this time."

"The balance was tipped against me by recent actions of this turncoat," the Logrus replied—a burst of fire occurring above my head, presumably to demonstrate the identity of the turncoat in question.

I smelled burning hair, and I warded the flame.

"Just a minute!" I cried. "I wasn't given much choice in the matter!"

"But there was a choice," wailed the Logrus, "and you made it."

"Indeed, he did," responded the Pattern. "But it served only to redress the balance you'd tipped in your own favor."

"Redress? You overcompensated! Now it's tipped in

your favor! Besides, it was accidentally tipped my way, by the traitor's father." Another fireball followed, and I warded again. "It was not my doing."

"You probably inspired it."

"If you can get the Jewel to me," Dworkin said, "I can put it out of reach of both of them until this matter is settled."

"I don't know whether I can get hold of it," I said, "but I'll remember that."

"Give it to me," the Logrus said to Ghost, "and I will take you with me as First Servant."

"You are a processor of data," said the Pattern. "I will give you knowledge such as none in all of Shadow possess."

"I will give you power," said the Logrus.

"Not interested," said Ghost, and the cylinder spun and vanished.

The girl, the Jewel, and everything were gone.

The Logrus wailed, the Pattern growled, and the Signs of both Powers rushed to meet, somewhere near Bleys's nearer room.

I raised every protective spell that I could. Behind me I could feel Mandor doing the same. I covered my head, I drew up my knees, I—

I was falling. Through a bright, soundless concussion. Bits of debris struck me. From several directions. I'd a hunch that I had just bought the farm and that I was about to die without opportunity to reveal my insight into the nature of reality: The Pattern did not care about the children of Amber any more than the Logrus did about those of the Courts of Chaos. The Powers cared, perhaps, about themselves, about each other, about heavy cosmic principles, about the Unicorn and the Serpent, of which they were very probably but geometric manifestations They did not care about me, about Coral, about Mandor, probably not even about Oberon or Dworkin himself. We were totally insignificant or at most tools or sometimes annoyances, to be employed or destroyed as the occasion warranted—

"Give me your hand," Dworkin said, and I saw him, as in a Trump contact. I reached and—

—fell hard at his feet upon a colorful rug spread over a stone floor, in a windowless chamber my father had once described to me, filled with books and exotic artifacts, lit by bowls of light which hung without visible means of support high in the air.

"Thanks," I said, rising slowly, brushing myself off massaging a sore spot in my left thigh.

"Caught a whiff of your thoughts," he said "There's more to it."

"I'm sure. But sometimes I enjoy being bleakminded. How much of that crap the Powers were arguing about was true?"

"Oh, all of it," Dworkin said, "by their lights The biggest bar to understanding is the interpretation they put on each other's doings. That, and the fact that everything can always be pushed another step backward —such as the break in the Pattern having strengthened the Logrus and the possibility that the Logrus actively influenced Brand into doing it. But then the Logrus might claim this was in retaliation for the Day of the Broken Branches several centuries ago."

"I haven't heard about that one," I said.

He shrugged.

"I'm not surprised. It wasn't all that important a matter, except to them. What I'm saying is that to argue as they do is to head into an infinite regression— back to first causes, which are always untrustworthy."

"So what's the answer?"

"Answer? This isn't a classroom. There are no answers that would matter, except to a philosopher—that is, none with any practical applications."

He poured a small cup of green liquid from a silver flask and passed it to me.

"Drink this," he said.

"It's a little early in the day for me."

"It's not refreshment. It's medication," he explained. "You're in a state of near shock, whether you've noticed or not."

I tossed the thing off, and it burned like a liquor but didn't seem to be one. I did feel myself beginning to relax during the next few minutes, in places I had not even realized I was tense.

"Coral, Mandor..." I said.

He gestured, and a glowing globe descended, drew nearer. He signed the air with a half-familiar gesture, and something like the Logrus Sign without the Logrus came over me. A picture formed within the globe.

That long section of hallway where the encounter had occurred had been destroyed, along with the stairs, Benedict's apartment, and possibly Gérard's as well. Also, Bleys's rooms, portions of my own, the sitting room I had been occupying but a short time before, and the northeast corner of the library were missing, as were the floor and ceiling. Below, I could see that sections of the kitchen and armory had been hit, and possibly more across the way. Looking upward—magic globes being wondrous accommodating—I could see sky, which meant that the blast had gone through the third and fourth floors, possibly damaging the royal suite along with the upper stairways and maybe the laboratory—and who knew what all else.

Standing on the edge of the abyss near what had been a section of Bleys's or Gérard's quarters was Mandor, his right arm apparently broken, hand tucked in behind his wide black belt. Coral leaned heavily upon his left shoulder, and there was blood on her face. I am not sure that she was fully conscious. Mandor held her about the waist with his left arm, and a metal ball circled the two of them. Diagonally across the abyss, Random stood on a heavy crossbeam near the opening to the library. I believe Martin was standing atop a short stack, below and to the rear. He was still holding his sax. Random appeared more than a little agitated and seemed to be shouting.

"Voice! Voice!" I said.

Dworkin waved.

"—ucking Lord of Chaos blowing up my palace!" Random was saying.

"The lady is injured, Your Highness," Mandor said.

Random passed a hand across his face. Then he looked upward.

"If there's an easy way to get her to my quarters, Vialle is very skilled in certain areas of medicine," he said in a softer voice. "So am I, for that matter."

"Just where is that, Your Highness?"

Random leaned to his side and pointed upward.

"Looks as if you won't need the door to get in, but I can't tell whether there's enough stairway left to get up there or where you might cross to it if there is."

"I'll make it," Mandor said, and two more of the balls came rushing to him and set themselves into eccentric orbits about him and Coral. Shortly thereafter they were levitated and drifted slowly toward the opening Random had indicated.

"I'll be along shortly," Random called after them. He looked as if he were about to add something, but then regarded the devastation, lowered his head, and turned away. I did the same thing.

Dworkin was offering me another dose of the green

medicine, and I took it. Some sort of trank, it seemed, in addition to whatever else it did.

"I have to go to her," I told him. "I like that lady, and I want to be sure she's all right."

"I can certainly send you there," Dworkin said, "though I cannot think of anything you could do for her which will not be done well by others. Perhaps the time were more profitably spent in pursuit of that errant construct of yours the Ghostwheel. It must be persuaded to return the Jewel of Judgment."

"Very well," I acknowledged. "But I want to see Coral first."

"Your appearance could cause considerable delay," he said, "because of explanations which may be required of you."

"I don't care," I told him.

"All right. A moment then."

He moved away and took down what appeared to be a sheathed wand from the wall, where it had hung suspended from a peg. He hung the sheath upon his belt, then crossed to a small cabinet and removed a flat leather-bound case from one of its drawers. It rattled with a faint metallic sound as he slipped it into a pocket. A small jewelry box vanished up a sleeve without any sound.

"Come this way," he told me, approaching and taking my hand.

He turned me and led me toward the room's darkest corner, where I had not noted that a tall, curiously framed mirror hung. It exhibited an odd reflective capacity in that it showed us and the room behind us with perfect clarity from a distance, but the closer we approached to its surface, the more indistinct all of its images became. I could see what was coming, coming. But I still tensed as Dworkin, a pace in advance of me by then, stepped through its foggy surface and jerked me after him.

I stumbled and regained my footing, coming to myself in the good half of the blasted royal suite in front of a decorative mirror. I reached back quickly and tapped it with my fingertips, but its surface remained solid. The short, stooped figure of Dworkin stood before me, and he still had hold of my right hand. Looking past that profile, which in some ways caricatured my own, I saw that the bed had been moved eastward, away from the broken corner and a large opening formerly occupied by a section of flooring. Random and Vialle stood on the near side of the bed, their backs to us. They were studying Coral, who was stretched out upon the counterpane and appeared to be unconscious. Mandor, seated in a heavy chair at the bed's foot, observing operations, was the first to notice our presence, which he acknowledged with a nod.

"How . . . is she?" I asked.

"Concussion," Mandor replied, "and damage to the right eye."

Random turned. Whatever he was about to say to me died on his lips when he realized who stood beside me.

"Dworkin!" he said. "It's been so long. I didn't know whether you were still alive. Are you . . . all right?"

The dwarf chuckled.

"I read your meaning, and I'm rational," he replied. "I would like to examine the lady now."

"Of course," Random answered, moving aside.

"Merlin," Dworkin said, "see whether you can locate that Ghostwheel device of yours, and ask it to return the artifact it borrowed."

"I understand," I said, reaching for my Trumps.

Moments later I was reaching, reaching . . .

"I felt your intent several moments ago, Dad."

"Well, do you have the Jewel or don't you?"

"Yes, I just finished with it."

" 'Finished'?"

"Finished utilizing it."

"In what fashion did you . . . utilize it?"

"As I understood from you that passing one's awareness through it would give some protection against the Pattern, I wondered whether it might work for an ideally synthesized being such as myself."

"That's a nice term, 'ideally synthesized.' Where'd it come from?"

"I coined it myself when seeking the most appropriate designation."

"I've a hunch it'll reject you."

"It didn't."

"Oh. You actually got all the way through the thing?"

"I did."

"What effect did it have upon you?"

"That's a hard thing to assess. My perceptions are altered. It's difficult to explain. . . . It's subtle, whatever it is."

"Fascinating. Can you move your awareness into the stone from a distance now?"

"Yes."

"When all of our present troubles have passed, I'm going to want to test you again "

"I'm curious myself to know what's changed."

"In the meantime, there is a need for the Jewel here."

"Coming through."

The air shimmered before me.

Ghostwheel appeared as a silver circlet, the Jewel of Judgment at its center. I cupped my hand and collected it. I took it to Dworkin, who did not even glance at me as he received it. I looked down at Coral's face and looked away quickly, wishing I hadn't.

I moved back near Ghost.

"Where's Nayda?" I asked.

"I'm not sure," he replied. "She asked me to leave her—there near the crystal cave—after I took the Jewel away from her."

"What was she doing?"

"Crying."

"Why?"

"I suppose because both of her missions in life have been frustrated. She was charged to guard you unless some wild chance brought her the opportunity of obtaining the Jewel, in which instance she was released from the first directive. This actually occurred; only I deprived her of the stone. Now she is bound to neither course."

"You'd think she'd be happy to be free at last. She wasn't on either job as a matter of choice. She can go back to doing whatever carefree demons do beyond the Rimwall."

"Not exactly, Dad."

"What do you mean?"

"She seems to be stuck in that body. Apparently she can't simply abandon it the way she could others she's used. It has something to do with there being no primary occupant."

"Oh. I suppose she could, uh, terminate and get loose that way."

"I suggested that, but she's not sure it would work that way. It might just kill her along with the body, now that she's bound to it the way she is."

"So she's still somewhere near the cave?"

"No. She retains her *ty'iga* powers, which make her something of a magical being. I believe she must simply have wandered off through Shadow while I was in the cave experimenting with the Jewel."

"Why the cave?"

"That's where you go to do clandestine things, isn't it?"

"Yeah. So how come I could reach you there with the Trump?"

"I'd already finished the experiment and departed. In fact, I was looking for her when you called."

"I think you'd better go and look some more."

"Why?"

"Because I owe her for favors past—even if my mother did sic her on me."

"Certainly. I'm not sure how successful I'll be, though. Magical beings don't track as readily as the more mundane sort."

"Give it a shot anyway. I'd like to know where she's gotten to and whether there's anything I can do for her. Maybe your new orientation will be of help —somehow."

"We'll see," he said, and he winked out.

I sagged. How was Orkus going to take it? I wondered. One daughter injured and the other possessed of a demon and wandering, off in Shadow. I moved to the foot of the bed and leaned against Mandor's chair. He reached up with his left hand and squeezed my arm.

"I don't suppose you learned anything about bonesetting off on that shadow-world, did you?" he inquired.

"Afraid not," I answered.

"Pity," he replied. "I'll just have to wait my turn."

"We can Trump you somewhere and get it taken care of right away," I said, reaching for my cards.

"No," he said. "I want to see things played out here."

While he was speaking, I noticed that Random seemed engaged in an intense Trump communication. Vialle stood nearby, as if shielding him from the opening in the wall and whatever might emerge therefrom. Dworkin continued to work upon Coral's face, his body blocking sight of exactly what he was doing.

"Mandor," I said, "did you know that my mother sent the *ty'iga* to take care of me?"

"Yes," he replied. "It told me that when you stepped out of the room. A part of the spell would not permit it to tell you this."

"Was she just there to protect me, or was she spying on me, too?"

"That I couldn't tell you. The matter didn't come up. But it does seem her fears were warranted. You were in danger."

"You think Dana knew about Jasra and Luke?"

He began to shrug, winced, thought better of it.

"Again, I don't know for certain. If she did, I can't answer the next one either: How did she know? Okay?"

"Okay."

Random completed a conversation, covering a Trump. Then he turned and stared at Vialle for some time. He looked as if he were about to say something, thought better of it, looked away. He looked at me. About then I heard Coral moan, and I looked away, rising.

"A moment, Merlin," Random said, "before you go rushing off."

I met his gaze. Whether it was angry or merely curious, I could not tell. The tightening of the brows, the narrowing of the eyes could indicate either.

"Sir?" I said.

He approached, took me by the elbow, and turned me away from the bed, leading me off toward the doorway to the next room.

"Vialle, I'm borrowing your studio for a few moments," he said.

"Surely," she replied.

He led me inside and closed the door behind us.

Across the room a bust of Gérard had fallen and broken. What appeared to be her current project—a multilimbed sea creature of a sort I'd never seen—occupied a work area at the studio's far end.

Random turned on me suddenly and searched my face.

"Have you been following the Begma-Kashfa situation?" he asked.

"More or less," I replied. "Bill briefed me on it the other night. Eregnor and all that."

"Did he tell you that we were going to bring Kashfa into the Golden Circle and solve the Eregnor problem by recognizing Kashfa's right to that piece of real estate?"

I didn't like the way he'd asked that one, and I didn't want to get Bill in trouble. It had seemed that that matter was still under wraps when we'd spoken. So, "I'm afraid I don't recall all the details on this stuff," I said.

"Well, that's what I planned on doing," Random told me. "We don't usually make guarantees like that—the kind that will favor one treaty country at the expense of another—but Arkans, the Duke of Shadburne, kind of had us over a barrel. He was the best possible head of state for our purposes, and I'd paved the way for his taking the throne now that that red-haired bitch is out of the picture. He knew he could lean on me a bit, though —since he'd be taking a chance accepting the throne following a double break in the succession—and he asked for Eregnor, so I gave it to him."

"I see," I said, "everything except how this affects me."

He turned his head and studied me through his left eye.

"The coronation was to be today. In fact, I was going to dress and Trump back for it in a little while. . . ."

"You use the past tense," I observed, to fill the silence he had left before me.

"So I do. So I do," he muttered, turning away, pacing a few steps, resting his foot on a piece of broken statuary, turning back. "The good Duke is now either dead or imprisoned."

"And there will be no coronation?" I said.

"*Au contraire*," Random replied, still studying my face.

"I give up," I said. "Tell me what's going on."

"There was a coup, at dawn, this morning."

"Palace?"

"Possibly that, too. But it was backed by external military force."

"What was Benedict doing while this was going on?"

"I ordered him to pull the troops out yesterday, right before I came home myself. Things seemed stable, and it wouldn't have looked good to have combat troops from Amber stationed there during the coronation."

"True," I said. "So somebody moved right in, almost as soon as Benedict moved out and did away with the man who would be king, without the local constabulary even suggesting that that was not nice?"

Random nodded slowly.

"That's about the size of it," he said. "Now why do you think that might be?"

"Perhaps they were not totally displeased with the new state of affairs."

Random smiled and snapped his fingers.

"Inspired," he said. "One could almost think you knew what was going on."

"One would be wrong," I said.

"Today your former classmate Lukas Raynard becomes Rinaldo I, King of Kashfa."

"I'll be damned," I said. "I'd no idea he really wanted that job. What are you going to do about it?"

"I think I'll skip the coronation."

"I mean, over a slightly longer term."

Random sighed and turned away, kicking at the rubble.

"You mean, am I going to send Benedict back, to depose him?"

"In a word, yes."

"That would make us look pretty bad. What Luke just did is not above the Graustarkian politics that prevail in the area. We'd moved in and helped straighten out something that was fast becoming a political shambles. We could go back and do it again, too, if it were just some half-assed coup by a crazy general or some noble with delusions of grandeur. But Luke's got a legitimate claim, and it actually is stronger than Shadburne's. Also, he's popular. He's young, and he makes a good appearance. We'd have a lot less justification for going back than we had for going in initially. Even so, I was almost willing to risk being called an aggressor to keep that bitch's homicidal son off the throne. Then my man in Kashfa tells me that he's under Vialle's protection. So I asked her about it. She says that it's true and that you were present when it happened. She said she'd tell me about it after the operation Dworkin's doing now, in case he needs her empathic abilities. But I can't wait. Tell me what happened."

"You tell me one more thing first."

"What is it?"

"What military forces brought Luke to power?"

"Mercenaries."

"Dalt's?"

"Yes."

"Okay. Luke canceled his vendetta against the House of Amber," I said. "He did this freely, following a conversation with Vialle, just the other night. It was then that she gave him the ring. At the time I thought it was to keep Julian from trying to kill him, as we were on our way down to Arden."

"This was in response to Dalt's so-called ultimatum regarding Luke and Jasra?"

"That's right. It never occurred to me that the whole thing might be a setup—to get Luke and Dalt together so they could go off and pull a coup. That would mean that even that fight was staged, and now that I think of it, Luke did have a chance to talk with Dalt before it occurred."

Random raised his hand.

"Wait," he said. "Go back and tell me the thing from the beginning."

"Right."

And so I did. By the time I'd finished we had both paced the length of the studio countless times.

"You know," he said then, "the whole business sounds like something Jasra might have set up before her career as a piece of furniture."

"The thought had occurred to me," I said, hoping he wasn't about to pursue the matter of her present whereabouts. And the more I thought of it, recalling her reaction to the information about Luke following our raid on the Keep, the more I began to feel not only that she had been aware of what was going on but that she'd even been in touch with Luke more recently than I had at that time.

"It was pretty smoothly done," he observed. "Dalt must have been operating under old orders. Not being certain how to collect Luke or locate Jasra for fresh instructions, he took a chance with that feint on Amber. Benedict might well have spitted him again, with equal skill and greater effect."

"True. I guess you have to give the devil his due when

it comes to guts. It also means that Luke must have done a lot of fast plotting and laid that fixed fight out during their brief conference in Arden. So he was really in control there, and he conned us into thinking he was a prisoner, which precluded his being the threat to Kashfa that he really was—if you want to look at it that way."

"What other way is there to look at it?"

"Well, as you said yourself, his claim is not exactly without merit. What do you want to do?"

Random massaged his temples.

"Going after him, preventing the coronation, would be a very unpopular move," he said. "First, though, I'm curious. You say this guy's a great bullshitter. You were there. Did he con Vialle into placing him under her protection?"

"No, he didn't," I said. "He seemed as surprised as I was at her gesture. He called off the vendetta because he felt that honor had been satisfied, that he had to an extent been used by his mother, and out of friendship for me. He did it without any strings on it. I still think she gave him the ring so the vendetta would end there, so none of us would go gunning for him."

"That is very like her," Random said. "If I thought he'd taken advantage of her, I was going to go after him myself. The embarrassment for me is unintentional then, and I guess I can live with it. I prime Arkans for the throne, and then he's shunted aside at the last minute by someone under my wife's protection. Almost makes it look as if there's a bit of divisiveness here at the center of things—and I'd hate to give that impression."

"I've got a hunch Luke will be very conciliatory. I know him well enough to know he appreciates all of these nuances. I'd guess he'd be a very easy man for Amber to deal with, on any level."

"I'll bet he will. Why shouldn't he?"

"No reason," I said. "What's going to happen to that treaty now?"

Random smiled.

"I'm off the hook. I never felt right about the Eregnor provisions. Now, if there's to be a treaty at all, we go at it *ab initio.* I'm not even sure we need one, though. The hell with 'em."

"I'll bet Arkans is still alive," I said.

"You think Luke's holding him hostage, against my giving him Golden Circle status?"

I shrugged.

"How close are you to Arkans?"

"Well, I did set him up for this thing, and I feel I owe him. I don't feel I owe him that much, though."

"Understandable."

"There would be loss of face for Amber even to approach a second-rate power like Kashfa directly at a time like this."

"True," I said, "and for that matter, Luke isn't officially head of state yet."

"Arkans would still be enjoying life at his villa if it weren't for me, though, and Luke really does seem to be a friend of yours—a scheming friend, but a friend."

"You would like me to mention this during a forthcoming discussion of Tony Price's atomic sculpture?"

He nodded.

"I feel you should have your art discussion very soon. In fact, it would not be inappropriate for you to attend a friend's coronation—as a private individual. Your dual heritage will serve us well here, and he will still be honored."

"Even so, I'll bet he wants that treaty."

"Even if we were inclined to grant it, we would not guarantee him Eregnor."

"I understand."

"And you are not empowered to commit us to anything."

"I understand that, too."

"Then why don't you clean up a bit and go talk to him about it? Your room is just around the abyss. You can leave through the hole in the wall and shinny down a beam I noticed was intact."

"Okay, I will," I answered, moving in that direction. "But one question first, completely off the subject."

"Yes?"

"Has my father been back recently?"

"Not to my knowledge," he said, shaking his head slowly. "We're all pretty good at hiding our comings and goings if we wish, of course. But I think he'd have let me know if he were around."

"Guess so," I said, and I turned and exited through the wall, skirting the abyss.

XI

No.

I hung from the beam, swung, and let go. I landed almost gracefully in the middle of the hallway in an area that would have been located approximately midway between my two doors, save that the first door was missing, also the section of wall through which it had provided entrance (or exit, depending on which side you happened to be), not to mention my favorite chair and a display case which had held seashells I'd picked up from beaches around the world. Pity.

I rubbed my eyes and turned away, for even the prospect of my ruined apartment took second place just now. Hell, I'd had apartments ruined in the past. Usually around April 30 . . .

As in "Niagara Falls," slowly I turned. . .

No.

Yes.

Across the hall from my rooms, where I had previously

faced a blank wall, there was now a hallway running to the north. I'd gotten a glimpse up its sparkling length as I'd dropped from my rafter. Amazing. The gods had just uptempoed my background music yet again. I'd been in that hallway before, in one of its commoner locations up on the fourth floor, running east-west between a couple of storerooms. One of Castle Amber's intriguing anomalies, the Corridor of Mirrors, in addition to seeming longer in one direction than the other, contained countless mirrors. Literally countless. Try counting them, and you never come up with the same total twice. Tapers flicker in high, standing holders, casting infinities of shadows. There are big mirrors, little mirrors, narrow mirrors, squat mirrors, tinted mirrors, distorting mirrors, mirrors with elaborate frames—cast or carved—plain, simply framed mirrors, and mirrors with no frames at all; there are mirrors in multitudes of sharp-angled geometric shapes, amorphous shapes, curved mirrors.

I had walked the Corridor of Mirrors on several occasions, sniffing the perfumes of scented candles, sometimes feeling subliminal presences among the images, things which faded at an instant's sharp regard. I had felt the mixed enchantments of the place but had somehow never roused its sleeping genii. Just as well perhaps. One never knew what to expect in that place; at least that's what Bleys once told me. He was not certain whether the mirrors propelled one into obscure realms of Shadow, hypnotized one and induced bizarre dream states, cast one into purely symbolic realms decorated with the furniture of the psyche, played malicious or harmless head games with the viewer, none of the above, all of the above, or some of the above. Whatever, it was something less than harmless, though, as thieves, servants, and visitors had occasionally been found dead or stunned and mumbling along that sparkling route, ofttimes wearing highly unusual expressions. And generally around the solstices and equinoxes—though it could occur at any season—the corridor moved itself to a new location, sometimes simply departing altogether for a time. Usually it was treated with suspicion, shunned, though it could as often reward as injure one or offer a useful omen or insight as readily as an unnerving experience. It was the uncertainty of it that roused trepidations.

And sometimes, I was told, it was almost as if it came looking for a particular person, bearing its ambiguous gifts. On such occasions it was said to be more dangerous to turn it down than to accept its invitation.

"Aw, come on," I said. "Now?"

The shadows danced along its length, and I caught a whiff of those intoxicating tapers. I moved forward. I extended my left hand past its corner and patted the wall. Frakir didn't stir.

"This is Merlin," I said, "and I'm kind of busy just now. You sure you wouldn't rather reflect someone else?"

The nearest flame seemed, for an instant, a fiery hand, beckoning.

"Shit," I whispered, and I strode forward.

There was no sense of transition as I entered. A long red-patterned runner covered the floor. Dust motes spun in the lights I passed. I was beside myself in many aspects, flickering flamelight harlequinading my garments, transforming my face within a dance of shadows.

Flicker.

For an instant it seemed that the stern visage of Oberon regarded me from a small high metal-framed oval—as easily a trick of the light as the shade of his late highness, of course.

Flicker.

I'd swear an animalistic travesty of my own face had leered at me for a moment, tongue lolling, from a mid-level rectangle of quicksilver to my left, framed in ceramic flowers, face humanizing as I turned, quickly, to mock me.

Walking. Footsteps muffled. Breathing slightly tight. I wondered whether I should summon my Logrus sight or even try that of the Pattern. I was loath to attempt either, though, memories of the nastier aspects of both Powers still too fresh within me for comfort. Something was about to happen to me, I was certain.

I halted and examined the one I thought must have my number—framed in black metal, with various signs from the magical arts inlaid in silver about it. The glass was murky, as if spirits swam just out of sight within its depths. My face looked leaner, its lines more heavily inscribed, the faintest of purple halos, perhaps, flickering about my head within it. There was something cold and vaguely sinister about that image, but though I studied it for a long while, nothing happened. There were no messages, enlightenments, changes. In fact, the longer I stared, the more all of the dramatic little touches seemed but tricks of the lighting.

I walked on, past glimpses of unearthly landscapes, exotic creatures, hints of memory, near subliminals of dead friends and relatives. Something within a pool even waved a rake at me. I waved back. Having so recently survived the traumas of my trek through the land between shadows, I was not as intimidated by these manifestations of strangeness and possible menace as I would likely have been at almost any other time. I thought I had sight of a gibbeted man, swinging as in a strong wind, hands tied behind his back, El Greco sky above him.

"I've had a rough couple of days," I said aloud, "and

there's no sign of any letup. I'm sort of in a hurry, if you know what I mean."

Something punched me in the right kidney, and I spun around, but there was no one there. Then I felt a hand upon my shoulder, turning me. I cooperated quickly. No one there either.

"I apologize," I said, "if the truth requires it here."

Invisible hands continued to push and tug at me, moving me past a number of attractive mirrors. I was steered to a cheap-looking mirror in a dark-stained wooden frame. It looked as if it might have come from some discount house. There was a slight imperfection in the glass, in the vicinity of my left eye. Whatever forces had propelled me to this point released me here. It occurred to me that the powers that be here might actually have been attempting to expedite things per my request, rather than simply hustling me in a peevish spirit.

So, "Thanks," I said, just to be safe, and I continued to stare. I moved my head back and forth and from side to side, producing ripple effects across my image. I repeated the movements while waiting for whatever might occur.

My image remained unchanged, but on the third or fourth ripple my background was altered. It was no longer a wall of dimly lit mirrors that stood behind me. It flowed away and did not return with my next movement. In its place was a stand of dark shrubbery beneath an evening sky. I continued to move my head slightly several times more, but the ripple effect had vanished. The bushes seemed very real, though my peripheral vision showed me that the hallway was intact in both directions and still seemed to possess its right-hand wall at both ends.

I continued to search the seemingly reflected shrubbery, looking for portents, omens, signs, or just a little movement. None of these became apparent, though a very real sensation of depth was there. I could almost feel a cool breeze upon my neck. I must have stared for several minutes, waiting for the mirror to produce something new. But it did not. If this was the best the mirror had to offer, it was time to move on, I decided.

Something seemed to stir in the bushes at my back then, causing reflex to take over. I turned quickly, raising my hands before me.

It was only the wind that had rustled them, I saw. And then I realized that I was not in the hallway, and I turned again. The mirror and its wall were gone. I now faced a low hill, a line of broken masonry at its top. Light flickered from behind that shattered wall. Both curiosity and my sense of purpose roused, I began climbing slowly, my wariness yet present.

The sky seemed to grow darker even as I climbed, and it was cloudless, a profusion of stars pulsing in unfamiliar constellations across it. I moved with some stealth amid stones, grasses, shrubs, broken masonry. From beyond the vine-clad wall I now heard the sounds of voices. Though I could not distinguish the words being spoken, it did not seem conversation that I overheard, but rather a cacophony—as if a number of individuals, of both genders and various ages, were delivering simultaneous monologues.

Coming to the hill's top, I extended my hand until it made contact with the wall's irregular surface. I decided against going around it to see what sort of activity was in progress on the other side. It could make me visible to I knew not what. It seemed so much simpler to reach as high as I could, hook my fingers over the top of the nearest depressed area, and draw myself upward—as I did. I even located toeholds as my head neared the top, and I was able to ease some of the strain on my arms by resting part of my weight upon them.

I drew myself carefully up those final few inches, peering past fractured stone and down into the interior of the ruined structure. It appeared to have been some sort of church. The roof was fallen, and the far wall still stood, in much the same condition as the one I clung to. There was an altar in bad repair in a raised area off to my right. Whatever had happened here must have happened long ago, for shrubs and vines grew in the interior as well as without, softening the lines of collapsed pews, fallen pillars, fragments of the roof.

Below me, in a cleared area, a large pentagram was drawn. At each of the star's points stood a figure, facing outward. Inward from them, at the five points where the lines crossed, flared a torch, its butt driven into the earth. This seemed a somewhat peculiar variation on the rituals with which I was familiar, and I wondered at the summoning and why the five were not better protected and why they were not about the work in concert, rather than each seeming off on a personal trip and ignoring the others. The three whom I could see clearly had their backs to me. The two who faced in my direction were barely within my line of sight, their faces covered over with shadows. Some of the voices were male; some, female. One was singing; two were chanting; the other two seemed merely to be speaking, though in stagy, artificial tones.

I drew myself higher, trying for a glimpse of the faces of the nearer two. This because there was something familiar about the entire ensemble, and I felt that if I were to identify one, I might well realize all of their identities.

Another question high on my list was, What was it they were summoning? Was I safe up here on the wall, this close to the operation, if something unusual put in an appearance? It did not seem that the proper constraints were in place below. I drew myself higher still. I felt my center of gravity shifting just as my view of affairs improved yet again. Then I realized that I was moving forward without effort. An instant later I knew that the wall was toppling, carrying me forward and down right into the midst of their oddly choreographed ritual. I tried to push myself away from the wall, hoping to hit the ground rolling and run like hell. But it was already too late. My abrupt push-up raised me into the air but did not really halt my forward momentum.

No one beneath me stirred, though rubble rained about them all, and I finally caught some recognizable words as I fell.

". . . summon thee, Merlin, to fall into my power now!" one of the women was chanting.

A very effective ritual after all, I decided, as I landed on my back upon the pentagram, arms flopping out to my sides at shoulder level, legs spread. I was able to tuck my chin, protecting my head, and the slapping of my arms seemed to produce a break-fall effect so that I was not badly stunned by the impact. The five high towers of fire danced wildly about me for several seconds, then settled once again into steadier blazing. The five figures still faced outward. I attempted to rise and found that I could not. It was as if I were staked out in that position.

Frakir had warned me too late, as I was falling, and now I was uncertain to what employment I might put her. I could send her creeping off to any of the figures with orders to work her way upward and commence choking. But so far I had no way of knowing which one, if any, might deserve such treatment.

"I hate dropping in without notice," I said, "and I can

see this is a private party. If someone will be good
enough to turn me loose, I'll be on my way——"

The figure in the vicinity of my left foot did an about-
face and stood staring down at me. She wore a blue
robe, but there was no mask upon her fire-reddened
face. There was only a tight smile, which went away
when she licked her lips. It was Julia, and there was a
knife in her right hand.

"Always the smartass," she said. "Ready with a flip-
pant answer to any situation. It's a cover for your unwil-
lingness to commit yourself to anything or anyone. Even
those who love you."

"It could just be a sense of humor, too," I said, "a
thing I'm beginning to realize you never possessed."

She shook her head slowly.

"You keep everyone at arms' distance. There is no
trust in you."

"Runs in the family," I said. "But prudence does not
preclude affection."

She had begun raising the blade, but she faltered for a
second.

"Are you saying that you still care about me?" she
asked.

"I never stopped," I said. "It's just that you came on
too strong all of a sudden. You wanted more of me than
I was willing to give just then."

"You lie," she said, "because I hold your life in my
hand."

"I could think of a lot worse reasons for lying," I said.
"But, unfortunately, I'm telling the truth."

There came another familiar voice then, from off to my
right.

"It was too early for us to speak of such things," she
said, "but I begrudge her your affection."

Turning my head, I saw that this figure, too, now

224

faced inward, and it was Coral and her right eye was covered by a black patch and she, too, held a knife in her right hand. Then I saw what was in her left hand, and I shot a glance back at Julia. Yes, they both held forks as well as knives.

"*Et tu,*" I said.

"I told you I don't speak English," Coral replied.

"Et by two," Julia responded, raising her utensils. "Who says I don't have a sense of humor?"

They spit at each other across me, some of the spittle not quite going the distance.

Luke, it occurred to me, might have tried settling matters by proposing to both of them on the spot. I'd a feeling it wouldn't work for me, so I didn't.

"This is an objectification of marriage neurosis," I said. "It's a projective experience. It's a vivid dream. It's—"

Julia dropped to one knee, and her right hand flashed downward. I felt the blade enter my left thigh.

My scream was interrupted when Coral drove her fork into my right shoulder.

"This is ridiculous!" I cried as the other utensils flashed in their hands and I felt fresh stabs of pain.

Then the figure at the star's point near my right foot turned slowly, gracefully. She was wrapped in a dark brown cloak with a yellow border, her arms crossed before her holding it closed up to her eye level.

"Stop, you bitches!" she ordered, flinging the garment wide and resembling nothing so much as a mourning cloak butterfly. It was, of course, Dara, my mother.

Julia and Coral had already raised their forks to their mouths and were chewing. There was a tiny bead of blood beside Julia's lip. The cloak continued to flow outward from my mother's fingertips as if it were alive, as if it were a part of her. Its wings blocked Julia and

ROGER ZELAZNY

Coral completely from my sight, falling upon them as
she continued to spread her arms, covering them, bearing
them over backward to become body-size lumps upon the
ground, growing smaller and smaller until the garment
simply hung naturally and they were gone from their
points of the star.

There came a slow, delicate clapping sound then, followed by a hoarse laugh from my left.

"Extremely well executed," came that painfully familiar voice, "but then you always liked him best."

"Better," she corrected.

"Isn't poor Despil even in the running?" Jurt said.

"You're being unfair," she told him.

"You liked that mad Prince of Amber more than you
ever cared for our father, who was a decent man," he told
her. "That's why Merlin was always your pet, isn't it?"

"That's just not true, Jurt, and you know it," she said.

He laughed again.

"We all summoned him because we all want him," he
said, "for different reasons. But in the end our desires all
come to this, do they not?"

I heard the growl, and I turned my head just in time
to see his face slide along the projective curve wolfward,
muzzle descending, fangs flashing as he fell to all fours
and slashed at my left shoulder, gaining himself a gory
taste of my person.

"Stop that!" she cried. "You little beast!"

He threw back his muzzle and howled, and it came out
the way a coyote's cry does, as a kind of mad laughter.

A black boot struck his shoulder, knocking him over
backward and sending him crashing into the uncollapsed
section of wall behind him, which promptly collapsed
upon him. He uttered but a brief whimper before being
covered over completely by the falling rubble.

"Well, well, well," I heard Dara say, and looking that

226

way, I saw that she also held a knife and fork. "What's a bastard like you doing in a nice place like this?"

"Keeping the last of the predators at bay, it would seem," replied the voice which had once told me a very long story containing multiple versions of an auto accident and a number of genealogical gaffes.

She lunged at me, but he stooped, caught me beneath the shoulders, and snatched me out of her way. Then his great black cloak swirled like a matador's, covering her. As she had done with Coral and Julia, she herself seemed to melt into the earth beneath it. He set me on my feet, stooped then, raised the cloak, and brushed it off. As he refastened it with a silver rose of a clasp, I studied him for fangs or at least cutlery.

"Four out of five," I said, brushing myself off. "No matter how real this seems, I'm sure it's only analogically or anagogically true. So how come you're not cannibalistically inclined in this place?"

"On the other hand," he said, drawing on a silver gauntlet, "I was never a real father to you. It's kind of difficult when you don't even know the kid exists. So I didn't really want anything from you either."

"That sure looks like Grayswandir you're wearing," I said.

He nodded.

"It seems to have served you, too."

"I suppose I should thank you for that. I also suppose you're the wrong . . . person to ask whether you really bore me from that cave to the land between shadows."

"Oh, it was me all right."

"Of course, you'd say that."

"I don't know why I should if I didn't. Look out! The wall!"

One quick glance showed me that another big section of wall was falling toward us. Then he pushed me, and I sprawled across the pentagram again. I heard the stones crashing behind me, and I half rose and threw myself even farther forward.

Something struck the side of my head.

I woke up in the Corridor of Mirrors. I was lying facedownward, my head resting on my right forearm, a rectangular piece of stone clutched in my hand, the aromas of the candles drifting about me. When I began to rise, I felt pains in both shoulders and in my left thigh. A quick investigation showed me that I bore cuts in all three of those places. Though there wasn't much I could do now to help demonstrate the veracity of my recent adventure beyond this, it wasn't something I felt like shrugging off either.

I got to my feet and limped back to the corridor that ran past my rooms.

"Where'd you go?" Random called down to me.

"Huh? What do you mean?" I responded.

"You walked back up the hall, but there's nothing there."

"How long was I gone?"

"Half a minute maybe," he answered.

I waved the stone I still carried.

"Saw this lying on the floor. Couldn't figure what it was," I said.

"Probably blown there when the Powers met," he said, "from one of the walls. There were a number of arches edged with stones like that at one time. Mostly plastered over on your floor now."

"Oh," I said. "See you in a bit, before I take off."

"Do that," he replied, and I turned and found my way through one of the day's many broken walls and on into my room.

The far wall had also been blasted, I noticed, creating

a large opening into Brand's dusty chambers. I paused and studied it. Synchronicity, I decided. It appeared there had once been an archway connecting those rooms with these. I moved forward and examined the exposed curve along its left side. Yes, it had been rendered from stones similar to the one I held. In fact—

I brushed away plaster and slid mine into a broken area. It fitted perfectly. In fact, when I gave it a small tug, it refused to be removed. Had I really brought it back from the sinister father-mother-brother-lovers ritual dream beyond the mirror? Or had I half-consciously picked it up on my return, from wherever it had been blasted during the recent architectural distress?

I turned away, removing my cloak, stripping off my shirt. Yes. There were punctures like fork marks on my right shoulder, something like an animal bite on my left. Also, there was dried blood on my left trouser leg in the area of a tear beyond which my thigh was tender. I washed up and brushed my teeth and combed my hair, and I put a dressing on my leg and left shoulder. The family metabolism would see me healed in a day, but I didn't want some exertion tearing them open and getting fresh garments gory.

Speaking of which . . .

The armoire was undamaged and I thought I'd wear my other colors, to give Luke a happy memory or two for his coronation: the golden shirt and royal blue trousers I'd found which approximated Berkeley's colors almost exactly; a leather vest dyed to match the pants; matching cloak with gold trim; black sword belt, black gloves tucked behind it, reminding me I needed a new blade. Dagger, too, for that matter. I was wondering about a hat when a series of sounds caught my attention. I turned.

Through a fresh screen of dust I now had a symmetrical view into Brand's quarters; rather than a jagged opening in the wall the archway stood perfect and entire, the wall intact at either hand and above. The wall to my right also seemed less damaged than it had been earlier.

I moved forward and ran my hand along the curve of stones. I inspected adjacent plastered areas, looking for cracks. There were none. All right. The stone had borne an enchantment. To what end?

I strode through the archway and looked around. The room was dark, and I summoned the Logrus sight reflexively. It came and served me, as usual. Perhaps the Logrus had decided against holding a grudge.

At this level I could see the residue of many magical experiments as well as a number of standing spells. Most sorcerers leave a certain amount of not normally visible magical clutter about, but Brand seemed to have been a real slob, though of course, he might have been rushed quite a bit near the end there when he was trying to take over control of the universe. It's not the sort of occupation wherein neatness counts the way it might in other endeavors. I passed on along my tour of inspection. There were mysteries here, unfinished bits of business and indications that he had gone farther along some magical routes than I had ever wished to go. Still, there was nothing here that I felt I could not handle and nothing representing grave and immediate danger. It was just possible, now I'd finally had an opportunity to inspect them, that I might want to leave the archway intact and add Brand's quarters to my own.

On the way out I decided to check Brand's armoire to see whether he had a hat to go with what I was wearing. I opened it and discovered a dark three-cornered one with a golden feather, which fitted me perfectly. The color was a little off, but I suddenly recalled a spell which altered it. As I was about to turn away, something to the rear of that top shelf which held the hats glinted for a moment within my Logrus vision. I reached in and withdrew it.

It was a long and lovely gold-chased sheath of dark green, and the hilt of the blade which protruded from it appeared to be goldplated, with an enormous emerald set in its pommel. I took hold of it and drew it partway, half expecting it to wail like a demon on whom one has dropped a balloon filled with holy water. Instead, it merely hissed and smoked a little. And there was a bright design worked into the metal of its blade—almost recognizable. Yes, a section of the Pattern. Only this excerpting was from the Pattern's end, whereas Grayswandir's was from a point near the beginning.

I sheathed it, and on an impulse I hung it from my belt. His old man's sword would make a neat coronation present for Luke, I decided. So I'd take it along for him. I let myself out into the side corridor then, made my way over a small section of collapsed wall from Gérard's quarters and back past Fiona's door to my dad's rooms. There was one thing more I wanted to check, and the sword had reminded me. I fished in my pocket for the key I'd transferred from my bloody trousers. Then I decided I'd better knock. What if . . .

I knocked and waited, knocked again and waited again. In that nothing but silence ensued I unlocked the door and entered. I went no farther than that first place. I'd just wanted to check the rack.

Grayswandir was gone from the peg where I'd hung it.

I backed out, closing and locking the door. The fact that the row of pegs had been empty was an instance of obtaining the knowledge one wanted and still not being certain what one had proved thereby. Yet it had been something I'd wished to know, and it did make me feel that final knowledge was nearer than it had been. . . .

I walked back, past Fiona's rooms. I reentered Brand's

rooms through the door I had left ajar. I hunted around till I spotted a key in a nearby ashtray. I locked the door and pocketed the key; that was almost silly because anyone could walk in from my room now and my room was missing a wall. Still . . .

I hesitated before crossing back to my sitting room with its Tabriz stained with *ty'iga* spit and partly covered by fallen wall. There was something almost restful about Brand's quarters, a kind of peaceful quality I hadn't really noticed before. I wandered a bit, opening drawers and looking inside magic boxes, studying a folder of the man's drawings. The Logrus sight showed me that something small and potent and magical was secreted in a bedpost, radiating lines of force every which way. I unscrewed the knob, found the compartment within it. It contained a small velvet bag which bore a ring. The band was wide, possibly of platinum. It bore a wheel-like device of some reddish metal, with countless tiny spokes, many of them hair-fine. And each of these spokes extended a line of power leading off somewhere, quite possibly into Shadow, where some power cache or spell source lay. Perhaps Luke would rather have the ring than the sword. When I slipped it on, it seemed to extend roots to the very center of my body. I could feel my way back along them to the ring and then out along those connections. I was impressed by the variety of energies it reached and controlled—from simple chthonic forces to sophisticated constructs of High Magic, from elementals to things that seemed like lobotomized gods. I wondered why he hadn't been wearing it on the day of the Patternfall battle. If he had, I'd a feeling he might have been truly invincible. We could all have been living on Brandenberg in Castle Brand. I wondered, too, why Fiona, in the next room over, had not felt its presence and come looking for it. On the other hand, I hadn't. For what it was, it didn't register well at all, beyond a few feet. It was amazing the treasures this place contained. Was it something about the private universe effect said to obtain in some of these rooms? The ring was a beautiful alternative to Pattern Power or Logrus Power, hooked in as it was with so many sources. It must have taken centuries to empower the thing. Whatever Brand had wanted it for, it had not been part of a short-range plan. I decided I could not surrender the thing to Luke—or to anyone with any familiarity with the Arts. I didn't even think I should trust a nonmagician with it. And I certainly didn't feel like returning it to the bedpost. What was that throbbing at my wrist? Oh, yes, Frakir. It had been going on for some small while, and I'd barely noticed.

"Sorry you lost your voice, old girl," I said, stroking her as I explored the room for threats both psychic and physical. "I can't find a damned thing here that I should be worried about."

Immediately she spiraled down from my wrist and tried to remove the ring from my finger.

"Stop!" I ordered. "I know the ring could be dangerous. But only if you use it wrongly. I'm a sorcerer, remember? I'm into these matters. There is nothing special about it for me to fear."

But Frakir disobeyed my order and continued her attack on the ring, which I could now only attribute to some form of magical artifact jealousy. I tied her in a tight knot around the bedpost and left her there, to teach her a lesson.

I began to search the apartment more diligently. If I were to keep the sword *and* the ring, it would be nice to find something else of his father's that I could take to Luke—

"Merlin! Merlin!" I heard bellowed from somewhere beyond my room.

Rising from a tapping of the floor and lower walls, where I had been seeking hollow spots, I returned to my archway and passed through into my own sitting room. I halted then despite another summons in what I now recognized to be Random's voice. The wall which faced upon the side corridor was more than half rebuilt since last I had viewed it—as if an invisible crew of carpenters and plasterers had been silently at work since I had positioned the dreamstone in the gateway to the kingdom of Brand. Amazing. I simply stood and stared, hoping for some betraying bit of business within the damaged area. Then I heard Random mutter, "I guess he's gone," and I called back, "Yeah? What is it?"

"Get your ass up here quick," he said. "I need your advice."

I stepped out into the corridor through the opening which remained in that wall, and I looked upward. Immediately I could feel the capabilities in the ring that I wore, responding like a musical instrument to my most immediate need. The appropriate line was activated as I assented to the suggestion, and I took the gloves from behind my belt and drew them on as I was levitated toward the opening in the ceiling. This, because it had occurred to me that Random might recognize the ring as having once been Brand's, and that could lead to a complicated discussion I'd no desire for at the moment.

I held my cloak close to my side as I came up through the hole into the studio, to keep the blade under wraps also.

"Impressive," Random said. "Glad you're keeping the magical muscle exercised. That's what I called you for."

I gave him a bow. Being dressed up made me feel vaguely courtly.

"How may I be of service?"

"Cut the crap and come on," he said, taking hold of my elbow and steering me back toward the demi-bedroom. Vialle stood at the door, holding it open.

"Merlin?" she said as I brushed by.

"Yes?" I answered.

"I wasn't certain," she said.

"Of what?" I asked.

"That it was you," she responded.

"Oh, it's me, all right," I said.

"It is indeed my brother," Mandor stated, rising from his chair and approaching us. His arm was splinted and slung, his face considerably relaxed. "If anything about him strikes you as strange," he continued, "it is likely because he has had a number of traumatic experiences since he left here."

"Is that true?" Random asked.

"Yes," I replied. "I didn't realize it was all that apparent."

"Are you all right?" Random asked.

"I seem to be intact," I said.

"Good. Then we'll save the particulars of your story for another time. As you can see, Coral is gone and Dworkin is, too. I didn't see them go. I was still in the studio when it happened."

"When what happened?" I asked.

"Dworkin finished his operation," Mandor said, "took the lady by the hand, drew her to her feet, and transported her away from here. It was most elegantly managed. One moment they stood at the bedside; the next their afterimages ran through the spectrum and winked out."

"You say that he transported them. How do you know that they weren't snatched away by Ghostwheel or one of the Powers?" I asked.

"Because I watched his face," he said, "and there was no surprise whatsoever upon it, only a small smile."

"I guess you're right," I admitted. "Then who set your arm, if Random was off in the studio and Dworkin occupied?"

"I did," Vialle said. "I've been trained in it."

"So you were the only eyewitness to their vanishment?" I said to Mandor.

He nodded.

"What I want of you," Random said, "is some idea where they flashed off to. Mandor said he couldn't tell. Here!"

He handed me a chain, from which a metal setting hung.

"What's this?" I asked.

"It was the most important of all the Crown Jewels," he said, "the Jewel of Judgment. This is what they left me. The Jewel part is what they took."

"Oh," I said. Then: "It must be secure if it's in Dworkin's care. He'd said something about putting it in a safe place, and he knows more about it than anyone else—"

"He may also have flipped out again," Random said. "I'm not interested in discussing his merits as its custodian, though. I just want to know where the hell he's gone with the thing."

"I don't believe he left any tracks," Mandor said.

"Where were they standing?" I asked.

"Over there," he said, with a gesture of the good arm, "to the right of the bed."

I moved to that area, feeling through the potencies I ruled after the most appropriate.

"A little nearer the foot."

I nodded, feeling it would not be all that difficult to look back a small distance through time within my personal space.

I felt the rainbow rush and saw their outlines. Freeze.

A power line moved forth from the ring, attached itself, ran rainbow with them, passed through the portal which closed with a mild implosion. Raising the back of my hand to my forehead, I seemed to look down the line—

—into a large hall hung with six shields to my left. To my right hung a multitude of flags and pennons. A fire blazed in an enormous hearth before me. . . .

"I see the place they went to," I said, "but I don't recognize it."

"Is there some way you can share the vision?" Random asked.

"Perhaps," I replied, realizing there was a way even as I said it. "Regard the mirror."

Random turned, moved nearer the looking glass through which Dworkin had brought me—how long ago? "By the blood of the beast on the pole and the shell that is cracked at the center of the world," I said, feeling the need to address two of the powers I controlled, "may the sight be cast!"

The mirror frosted over, and when it cleared, my vision of the hall lay within it.

"I'll be damned," Random said. "He took her to Kashfa. I wonder why."

"One day you'll have to teach me that trick, brother," Mandor commented.

"In that I was about to head for Kashfa," I said, "is there anything special I should do?"

"Do?" Random said. "Just find out what's going on and let me know, will you?"

"Of course," I said, uncasing my Trumps.

Vialle came up and took my hand as if in farewell.

"Gloves," she commented.

"Trying to look a little formal," I explained.

237

"There is something in Kashfa that Coral seems to fear," she whispered. "She muttered about it in her sleep."

"Thanks," I said. "I'm ready for anything now."

"You may say that for confidence," she said, "but never believe it."

I laughed as I held a Trump before me and pretended to study it while extending the force of my being along the line I had sent to Kashfa. I reopened the route Dworkin had taken and stepped through.

XII

Kashfa.

I stood in the gray stone hall, flags and shields on the walls, rushes strewn about the floors, rude furniture about me, a fire before me which did not completely dispel the dampness of the place, cooking smells heavy on the air. I was the only person in the room, though I could hear voices from many directions; also the sounds of musicians tuning and practicing. So I had to be fairly near the action. The disadvantage of coming in the way I did rather than using a Trump was that there was no one on the spot to show me around and tell me what was going on. The advantage was the same——that is, if there were any spying I wanted to do, now was the time. The ring, a veritable encyclopedia of magics, found me an invisibility spell in which I quickly cloaked myself.

I spent the next hour or so exploring. There were four large buildings and a number of smaller ones within this central walled area. There was another walled sector

239

beyond it and another beyond that—three roughly con-
centric zones of ivy-covered protection. I couldn't see
any signs of heavy damage, and I got the feeling Dalt's
troops hadn't met with much resistance. No indications
of pillaging or burning, but then they'd been hired to
deliver a property, and I'd a feeling Jasra had stipulated
that it remain relatively intact. The troops occupied all
three rings, and I got the impression from a bit of eaves-
dropping that they'd be around till after the coronation.
There were quite a few in the large plaza in the central
area, making fun of the local troops in their fancy livery
as they waited for the coronation procession. None of
this was in particular bad nature, however, possibly because Luke was popular with both groups, though it did
also seem that many individuals on both sides seemed
personally acquainted.

The First Unicornian Church of Kashfa, as one might
translate its title, was across the plaza from the palace
proper. The building in which I'd arrived was an ancil-
lary, all-purpose adjunct, at this time being used to house
a number of hastily summoned guests, along with servants, courtiers, and hangers-on.

I'd no idea exactly when the coronation was to take
place, but I decided I'd better try to see Luke in a hurry,
before he got too swept up into the course of events. He
might even have an idea where Coral had been delivered,
and why.

So I found me a niche with a blank-walled, neutral
background even a native probably couldn't recognize out
of context, dropped my invisibility spell, located Luke's
Trump, and gave him a call. I didn't want him to think
I was already in town because I didn't want him to know
I possessed the power to drop in the way I had. This
under the theory that you never tell anybody everything.

"Merlin!" he announced, studying me. "Is the cat out of the sack or what?"

"Yeah, the kittens, too," I said. "Congratulations on your coronation day."

"Hey! You're wearing the school colors!"

"What the hell. Why not? You won something, didn't you?"

"Listen. It's not as festive a thing as all that. In fact, I was about to call you   I need your advice before this goes any further. Can you bring me through?"

"I'm not in Amber, Luke."

"Where are you?"

"Well . . . downstairs," I admitted. "I'm on the side street between your palace and the building next door that's sort of like a hotel at the moment."

"That won't do," he said. "I'd get spotted too quick if you bring me down. Go on over to the Unicorn Temple. If it's relatively empty and there's a dark, quiet corner where we can talk, call me and bring me through. If there isn't, figure something else, okay?"

"Okay."

"Hey, how'd you get here anyway?"

"Advance scout for an invasion," I said. "One more take-over would be a coup-coup, wouldn't it?"

"You're about as funny as a hangover," he said. "Call me."

Break.

So I crossed the plaza, following what seemed marked out as the route of the procession. I thought I might meet some trouble at the House of the Unicorn and need a spell to get in, but no one barred my way.

I entered. It was big and all decked out for the ceremony, with a great variety of pennons on the walls and flowers all over the place. The only other inhabitant was a muffled woman up near the front who appeared to be praying. I moved off to the left into a somewhat darker section.

"Luke," I addressed his Trump. "All clear. Do you read me?"

I felt his presence before I caught the image. "Okay," he said. "Bring me through," and we clasped hands, and he was there.

He clapped me on the shoulders.

"Well, now, let me look at you," he said. "Wonder whatever became of my letter sweater?"

"I think you gave it to Gail."

"I think you may be right."

"Brought you a present," I said, tossing back my cloak and fumbling at the side of my sword belt. "Here. I turned up your father's sword."

"You're kidding."

He took it into his hands, examined the sheath, turned it over many times. Then he drew it partway, and it hissed again and sparks danced along its tracery and a bit of smoke drifted upward from it.

"It really is!" he said. "Werewindle, the Daysword— brother to the Nightblade, Grayswandir!"

"What's that?" I said. "I didn't know there was any connection."

"I'd have to think hard to remember the full story, but they go back a long way. Thank you."

He turned and took several paces, slapping the weapon against his thigh as he walked. Abruptly he returned.

"I've been had," he said. "That woman has done it again, and I am peeved to the extreme. I don't know how to handle this."

"What? What are you talking about?"

"My mother," he explained. "She's done it again. Just when I thought I'd taken the reins and was riding my own course, she's come along and messed up my life."

"How'd she do that?"

"She hired Dalt and his boys to take over here."

"Yeah, we sort of figured that out. By the way, what happened to Arkans?"

"Oh, he's okay. I've got him under arrest, of course. But he's in good quarters and he can have anything he wants. I wouldn't hurt him. I always kind of liked the guy."

"So what's the problem? You win. You've got your own kingdom now."

"Hell," he said, then glanced furtively toward the sanctum. "I think I was conned, but I'm not exactly sure. See, I never wanted this job. Dalt told me we were taking over for Mom. I was coming in with him to establish order, claim the place for the family again, then welcome her back with a lot of pomp and crap. I figured once she had her throne back, she'd be off my case for good. I'd hit it out of here for more congenial turf, and she'd have a whole kingdom to occupy her attention. Nothing was said about me getting stuck with this lousy job."

I shook my head.

"I don't understand at all," I said. "You got it for her. Why not just turn it over to her and do as you planned?"

He gave a humorless laugh.

"Arkans they liked," he said. "Me they like. Mom they're not so fond of. Nobody seems that enthusiastic about having her back. In fact, there were strong indications that if she tried it, there would indeed be a coup-coup."

"I suppose you could still step aside and give it to Arkans."

Luke punched the stone wall.

"I don't know whether she'd be madder at me or at herself for having paid Dalt as much as she did to throw Arkans out. But she'd tell me it's my duty to do it, and I don't know—maybe it is. What do you think?"

"That's a hard one to answer, Luke. Who do you think would do a better job, you or Arkans?"

"I honestly don't know. He's had a lot of experience in government, but I did grow up here, and I do know how the place is run and how to get things done. The only thing I'm sure of is that either of us would be better at it than Mom."

I folded my arms, and I thought hard.

"I can't make this decision for you," I said. "But tell me, what would you most like to do?"

He chuckled.

"You know I've always been a salesman. If I were going to stick around and do something for Kashfa. I'd rather represent her industries abroad, which would be sort of undignified for a monarch. Probably what I'd be best at, though. I don't know."

"It's a problem and a half, Luke. I don't want the responsibility of telling you which way to go."

"If I'd known it was going to come to this, I'd have smeared Dalt back in Arden."

"You really think you could take him?"

"Believe it," he said.

"Well, that doesn't solve your present problem."

"True. I've a strong feeling I may have to go through with this."

The woman up front glanced our way several times. I guess we were talking kind of loud for the surroundings.

"Too bad there are no other good candidates," I said, lowering my voice.

"This must seem like pretty small beer to someone from Amber."

"Hell, it's your home. You've got a right to take it seriously. I'm just sorry it's doing such a job on you."

"Yeah, most problems seem to start at home, don't they? Sometimes I just feel like taking a walk and not coming back."

"What would happen if you did?"

"Either Mom would restore herself to the throne with Dalt's gang to back her up, which would require a mess of executions of people I can think of who'd be against it, or she'd say the game isn't worth the candle and settle for the Keep. If she decided to enjoy her retirement, then the coalition which backed him in the first place would probably spring Arkans and continue things from where they'd had to leave off."

"Which course of action seems most likely to you?" I said.

"She'd go for it and there'd be a civil war. Win or lose, it would mess up the country and doubtless keep us out of the Golden Circle this time around, too. Speaking of which——"

"I don't know," I said quickly. "I'm not empowered to talk Golden Circle Treaty with you."

"I'd kind of guessed that," Luke said, "and that wasn't what I wanted to ask. I was just curious whether anyone back in Amber might have said, 'They just blew it,' or 'Maybe we'll give them another crack at it a little farther down the road,' or 'We'll still deal, but they can forget the Eregnor guarantees.'"

He gave me an artificial grin, and I returned it.

"You can forget Eregnor," I said.

"Figured that," he said. "What about the rest?"

"I get the impression it's 'Let's wait and see what happens.'"

"Guessed that much, too. Give me a good report, even if they don't ask, okay? By the way, I don't suppose your presence here is technically official?"

"Personal," I said, "from a diplomatic standpoint."

The lady up front rose to her feet. Luke sighed.

"Wish I could find my way back to Alice's restaurant. Maybe the Hatter would see something we're missing," he said. Then: "Hey! Where'd he come from? Looks just like you but—"

He was staring past me, and I could already feel the disturbance. I didn't even bother to summon the Logrus, though, because I felt ready for anything.

I turned, smiling.

"Are you ready to die, brother?" Jurt asked. He had either managed to regrow his eye or was wearing an artificial one, and he now had sufficient hair that I could no longer tell about the ear. His little finger was partly regrown also.

"No, but I'm ready to kill," I said. "I'm glad you happened by."

He bowed, mockingly. There was a faint glow about him. I could feel the power that flowed through and around his person.

"Have you been back to the Keep for your final treatment?" I inquired.

"I don't believe that will be necessary," he said. "I am more than adequate for any task I've set myself, now I've control of these forces."

"This is Jurt?" Luke asked.

"Yes," I replied. "This is Jurt."

Jurt cast a quick glance Luke's way. I could feel him focusing on the blade.

"Is that a power object you bear?" he inquired. "Let me see it!"

He extended his hand, and the weapon jerked within Luke's grip but did not come loose.

"No, thanks," Luke said, and Jurt vanished. A moment later he appeared behind Luke, and his arm went around Luke's neck in a choke. Luke gripped it with one hand, bowed, and turned and threw him over his shoulder.

Jurt landed on his back before him, and Luke made no move to follow up on his action.

"Draw that blade," Jurt said, "and let me see it." Then he shook himself like a dog and rose to his feet. "Well?" he said.

"I see no need for a weapon in dealing with the likes of you," Luke told him.

Jurt raised both hands above his head and formed them into fists. They met, remained in contact for a moment. Then he drew them apart, his right hand somehow drawing a long blade out of his left.

"You ought to take that show on the road," Luke said, "now."

"Draw it!" Jurt said.

"I don't like the idea of fighting in a church," Luke told him. "You want to step outside?"

"Very funny," Jurt replied. "I know you've got an army out there. No thanks. I'll even take a certain pleasure in bloodying a Unicorn shrine."

"You ought to talk to Dalt," Luke said. "He gets his kicks in weird ways, too. Can I get you a horse—or a chicken? Maybe some white mice and aluminum foil?"

Jurt lunged. Luke stepped backward and drew his father's blade. It hissed and crackled and smoked as he parried lightly and drove it forward. There was a sudden fear on Jurt's face as he threw himself backward, batting at it, stumbling. As he fell, Luke kicked him in the stomach and Jurt's blade went flying.

"That's Werewindle!" Jurt gasped. "How did you come by the sword of Brand?"

"Brand was my father," Luke said.

A momentary look of respect passed over Jurt's face.

"I didn't know..." he muttered, and then he vanished.

I waited. I extended magical feelers all over the place. But there was just Luke, myself and the lady, who had halted some distance from us, watching, as if afraid to come any nearer on her way out.

Then Luke collapsed. Jurt was standing behind him, having just struck him on the back of the neck with his elbow. He reached then for Luke's wrist, as if to seize it and wrench the blade from his hand.

"It must be mine!" he said as I reached through the ring and struck him with a bolt of pure energy which I thought would rupture most of his organs and leave him a bleeding mass of jelly. Only for an instant had I considered using anything less than lethal force. I could see that sooner or later one of us was going to kill the other, and I'd decided to get it over with before he got lucky.

But he was already lucky. His bath in the Fount must have toughened him even more than I'd thought. He spun around three times, as if he'd been clipped by a truck, and was slammed up against the wall. He sagged. He slipped to the floor. Blood came out of his mouth. He looked as if he were about to pass out. Then his eyes focused and his hands extended.

A force similar to the one I'd just thrown at him struck at me. I was surprised by his ability to regroup and retaliate at that level with that speed. Not so surprised that I wasn't able to parry it, though. I took a step forward then and tried to set him afire with a beautiful spell the ring suggested. Rising, he was able to shield against it within moments of his clothes' beginning to smolder. I kept coming, and he created a vacuum around me. I pierced it and kept breathing. Then I tried a battering ram spell which the ring showed me, even more forceful than the first working with which I'd hit him.

He vanished before it hit, and a crack ran up three feet of the stone wall which had been behind him. I sent sense-tendrils all over and spotted him seconds later, crouched on a cornice high overhead. He launched himself at me just as I looked up.

I didn't know whether it would break my hand or not, but I felt it would be worth it, even so, as I levitated. I contrived to pass him at about the midway point, and I hit him with a left, which I hoped broke his neck as well as his jaw. Unfortunately it also broke my levitation spell, and I tumbled to the floor along with him.

I heard the lady cry out as we fell, and she came rushing toward us. We lay stunned for several heartbeats. Then he rolled over onto his stomach, reached, hunched and fell, reached again.

His hand fell upon the haft of Werewindle. He must have felt my gaze as his fingers tightened about it, for he glanced at me and smiled. I heard Luke mutter a curse and stir. I threw a deep freeze spell at Jurt, but he trumped out before the cold front hit.

Then the lady screamed again, and even before I turned, I knew that the voice had been Coral's.

Reappearing, Jurt half collapsed against her from the rear, finding her throat with the edge of that bright, smoldering blade.

"Nobody," he gasped, "move . . . or I'll carve her . . . an extra smile."

I sought after a quick spell that would finish him without endangering her.

"Don't try it, Merle," he said. "I'll feel it . . .

coming. Just leave me...alone...for half a minute
...and you'll get to live...a little longer. I don't know
where you picked up...those extra tricks...but they
won't save you——"

He was panting and covered with sweat. The blood
still dripped from his mouth.

"Let go of my wife," Luke said, rising, "or there'll
never be anyplace you'll be able to hide."

"I don't want you for an enemy, son of Brand," Jurt
said.

"Then do as I say, fella. I've taken out better men than
you."

And then Jurt screamed as if his soul were on fire.
Werewindle moved away from Coral's throat, and Jurt
backed off and began jerking, like a puppet whose
joints have seized up but whose strings are still being
yanked. Coral turned toward him, her back to Luke
and me. Her right hand rose to her face. After a time
Jurt fell to the floor and curled into a fetal position. A
red light seemed to be playing upon him. He was
shaking steadily, and I could even hear his teeth
chattering.

Abruptly, then, he was gone, trailing rainbows, leaving blood and spittle, bearing Werewindle with him. I
sent a parting bolt after, but I knew that it did not reach
him. I'd felt Julia's presence at the other end of the
spectrum, and despite everything else, I was pleased to
know that I had not slain her yet. But Jurt——Jurt was
very dangerous now, I realized. For this was the first
time we'd fought that he hadn't left a piece of himself
behind, had even taken something away with him.
Something deadly. He was learning, and that did not
bode well.

When I turned my head, I caught sight of the red
glow before Coral lowered her eyepatch, and I realized

what had become of the Jewel of Judgment, though not, of course, why.

"Wife?" I said.

"Well, sort of . . . Yes," she replied.

"Just one of those things," Luke said. "Do you two know each other?"

NEW BESTSELLERS
IN THE *MAGIC OF XANTH* SERIES!

PIERS ANTHONY

VALE OF THE VOLE

75287-5 / $4.95 US / $5.95 Can

HEAVEN CENT

75288-3 / $4.95 US / $5.95 Can

MAN FROM MUNDANIA

75289-1 / $4.50 US / $5.50 Can

Magic...Mystery...Revelations
Welcome to
**THE FANTASTICAL
WORLD OF AMBER!**

**ROGER ZELAZNY'S
VISUAL GUIDE to
CASTLE
AMBER**

by Roger Zelazny and Neil Randall
75566-1/$8.95 US/$10.95 Can
AN AVON TRADE PAPERBACK

Tour Castle Amber—
through vivid illustrations, detailed floor plans,
cutaway drawings, and page after page
of never-before-revealed information!

ROGER ZELAZNY

"One of science fiction's brightest lights...
His worlds are imaginative,
his plots tightly presented,
and his characters believably alive."
Library Journal

"It is impossible to find fault
with Zelazny's writing.
He is one of the prose masters of SF."
Denver Post

"I envy those who encounter Roger Zelazny!"
Theodore Sturgeon, *The New York Times*

AMBER

"Few works of science fiction are as satisfying...
Wickedly crafted and thoroughly engrossing."
Boston Herald

"Zelazny has us all hooked and at his mercy."
St. Louis Post Dispatch

KNIGHT OF SHADOWS